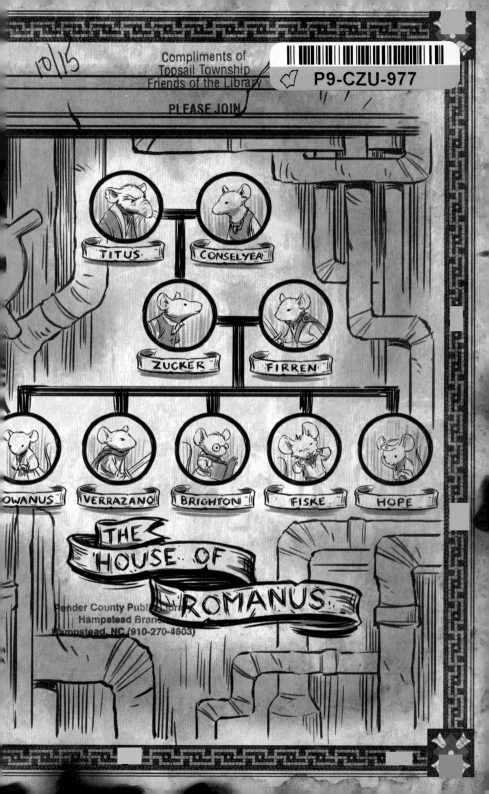

MOUSEHEART

RETURN OF THE FORGOTTEN

MOUSE

LISA FIEDLER

With illustrations by VIVIENNE TO

MARGARET K. McELDERRY BOOKS

HEART

VOL. 3

RETURN
OF THE
FORGOTTEN

New York London Toronto Sydney New Delhi

Also by Lisa Fiedler
Mouseheart

Mouseheart vol. 2:
Hopper's Destiny

MARGARET K. MCELDERRY BOOKS
An imprint of Simon & Schuster Children's Publishing Division
1230 Avenue of the Americas, New York, New York 10020
For information about special discounts for bulk purchases, please contact Simon & Schuster Special Sales at 1-866-506-1949 or business@simonandschuster.com.
The Simon & Schuster Speakers Bureau can bring authors to your live event. For more information or to book an event, contact the Simon & Schuster Speakers Bureau at 1-866-248-3049 or visit our website at www.simonspeakers.com.
Book design by Lauren Rille
The text for this book is set in Absara.
The illustrations for this book are rendered digitally.
Manufactured in the United States of America
0915 FFG
10 9 8 7 6 5 4 3 2 1
Library of Congress Cataloging-in-Publication Data
Fiedler, Lisa.
Return of the forgotten / Lisa Fiedler ; Vivienne To.—First edition.
p. cm.—(Mouseheart ; 3)
Summary: Although Felina the cat queen is gone, the subway tunnels are still dangerous, not only because of Hopper's rogue brother Pup and his arachnid companion Hacklemesh, but also due to a secret Firren has been hiding that worries her more than the disappearance of her daughter, Hope. Includes a bonus story, "Atlantia Rising: How It All Began."
ISBN 978-1-4814-2092-1 (hardback)
ISBN 978-1-4814-2094-5 (eBook)
[1. Adventure and adventurers—Fiction. 2. Mice—Fiction. 3. Rats—Fiction. 4. Utopias—Fiction. 5. Fate and fatalism—Fiction.] I. Title.
PZ7.F457Ret 2015
[Fic]—dc23
2015000179

To Shannon and Ricky.
My very best friends.

PROLOGUE

THE JOURNEY TO ATLANTIA FROM the upland world had been grueling. But the four brown mice pups had not questioned their father's plan. He'd been telling them about his dream to colonize the Forgotten Place, a splendid and magnificent wonderland, for so long that it had become their dream too.

And their mother had been just as excited to begin their new life below the city as their father had ... until the trap had taken her away.

The pups had been heartbroken, of course. But their father had told them they would have to be strong, and carry on. It was the best tribute their mother could have asked for. So they'd mustered their courage and went on with the plan.

And now they'd made it. All the way to the famed underground city of Atlantia.

They'd had a frightening moment at the entry gate, though, when a large cat had threatened to eat them for breakfast, but their father, Fiorello, was a gifted politician and he'd talked the cat into allowing them entrance not only to the city but the palace as well.

"I-I-I don't l-l-like it here," the smallest of the litter, Ira, stammered to his brother as the four siblings followed their father up the steps to the sprawling home of Emperor Titus.

Their sister, Celeste, put a paw on Ira's shoulder. "Don't be afraid," she said sweetly. "When Father gets permission from the emperor to colonize the Forgotten Place, we'll have the best home in all of the tunnels."

"She's right," said Hazel as she flicked her tail back and forth.

"I liked our old h-h-home, upland, where I could p-p-play under the mayor's desk," Ira protested.

"Shhh," hissed the oldest of the siblings. "Don't let Father hear you. This new city is his dream. We must help him realize it. And besides"—he gave his nervous brother a smile—"if it works, you and I will be princes, and Hazel and Celeste will be princesses. Royalty!"

At this, Ira smiled.

When they entered the grand lobby of the Atlantian palace, a uniformed rat escorted them to the doors of the throne room. The towering doors were slightly ajar, open just enough for the oldest pup to peek inside. A lavish room and a gilded chair, and upon it, an imposing rat with a scarred snout. Emperor Titus, who, it would seem, held this little mouse's future in his paws.

Looking up at Titus was his empress, wearing a shimmering gown, a tiara, and a chain of blue stones. Beside her was a pup. He had a rugged look about him, despite the elegant purple vest and fancy britches he wore. No doubt he was a royal prince, the Romanus heir. He was young, but his strength and pride were already beginning to show in his carriage. He held a handsome sword but squirmed and fidgeted in those ridiculous trousers. The mouse couldn't help but laugh; the rat prince looked as though he really hated those pants.

The mouse also noticed that not only did the prince look uncomfortable, but he was the only young rodent present. *I wonder where the rest of the emperor's litter is,* the mouse wondered.

"The emperor is just finishing a meeting with his family," the servant explained. "He will see you shortly."

The mouse leaned closer to the door, straining to hear.

"Titus, I am beginning to have some suspicions," the empress said. "I know your politics, mysterious as they are, have brought us prosperity and safety. But something has changed. Something feels wrong to me."

"I feel it too, Pop," the rat prince piped up.

The emperor made a *tsk tsk* sound and shook his head. "Prince Zucker, you forget yourself. I may be your father, but I am also the royal liege. You should remember to address me as such."

The prince rolled his eyes. "Fine . . . *Your Highness.* I agree with Mother. This whole treaty stinks! If you would only let *me* go out into the tunnels . . ."

"I forbid it! You are only a child."

The prince ground his teeth. "Well, I won't be a child forever. And someday I'm going to do it! Someday, when I'm older, I'm going to get out of this city and—"

"Silence!" Titus turned a cool look to his wife. "Perhaps your time would be better spent, Conselyea, teaching our only son some manners, instead of worrying your pretty little head over things like treaties and politics."

"Titus," the empress said, more desperate this time. "Let me go to Queen Felina. Let me talk to her. I think perhaps she has not been honest with you. I think there might be things you do not know."

"I know everything!" the emperor assured her. Then the intimidating rat turned back to his son. "You are never to leave the walls of this city, is that understood? You are never to venture into the Great Beyond."

The prince hesitated, then nodded. But his expression said that he did not intend to keep that promise for very long. The mouse suspected the rat pup would bide his time; he'd wait until he'd grown just a little bit larger—and perhaps braver—but eventually he would slip outside Atlantia's walls against his father's wishes.

"And you, my lady," Titus said, smiling at his wife. "I urge you not to bother yourself with these 'suspicions,' as you call them. And do not, under any circumstances, attempt to make contact with Queen Felina."

"Why?" the prince huffed. "Because she's a vicious, untrustworthy beast?"

"Because she is a busy monarch!" the emperor shot back. "Just like I am. Which is why I am going to ask you to leave me to my business now." He frowned at his son. "Zucker, to the schoolroom. And then to sword practice. I will be checking with your teachers regarding your progress."

With a wave the emperor rat sent his family on their way.

As the empress and the prince exited the throne room, the prince (stomping indignantly) bumped into the oldest mouse pup, knocking him off his feet.

He gave the mouse an apologetic look and offered a paw. "Sorry," he said. "I wasn't looking where I was going."

But the mouse did not accept the paw. *Knock me down, will you?* he thought, scrambling to his feet unaided. *Soon I'm going to be just as much a prince as you are. Then you'll think twice about bumping into me!* The mouse pup gave the rat prince a steely look, then turned away.

"Fine, whatever," grumbled Prince Zucker with a shrug. After offering a polite bow to the rest of the mouse litter, he left.

"He's *so* handsome," Hazel whispered to Celeste.

"And r-r-regal," Ira added.

The palace servant nodded to Fiorello. "The emperor will see you now."

Fiorello smiled at his litter. "You pups wait for me out here," he said, his eyes dancing with anticipation and hope. "This is going to be the beginning of something big, kids!"

The sisters squealed with delight; even little Ira looked excited. "B-b-big!" he stuttered, smiling.

Fiorello drew himself up and strode into the audience chamber. Again, the eldest peered around the edge of the door to listen.

"Welcome, mouse," said Titus in a haughty tone. "I hear you have come from the daylight world to request my assistance in colonizing an abandoned station somewhere far across the water."

"Yes, Your Majesty," Fiorello said with a deep, respectful bow. "And I believe that if you and I work together, we can accomplish truly marvelous things."

Titus was silent for a long moment, strumming his gnarled paws on the arm of his luxurious throne. "Tell me your plans, sir. I find I am very interested in what you have to say."

As his father began to explain his careful strategy to

the rat liege, the mouse pup felt a surge of pride.

Because he knew that his father was about to change their lives forever. He knew that, from this moment forward, nothing would ever be the same.

CHAPTER ONE

THEY STOOD ON A LEDGE far above the city with Atlantia sparkling below.

Sparkling and growing still, thought Hopper; the metropolis was improving and expanding, it seemed, every minute of every day.

"Tell me again how Atlantia came to be," came a sweet voice from beside him.

Hopper smiled and looked down into the snapping black eyes of his goddaughter, the princess Hope.

"Well," he began, delighted by the tiny rat's interest in learning her own history, "Atlantia was the dream of your grandfather, the late emperor Titus. He was an ambitious upland rat from Brooklyn, New York."

Hope shuddered. "But he was nasty!"

"He was misguided," Hopper corrected, but this was being generous. The truth was that as emperor, Titus had made a host of extremely poor choices, and countless innocent rodents had suffered because of his politics. It was also true that Titus had taken a forgotten subway platform deep beneath the borough of Brooklyn and transformed it into the spectacular city that lay before them now. But to maintain this prosperity, he had been forced to spend most of his reign sacrificing unsuspecting tunnel wanderers to the evil cat Queen Felina. Titus justified his own evil as being necessary to buy peace for Atlantia.

In the end, he paid a much greater price.

But Hopper did not like to discuss such gruesome details with his little friend. Instead he told her a far more palatable version of the story.

"Long ago, Titus happened upon this abandoned platform and chose it as the site on which to build his dazzling city. Under Titus's leadership, Atlantia bloomed into a great civilization."

"But my grandfather was hiding a dark secret," Hope cried, knowing the story by heart.

"Yes he was." Hopper gave her a solemn nod. "A secret that brought a great deal of pain to many . . . including himself. But thanks to your mother and father . . ."

"And you! The Chosen One!"

Hopper blushed slightly. "Right . . . thanks to all of us, and the rebels and the refugees, Titus was overthrown, and then, not long after, Felina, too, was defeated, putting an end to the brutality and the tyranny."

"But in the aftermath of battle Atlantia fell to ruins," Hope gushed, her eyes brimming with intelligence and excitement. "Now you and the emperor and empress—"

Hopper grinned. "Otherwise known as your mommy and daddy. You know they do not wish to be called by such titles anymore, now that Atlantia's government is shifting away from a monarchy to something more democratic and fair."

Hope rolled her eyes and pouted. "I know. I also know that *that* means they don't want me to wear beautiful crowns and gowns and jewels, like my grandmamma, the empress Conselyea, did."

"In the scheme of things, crowns and gowns don't count for much," Hopper reminded her.

"But *I like being a princess*."

"I know, little one, but your parents would much rather you liked being a good and wise leader instead." Hopper patted her between the ears. "They are determined to see Atlantia rise again, so it can welcome all rodents and offer them protection within its walls. And without any dark secrets this time. Come along, now."

As they started toward the palace, Hopper turned his attention back to the bustle of the city below. There he saw progress. Mice working beside rats working beside squirrels working beside chipmunks. Atlantia was on its way to once again becoming the magnificent place it had been the first time he'd seen it. After many long months of thrilling innovation and intensive labor, the underground urban masterpiece was nearly complete; the city was thriving again.

But it was more than just structural and commercial changes that Emperor Zucker and Empress Firren were striving for. They had an entirely new vision of the way Atlantia should be governed, and to this end, their empire was in the midst of great political improvements as well.

Citizens could now vote on civic decisions, and express their ideas at public hearings. Zucker had gotten the idea from a book in Titus's library. He called it a "republic," and together he and Firren were determined to make it a reality for Atlantia.

But they understood that even positive change took time, and they respected the fact that their subjects needed to get used to the idea.

So they stopped wearing their opulent jewels and elegant clothing. Zucker wore the same workaday attire his subjects did (which he found far more comfortable than his royal garb), and Firren always donned her beloved Rangers tunic. They requested that the Atlantians call them by name, not title.

Even still, the rodents insisted on bowing and curtsying to them and calling them His and Her Highness. The habit, it seemed, was difficult to break.

It seemed strange to Hopper that the rodents needed to be convinced of something that was in their own best interests, but there it was. He wondered: Did they believe that outward finery and glitz represented ability and competence? That was *exactly* the kind of superficiality Titus had relied upon to justify his authority. And look how *that* turned out!

In truth, when it came to governing, Hopper knew

that it was what was *inside* a rodent that counted. The character, not the crown, was what defined a ruler.

Sadly, little Hope did not yet understand this particular truth, but Hopper wasn't worried. She was still very young and she had many things to learn. At the moment, his darling godchild might be easily dazzled by her empress grandmamma's old tiaras and dresses (which she'd determinedly dug out of the palace basement and claimed for her own), but he truly believed she'd come to understand the value of invisible things like honesty, loyalty, and integrity. He was confident that she and her four littermates would one day step up to take part in the wonderful new government their parents were working so hard to set in motion.

This gave Hopper great joy indeed.

But mingled with his joy was the faintest prickle of sadness. It brought to mind his own littermates . . . his brother and sister. The last time he'd stood upon this ledge, he'd had no idea what his own future held and he'd been desperate to know what had become of Pinkie and Pup.

He knew well enough where Pinkie was *now*—safe behind the gray wall of their ancestral village, ruling the Mūs citizens with her newfound wisdom and benevolence. To Hopper's great relief, Pinkie had undergone a change of heart after discovering that their father, the legendary rebel Dodger, was still alive. She was still given to grumbling and bossiness, but she was no longer angry or unkind. Dodger split his time between assisting Pinkie in ruling the Mūs, and advising Zucker here in Atlantia. Hopper was thrilled about Pinkie's new outlook.

But Pup. Pup was another story entirely.

Where in these vast tunnels their diminutive sibling had taken himself off to still remained a mystery. And what Pup might be up to was anybody's guess.

"Uncle Hopper! Look!"

"What is it, Hope?" Hopper asked, shaking off his dark thoughts. "What do you see?"

"Over there!" Hope leaned so far toward the rim of the ledge that Hopper had to lunge forward to grasp the hood of her tiny pink cloak (a gift from Pinkie, of course). "In the market square! That chipmunk is selling whirligigs! Can I please have a whirligig? I can, can't I? I can have anything I want—after all, I am a crown princess of Atlantia!"

"Hope," said Hopper, gently but firmly, "it's wrong to demand things just because you happened to be born to Zucker and Firren. You should focus on *earning* the things you want."

Hope gave him a pout. "But I *didn't* demand. I asked politely." She gave a heavy sigh. "So . . . no whirligig, then?"

Hopper chuckled. "I didn't say *that*. I only meant that if you *do* get one, it won't be because you are entitled to it as a princess. It will be because your parents and I like to see you happy and because you've earned it. But for now the whirligig will have to wait. You know you're expected in the schoolroom."

Hope let out a little snort. "Do I have to go? The tutor smells funny and my brothers and sisters pick on me. And there's no one else to play with."

Hopper smiled. "Well, I'm sorry to hear that, but you can take comfort in the fact that soon you'll all be enrolled in the public school," he promised. "Your mama is determined to see that happen sooner than later. It's just a matter of getting it built."

"Well, it can't happen soon enough for me!" she huffed. "My siblings all think they're so smart!"

"You're just as smart as they are."

She smiled at the compliment, then frowned again. "Not as smart as Brighton is. She's a genius. They call *her* Bright-one. Of course, *she* never has any fun."

Hopper laughed. "She is the serious one of the litter, isn't she?"

"Yes," Hope agreed. "And Verrazano is the great leader and talented swordsman. Fiske is the clown but also a philosopher, and Go-go is the one who all the little boy rats of the city fawn over and make goofy eyes at." She frowned. "Princess Gowanus, the royal heartbreaker."

"Go-go has her good points," Hopper said, biting back another chuckle. "You all do. Which is why

Zucker and Firren and all the rest of us are so proud of each and every one of you. You're a wonderful little bunch of future upstanding politicians."

"I prefer princes and princesses," Hope teased.

"Royal heirs," said Hopper, compromising by using the commonly accepted term for referring to Firren and Zucker's offspring. "Will you settle for that?"

"I guess," said Hope, placing her paw in Hopper's.

Hopper recalled the night he'd sat down with Firren and Zucker to discuss recasting the public's impression of their babies by coming up with a better, more down-to-earth term than the "royal heirs."

"You can call them the Patriot Pups," he'd suggested. "That has a nice ring to it."

"It's not bad," Zucker had allowed. "But how about the Children of Democracy?"

"That's still a bit lofty," Firren had observed with a grin. She'd thought for a moment, then clapped her hands. "We can continue to refer to them as royal heirs, as long as we're very clear about the fact that what they are heir *to* is responsibility and purpose, and *not* riches and unqualified adoration."

Zucker had smiled, his eyes twinkling. "I like it," he'd pronounced. "They'll be the heirs to our best intentions and our most worthy efforts."

Hopper had thought that was the perfect way to look at it, but in truth he would have loved the little rats no matter what anyone called them.

Now Hope was tugging at the sleeve of his tunic, giving him her most glowing smile. "Of all us royal heirs, *I'm* your *favorite*, aren't I, Uncle Hopper?"

Hopper beamed at her. It was true that Hope held a special place in her godfather's heart. And with very good reason:

When the royal litter had arrived, Hopper and Pinkie had both been there to provide Zucker, the nervous first-time father, some much-needed support and distraction. Marcy, back in the palace on one of her rare visits, had skillfully assisted the midwife, Maimonides, who'd come all the way from the Mūs village to lend her experience and expertise. When Mamie, as the midwife was called, handed Zucker his firstborn—a daughter—he'd kissed the squirming infant on her forehead and promptly named her Gowanus.

Marcy gave the second pup, a boy, to Pinkie to hold.

"We'll call him Verrazano," Zucker decreed. "Raz for short."

Little Raz's first royal act was to spit up all over Pinkie's golden cape. Hopper took some brotherly pleasure in seeing that.

Two more pups arrived, mewling and cooing— twins, one male, one female. They were christened Fiske and Brighton, and handed to Dodger to snuggle. At last the fifth and final royal rat-ling entered the world. Yet another precious baby girl.

"Hope," Firren whispered, exhausted but happy. "Her name is Hope. After your mother, Hopper."

Hopper had been too choked up to speak at first, so touched was he by such a tribute. "It's a lovely name," he whispered at last, when Marcy placed the babe in his arms. The rush of love he'd felt was nearly indescribable. *Such innocence*, he thought, gazing down at her scrunched-up little face. *Such possibility and promise.*

But it was immediately clear that Princess Hope was by far the smallest of Firren's litter—the runt, as Pinkie might have said in the old days. It was also evident that the newborn princess was in great distress. She struggled to catch her breath, writhing and squirming, as though the act of living was simply beyond her capability.

Marcy had given Hopper a somber look. "Keep her warm," she advised softly. "And think good thoughts."

While the other four robust heirs had snuggled up to their empress mother in peaceful slumber, poor little Hope wheezed and gasped and shuddered, fighting for her life.

As the night wore on, Hope's condition worsened. Zucker was inconsolable, sick with worry. For hours he paced the palace floor, stomping his paws in anger, crying out in frustration and sending off muttered wishes to La Rocha (something Zucker rarely did) that his infant daughter might be spared.

Hopper saw in Hope's pale little features how much she resembled her father, the friend and comrade he loved so dearly; he simply could not stand the thought of what it would do to Zucker and Firren if they lost this precious bundle. So the Chosen One had held the shivering pup while murmuring words of encouragement and hope, humming to her gently and keeping her warm all through that endless night.

"I don't know what else to do," he'd said to Marcy, his voice trembling.

Marcy had smiled. "Tell her a story. Tell her *your* story. I can't imagine a better pep talk."

So Hopper did. He told the sickly baby about his brave escape from the pet shop, his fall into the tunnels, and his journey to becoming the Chosen One. He cradled the baby close to his heart, hoping the powerful beat of it would somehow transfer to her and give her the strength she needed. Her own tiny heart was beating quickly but quietly . . . much too quietly for Hopper's comfort; still, he continued to whisper in her dainty, translucent ear:

"I know it's hard to be strong, and even harder to be brave," he confided. "When I thought I couldn't carry on a moment longer, I found the strength in my own little mouse heart to do it. You must do the same, Hope! You must find the courage in your heart to be strong." He cuddled her even more snugly to his chest, hoping the steady rhythm of his heartbeat would calm her, inspire her, make her well.

And suddenly she opened her eyes—two miniature black jewels they were, glittering with curiosity and determination as they stared up into the weary but grateful face of her protector.

Hopper's relieved and joyful countenance, with its distinctive white circle of fur around the right eye, had been the first thing Hope had ever seen. The two had been best pals ever since.

Sometimes Hopper imagined he could still feel the wispy flutter of her newborn heartbeat against his chest. He understood that part of the reason he adored Hope so much was that she reminded him of Pup back in the days when they'd lived together in the cage in Keep's shop. Back then, Pup had been helpless and trusting and sweet. But now . . .

In Hopper's mind's eye, he could still see the last missive dispatched by La Rocha:

BEWARE THE TINY VILLAIN
RINGED IN A CIRCLE OF GLOOM
FOR HE IS THE THIEF WHO STEALS OUR HOPE
AND THE LOSS OF HOPEFUL IS DOOM

Now into the frame of his imagination floated an image of his brother the last time he'd seen him; in this recollection Pup had a menacing scowl on his once-sweet face. And his eye! Like Hopper's and

Pinkie's, one of Pup's eyes was outlined with a circle. But this was no natural birthmark of soft white fur. This coal-black circle had been added by Pup himself with a sooty stone—an angry tattoo. A self-inflicted stain meant to reflect outwardly the darkness that had overtaken him from within.

Again, Hopper pushed aside his grim thoughts and gave Hope's paw a squeeze.

"Come on now, back to the palace."

She gave him a coy flutter of her eyelashes. "Just out of curiosity, *how* exactly might a princess earn herself a whirligig?"

"Well . . ." Hopper threw her a wink. "Perhaps by working hard at your lessons. If you do that, not only will you show Brighton that you are just as smart as she is, but I will personally take you out to the market square to buy you whichever whirligig you choose. Okay?"

Hope nodded hard, her eyes shining. "Okay. But tell me again about the time you went upland in a Windbreaker and met a cat named Ace and a white lab mouse named Carroll and ate eggplant parmigiana at Bellissimo's Deli."

"Again?" Hopper laughed. "You've heard it a million times already."

"I know, but I like to hear about the daylight world. Tell me everything about Brooklyn, New York!"

So Hopper retold the whole incredible story of the

enormous Barclays Center, and the sprawling grass-lands where his friend Valky the bespectacled chip-munk lived, and the Italian delicatessen where a stout bulldog named Capone lolled contentedly on a plump pillow by the back door.

Hope gasped at the part where Hopper found himself hanging off the edge of the Brooklyn Bridge, and she sighed dreamily when he told her how he'd gone weak in his little mouse knees the moment he'd first laid eyes on Carroll.

"I would like to meet her someday," Hope said.

Hopper felt a flutter in his belly. He wouldn't mind seeing Carroll again himself.

"Well, I'd be happy to introduce you, but only good students get to go upland," he explained. "So . . . let's get you to that schoolroom."

Together the unlikely pair—the pet-store mouse and the princess rat—made their way back down the long flight of stairs and into the palace.

Neither had any idea they were being watched.

CHAPTER TWO

PUP HAD HEARD EVERYTHING.

Thanks to his eight-legged friend, Hacklemesh, Hopper's little brother had been present during the entire conversation, hovering . . . listening.

Hack was not only a loyal companion but a powerful weaver as well. He'd wrapped Pup in a snug cocoon of spider silk and slowly lowered him to dangle above the ledge while clinging with his craggy legs to a high spot on the outer wall of the tunnel.

Hopper had had no idea that Pup was looming overhead the entire time he and Hope had been talking . . . which was precisely how Pup had planned it. He couldn't proceed with his plan until he determined Hopper's (and the city's) current mood. Hanging there like a caught fly, Pup had been closer to his brother than he'd been in what felt like ages. It had taken all he had to keep from reaching out for Hopper with both paws; he'd wanted to grasp him with all his strength . . .

And say . . .

Well, he did not know exactly *what* he would have said to his brother at this point. There were so many feelings inside him; feelings that were, it seemed, almost beyond expression.

Now, as Pup regained his footing on the narrow

blister of tile that buckled out from the tunnel wall, he swept away Hack's silk from his belly and shoulders. He wished he could sweep away his mistakes as easily.

And oh, what monumental mistakes Pup had made! Who would have believed that such a tiny creature could err so enormously?

"Look at this place, Hack," he said, gesturing with a paw at the bustling city below. "So much is happening. Rodents are accomplishing things. All kinds of things! Every individual has his own piece of the power."

Hacklemesh blinked all eight of his eyes at once.

Pup took this as a sign of agreement. He continued to survey the activity of Atlantia, overwhelmed by the pace of its commerce, the sense of its purpose. Here was an entire society of well-meaning rodents, united in their common goal of peace and prosperity. And for the last several weeks Pup had skulked around the dank tunnels thinking of only one thing: how to destroy it.

It was an obsession that had very nearly destroyed him.

For so long, Hopper and their sister, Pinkie, the celebrated Chosen Ones, had refused to give Pup the responsibility and stature he craved. They'd been far more intent on sheltering and protecting him. He had to admit, after creeping around in these unpredictable tunnels, he had come to understand just how much there was to be protected from. Still, his escape from the *Mūs* village had given him the autonomy and independence he'd believed he deserved.

But independence was scary.

Not to mention exhausting.

And lonely.

He closed his eyes now (one of them still stained with the dark, chalky marking with which he'd encircled it) to picture Hopper and the rat child standing together on the ledge. The warmth and affection in the Chosen One's voice had been impossible to miss. He was *her* protector now.

Pup wasn't exactly sure how he felt about that.
But he *was* sure of this . . .
It was time to finish what he'd come here to do.
All he needed was the guts.

Chapter Three

The battle raged.

Rats pounced, dove, and ducked for cover in a riot of tails, ears, and whiskers. There were screams of fury and shouts for mercy. At last a sword came slashing to rest with its tip poised against a swiftly beating heart.

All went silent as the attacker and his victim stared each other down.

"Remove that blade, sir," the victim demanded.

The swordsman laughed, twirling his weapon carelessly. "You aren't the boss of me. And besides, it ain't even real."

"'Ain't' is not a word," someone corrected from the far side of the battlefield. "The proper grammar is 'it's *not* even real.'"

"Oh yeah?" snapped the swordsman, Fiske, who had his paw planted firmly on his victim's tail. "Well, neither are your eyeglasses, Brighton. Everybody knows you only wear 'em to make yourself look smart!"

"Smart-*er*," Brighton huffed, pushing her round-rimmed spectacles up higher on her snout.

"I captured Gowanus fair and square," Fiske insisted. "She's my prisoner."

Before Brighton could comment, Gowanus—despite still having a sword aimed at her chest—raised her chin and glared with flashing eyes.

"I'm going to tell you one more time, Fiske of Romanus. Remove that silly toy blade this instant before you mess up my fur. I just combed it!"

Fiske huffed but obeyed his slightly older sister, grudgingly slipping the wooden sword back into its sheath. "You're such a priss, Go-go, ya know that?"

"She is *not* a priss," Brighton defended.

"Oh no?" Fiske, the self-proclaimed jester of the royal brood, gave each of his sisters a wicked grin. "Well, if she's not, then she won't care if I do *this!*" With that, he flung out a paw and snatched the pretty ribbon right off Go-go's head.

"Give that back!" Go-go commanded.

"Give it back, Fiskey!" shrieked Brighton to her twin.

"Hah!" cried Fiske. "Make me!"

The scuffle resumed in full force. From the doorway, Hopper and Hope watched in amazement as the three heirs tumbled over one another, squirming, pounding, nipping, and kicking.

"*Now* do you see why I don't like the schoolroom?" Hope asked with a sigh.

Hopper had to admit, he didn't blame her. "It is a bit rowdy."

Fiske had now succeeded in maneuvering his weapon so that it was pressed to the tip of Brighton's nose. Brighton pinched him hard on the snout, and Go-go used this distraction as her opening to surprise Fiske, grabbing her ribbon out of his thieving claws.

Unfortunately, Fiske was fast and spry; he released Brighton but sprung at Go-go and wrestled her to the ground. Brighton flung herself on top of the brawling pair so that the three of them were once again fighting with all their might.

"Enough!" came a bold voice from the corner.

The word brought the action to an instantaneous halt, even before the echo of this confident command had faded to silence. With guilty expressions the siblings untangled themselves and scrambled to their feet, brushing off jerkins, straightening petticoats, and righting bent whiskers.

"Now they're in for it," Hope whispered.

But the cease-fire directive had not come from the siblings' schoolmaster. Nor had it come from their father, Zucker, or their mother, the fierce and lovely Firren. The demand had been uttered by Verrazano, the second oldest royal sibling, who was now strutting out of his shadowy corner to frown at his littermates. Raz proudly donned a smaller version of the purple-and-silver tunic worn by Zucker's soldiers. He had inherited his father's height and bulk, as well as his mother's intensity. Young as he was, he cut an imposing figure there among the rest of the rumpled heirs, who had now fallen into a crooked line and were all staring down at their paws or flicking their tails in nervous anticipation of a much-deserved scolding.

Raz folded his arms and walked slowly along the line, sizing up his siblings like a five-star general examining his troops. Then he made a *tsk tsk* sound and shook his head. "This conduct is unbecoming," he declared. "How will we ever defeat our enemies if we can't keep peace amongst ourselves?"

"What enemies?" Gowanus asked. "Everybody loves us!"

Verrazano rolled his eyes. "The schoolmaster will be here any minute," he continued. "Now, all three of you to your desks. When he arrives, we will stand and greet him in a polite and civilized manner. Is that understood?"

"Understood," his siblings mumbled. They shuffled off to their respective seats and bent their heads low over their books and lessons. Raz gave a satisfied nod.

Then he noticed Hopper and Hope in the doorway. He immediately executed an elegant bow.

"Chosen One," he said in a noble tone. "It is inspiring indeed to have such a valiant mouse in our humble schoolroom."

From her desk, Brighton made a face. "Oh, brother."

Hopper had to laugh.

A commotion in the hallway announced the arrival of another visitor: their father. Hopper could hear the flurry of salutations, the clicking of heavy boots, and the rustle of skirts as soldiers stood at attention and maids curtsied to their liege. Zucker's own booming voice rang along the corridor as he greeted his staff, replied to queries, and granted favors.

"Daddy's here!" cried Go-go.

"Don't you think you should call him 'Highness'?" Raz admonished.

"Don't you think you should mind your own business?" Go-go shot back.

When Zucker strode into the schoolroom, Hope jumped into his arms and he caught her effortlessly.

"I see you've been playing dress-up in your grandmamma's old wardrobe again," he said, watching as she adjusted her tiara, which had slipped down over her eye.

"It's not *playing* dress-up when you're an actual princess," she informed her father sweetly. "It's just being dressed."

"Honestly, Hope, the way you and Raz cling to the old ways is positively archaic," Brighton challenged. "You pretend to be so fancy and regal!"

"Be nice, Brighton," Zucker chided. "Your brother and sister are entitled to their opinion. If they want to play prince and princess, there's nothing wrong with that. As long as they know our real government functions differently now."

"Yes, but how am I supposed to concentrate with all those diamonds and ruffles all over the place?" Brighton huffed. She removed her faux eyeglasses and polished them on the hem of her simple cotton school dress. "It's impossible to focus without all that . . . what do you call it, Hope? *Zing*?"

"Bling," Hope corrected. "And speak for yourself! I like my bling!"

"It's not yours, it's grandmamma's, dumb-dumb!" said Go-go.

Furious, Hope flung out a paw and pointed accusingly at her siblings. "They were fighting, Daddy!" she reported.

"Were they, now?" Zucker tried to frown but couldn't quite manage it. Hopper knew the emperor was never happier than when he was in the presence of his family—even if they were misbehaving. Sometimes Hopper thought his friend was secretly amused when the children showed their mischievous streak. After all, the Zuck-meister had always been something of a misbehaver himself.

"You know your mother and I don't approve of fighting in the classroom," said Zucker.

"We're sorry, Pop," mumbled Fiske, tossing Hope a withering look. "Tattletale!"

"She's only telling the truth," Verrazano pointed out. "You *were* breaking the rules."

"Then why didn't you tell on them?" Hope asked.

"Well . . ." Raz squirmed. "Because *I'm* not a tattletale. Nobody likes a tattletale."

Hope stuck out her tongue.

"Oh, that's nice," scoffed Raz. "Way to not act like a princess!"

"Even so…," Zucker went on, his gaze sweeping over the classroom. "Perhaps an extra-long and difficult lesson in sword craft is in order today." He suggested this in a reproachful tone that, to Hopper, sounded incredibly forced. "Ya know . . . as punishment for your shenanigans."

A grumble of misery rolled through the room. Only Raz looked pleased.

"That would be punishment for everyone but Verrazano," Hope reminded her father.

"Then Raz will get an extra-long and difficult lesson in tunnel geography," Zucker pronounced.

Raz gave Hope a look of pure fury.

"And another thing, Daddy," Hope added. "Go-go sent a love letter to a boy she met last week at one of mother's speeches at the new school site. And guess what else! Brighton helped her write it and Fiske delivered it for her because—"

"All right, little one," said Zucker, placing a gentle paw to Hope's lips. "I know you're trying to be helpful, but I agree with Raz. Nobody likes a tattletale."

"But I wasn't being a tattletale," she said, waylaid by the accusation. "I was just being a truth teller."

"Same thing," Fiske huffed under his breath.

"Not *exactly*," said Raz, taking pity on Hope. "But it's still annoying."

"Hope's a baby," Go-go whispered to Fiske. "A big *hope*less baby. I wish she'd just go away and leave us alone."

Hopper felt the words pierce his heart like the point of a dagger. His own sister, Pinkie, used to say similarly cruel things to him.

Lip trembling, Hope pressed her face into Zucker's shoulder.

"That was unkind, Gowanus," Zucker said sternly.

"I'm sorry," Go-go mumbled. "But that little runt is always getting us in trouble!"

"She's so annoying!" Brighton agreed.

With Hope's face still buried in her father's fur, her shoulders began to shake.

"She always sneaks around and hides and watches us," Fiske complained, "and we don't notice because she's so much littler than we are. Then she goes back and tells you and Mother what we've been doing."

"She's practically a spy!" Brighton confirmed.

"Well, then," said Zucker, "perhaps one day our little Hope can put her espionage talents to good use as a member of the Atlantian Intelligence Agency, like my pal Ketchum."

Hope's head popped up from Zucker's shoulder, her eyes wide. "Really, Father?" she asked, wiping the tears from her sweet, furry face. "I can work for Uncle Ketch and be a secret agent? I can be a spy?"

"You can't be anything," Brighton interrupted, "if

you don't study. So can we all please quiet down and get on with our assignments?"

"That sounds like an excellent idea," said Hopper, hoping to be helpful.

At that moment, the stooped and quivery old rat who was their tutor toddled into the room.

As Raz had instructed, the students stood up and offered a polite greeting.

Zucker placed Hope back on her feet and gave her a gentle nudge toward the one empty desk. "Go along, now," he said softly.

And don't let them push you around, Hopper added silently as his godchild scampered to her seat.

Now Zucker turned a serious look to the Chosen One. "Let's go, kid," the emperor said. "You and I have an appointment in the Strategic Planning Area."

"We do?" This was the first Hopper was hearing of it. "An appointment with whom?"

Zucker let out a long sigh. "A certain testy, golden-caped leader of the Mūs, that's who." He gave Hopper's shoulder a comforting pat. "Also known as . . . your sister."

CHAPTER FOUR

I ARRIVE AT THE FOOT *of the palace steps with a note of great significance—a message for the Chosen One with important news about his brother. I would go in, but my comings and goings about the palace are complicated now, to say the least, and lately I am forced to time my visits carefully to avoid suspicion. So I wait, clutching my letter and hoping that an opportunity to deliver it will present itself.*

This note explains what I have only recently learned: that the outlaw Pup is nearby and prepared to make a move. The particular details of this move I have outlined with great care, as I want the Chosen One and the Emperor to be very clear about Pup's present frame of mind. Much depends on it.

I do not have to wait long. Soon a contingent of four pink-clad Mūs soldiers march up, their leader being the honorable General DeKalb. There is a female soldier among them, and she carries a sketch (for reference and comparison, I would imagine) of the one I myself coined the "tiny villain." The black marking around his eye is visible in the drawing, the one I described in that same prophecy as the "circle of doom."

The Mūs presence here indicates that the powers that be have at last decided to double their efforts with regard to Pup's threat. All the more reason for me to bring my new intelligence to their attention (oh, how I wish I could do it in person, but that is too risky). While they have been patiently waiting for Pup to make his intentions known, I have taken a more proactive (albeit surreptitious) approach. I have been tailing him. And I have been listening.

It is all explained in my letter, and as the Mūs soldiers mount the stairs, I realize that my timing could not have been better. I pull my hooded cloak close around me and approach the last soldier in line—one who is slightly darker in color than the others, and who has a most determined expression on his face.

"If you please, Private," I say, disguising my voice out of habit. "Are you here to see the emperor and empress of Atlantia?"

"I am."

"Might I impose upon you, then, to deliver this missive? It is of a dire nature, to be sure, and I know I can trust you to deliver it safely into their paws. The Chosen One, too, will take an interest in the contents of this note, so please do see to it that he is made aware of it."

The Mūs soldier eyes me with great interest, attempting to peer into the shadow of my hood. Then he unfolds my note and reads it but shows no emotion. I can't quite translate his reaction; he appears to be thinking. After a moment, he tucks the note into the breast pocket of his pink uniform jacket.

"Thank you," he says. "This information will be more useful than you know."

With that, he hurries to follow his compatriots into the palace.

I linger there at the foot of the steps, anxious to see what, if anything, will come of the news.

CHAPTER FIVE

WHEN THEY ARRIVED AT THE Strategic Planning Area—a room in the palace dedicated to military concerns—Hopper was pleasantly surprised to see that Pinkie had not come to Atlantia alone. She'd brought their father, the bold and virtuous Dodger, along with her.

"Father!" Hopper ran to accept a hug from the mouse who, like Hopper, boasted a pure white circle of fur around his right eye. Pinkie had a white marking as well, though hers encircled her left eye. It was a unique family trait that announced them to the world as a trio of very special rodents.

Hopper glanced beyond his father to where his sister sat, strumming her claws on the arm of a chair. As Zucker had mentioned, her shoulders were draped in a shimmering gold cape. To Hopper's surprise (and amusement), she was also wearing a round woolen hat perched between her ears at a jaunty angle. In addition, a gilded chain hung around her neck and from it dangled a burnished charm.

Pinkie had never been one to accessorize before. But what was even stranger to Hopper was her overall bearing. There was something different about Pinkie. . . . She seemed more . . . worldly, somehow.

Seasoned. As though she was seeing the world in a whole new light.

"Hi, Pinkie."

"Greetings, Hopper."

"I like your hat."

"*Merci beaucoup.* It's called a beret, and I had it made for myself after I saw a drawing of one in an old human book I found on one of my recent trips."

"Trips?"

Pinkie nodded.

So she was taking trips now? The bossy little mouse who'd seemed so content to ensconce herself behind the big gray wall of the Mūs village and lord it over the tribe had suddenly developed a yen for travel.

"I've been riding the slithering subway beast far and wide," she informed her brother. "You can't imagine the great distances those monsters are able to travel. Now that Father is helping me oversee the village, I have a little extra time on my paws. So I've been exploring the tunnels. Searching."

"Searching for hats?" Hopper eyed the chain around her neck. "And trinkets?"

"Searching for Pup," Pinkie corrected. "The trinkets are just a bonus." Her paw went to the pendant. "I found this amulet buried deep in a tunnel that runs beneath a borough called Queens."

"Queens, huh?" The only queen Hopper was familiar with was Felina. He imagined an entire city filled with evil white cats and shuddered.

"I have concluded that ancient travelers once believed this to be a lucky charm," Pinkie explained. "An amulet, or a coin, that they offered up to the Great Spirits of Transportation every time they set out on a journey."

"Neat," said Hopper.

"Yeah," said Pinkie, nodding.

But Hopper knew this meeting had nothing to do with Pinkie's new penchant for jewelry and headwear.

He felt a sudden pang of worry as the emperor took a step toward Pinkie, but his concern subsided quickly enough. Although Pinkie and Zucker were once bitter enemies, they had buried the hatchet and were now allies—friends, in fact. Sometimes Hopper still had to remind himself that since reuniting with their father, his sister had become almost likable.

"Have you discovered anything regarding Pup's whereabouts?" Zucker asked.

Pinkie shook her head. "No. Which is why I have decided to send out a search party." Her eyes shot briefly to the solemn Dodger. "The party will be led by General DeKalb, and will include three of my most promising soldiers."

Pinkie clapped her paws once; in the next second the general and his mice were marching into the room. A vision in pink they were, and Hopper had to bite down hard to keep from giggling at the sight of their pastel uniforms. He remembered DeKalb from his first visit to the Mūs village, long before Pinkie redesigned the military regalia to reflect her own colorful name.

The other three soldiers were unfamiliar to Hopper, but for the most part they were all built just like he was: small of stature and plump around their middles with large oval ears and long tails.

Zucker nodded at DeKalb. "Welcome to Atlantia."

"Thank you," said the general, who, being a Mūs, barely came up to Zucker's shoulder. "It will be an honor to serve you."

"Hmmm." Zucker bent a grin at his guest and patted his own chest, where (Hopper knew) a jagged scar lay hidden beneath the indigo-colored jerkin. "That's good to hear, considering the last time we met, you guys tried to kill me."

That was a battle Hopper would never forget. Firren, along with DeKalb and a contingent of Mūs soldiers, had been leading the Chosen One back to Atlantia when Zucker and his soldiers had ambushed them. Zucker had nearly died from the wound he had received.

"A misunderstanding, to be sure," said DeKalb, a slight chuckle in his voice.

"To be sure," echoed Zucker. "I'm just glad to have you on my side this time."

The rat liege and the Mūs general shook paws and laughed.

"I should mention that I have given General DeKalb and his team very specific orders for this mission," said Pinkie, her voice grim.

"Specific?" Hopper gulped. "How specific?" A knot of dread was beginning to form in his stomach.

"I have ordered them to comb every inch of these tunnels in pursuit of Pup. They have my permission to detain any wandering creature for questioning, and anyone who has knowledge of the outlaw's whereabouts or worse, admits to aiding and abetting said outlaw, will be taken into custody for further interrogation."

"That 'outlaw' you speak of happens to be our brother," Hopper reminded her.

"I know that," said Pinkie calmly. "Which is why I have directed the soldiers to refrain from causing him harm." She paused. "Unless absolutely necessary."

"And if it should become 'absolutely necessary,' as you say?" Dodger asked, sounding more sad than angry. "If Pup puts up a fight?"

Hopper could tell that Pinkie took no joy in what she said next:

"Their orders are to bring him back to Atlantia," she said quietly. "Dead or alive."

The room fell silent. Hopper took a step closer to Dodger. He so very much wanted to voice his disapproval, to squeak his complete disagreement with Pinkie's grave directive.

Dead or alive. The words seemed to rumble in the air like thunder.

But deep down, Hopper knew that Pinkie's instructions were sound. If Pup had allowed his soul to harden to ice, if his only objective was to destroy the peace and safety of Atlantia and the Mūs village, then he would have to be stopped by any means necessary.

Hopper felt queasy just thinking about it.

Dodger broke the silence with a heavy sigh. "It pains me to say it, but this is the most appropriate course of action."

"But only if Pup resists," Hopper clarified. "You will take him alive if you possibly can, right, General?"

The Mūs officer gave Hopper a kind smile. "I

promise, Chosen One, that I will do everything in my power to bring your brother back to you unharmed."

The sincerity of DeKalb's promise calmed Hopper a bit. But only a bit.

Now Pinkie introduced the other three soldiers, pointing to each in turn. "This is Pitkin," she announced, indicating the first in line.

Pitkin was slightly burlier than the others; he had a thicker neck and arms. His bulk strained at the seams of his pink military jacket. To Hopper he looked solid and strong, which of course is a very desirable quality in a soldier . . . unless that soldier is going out after one's little brother.

"And this is Wyona," Pinkie continued.

Wyona stood proudly, shoulders pushed back, hind paws firmly planted, her sword shining in its sheath. Hopper liked the way her whiskers curled up at the ends. There was a courageous air about her that made him think of Carroll, and a confidence that rivaled Firren's.

At that moment, as if just thinking about the warrior empress had the power to conjure her, Firren strode into the room.

"Good day to you all," she said as everyone (even Pinkie) bowed to her majesty.

"It is an honor to see you again, Highness," said DeKalb, holding his bow.

"Oh," said Firren with a smile and an embarrassed

little wave. "You don't have to do that. Really. I'm fine with just a friendly hello."

Hopper thought he noticed the third soldier, who had yet to be introduced, stiffen slightly at Firren's arrival; his bow was more of a sudden jerky movement than a graceful show of actual respect. Perhaps he was just nervous, likely having never been in the presence of an empress before, even one who didn't care much for bowing.

"Good day, my darling," said Zucker, kissing the back of Firren's paw. "Pinkie was just filling us in on her plan to send out a search-and-rescue party for Pup."

Hopper knew his friend had chosen to add the word "rescue" for his benefit, and he was grateful.

Zucker held out a chair for his wife. When Firren was settled in her seat, Pinkie nodded toward the third and final soldier.

"Last but not least is Devon. He goes by Dev, and he is the newest member of my personal guard."

Devon stepped forward, beaming under the praise of his leader. "I am most humbled to be here in the esteemed presence of your father, the great Dodger, his friend the emperor Zucker, and most of all . . ." Devon turned slowly until his eyes locked on Firren's. "The legendary and incomparable warrior Firren."

Hopper thought he noticed Wyona roll her eyes. He had to admit, it did sound a bit schmaltzy. Clearly, Dev was something of a suck-up.

"Thank you, Private Devon," said Firren. "That's very nice of you to say." She was smiling, but Hopper noticed how her eyes narrowed slightly as she studied the young solider.

Hopper, too, gave the soldier a closer look. The first thing he noted were his sharp, intelligent eyes, sparking with intensity. Like the others, Devon was small and roundish, but his ears were different. While Pitkin's and Wyona's (and Hopper's own) tilted outward and up, Devon's ears seemed to droop a bit. And his fur was a slightly darker brown. Of course, Hopper didn't think much of this variance in pelt color, since he and his family had become practically synonymous with the highly unusual white markings in their own fur.

When Firren spoke again, her curious gaze was still focused on Devon. "I'm sorry, soldier, but . . . do I . . . *know* you?"

Devon chuckled. "Oh, I think that is highly unlikely, Highness," he said easily. "I would certainly remember crossing paths with royalty."

At this, Firren seemed to relax a bit. She even laughed. "Well, I wasn't always royalty, you know."

"Yes, I know," said Dev. He offered Firren a broad smile that didn't quite reach his eyes.

Just then something outside the window caught Hopper's eye. The old schoolmaster was leading Zucker and Firren's royal brood down the palace steps toward the heart of Atlantia.

Must be a class field trip, Hopper thought absently. He knew Firren was adamant about her children learning all they could about the city they would one day govern, so the occasional walking tour was an important part of their curriculum.

"Now," said Zucker, slapping a crumpled scrap of paper onto the center of the strategic planning table. "Let's talk about Pup."

Hopper looked at the scrap: It was a note from La Rocha, a note Hopper had received right after his encounter with a bleeding Pup in an abandoned wingtip loafer, the day Felina met her tragic but befitting end. The ominous verse contained in the note had forewarned them all that Pup was a villain intent on destroying whatever peace might be restored to the tunnels. It was a prophecy, predicting that this new and vindictive Pup with the dark circle staining his face would surely do everything he could to steal away their hope.

"We've all worked long and hard to get this city up and running again," said Zucker. "We've promised our citizens prosperity and safety, and I for one am not about to go back on that promise. Pinkie has put a terrific strategy in motion with her plan to send these soldiers into the tunnels to find Pup. I only wish we knew where to start looking." He turned to Hopper's father. "Dodge, any ideas?"

Dodger nodded. "A few. I suggest we go back to

that smelly old shoe he'd commandeered the last time he was seen. A sweep of the subway tracks leading from the Mūs village would be wise as well. I would suggest checking the abandoned hunting ground, except the soldiers have done an admirable job of decimating it since the dissolution of Felina's treaty."

At the mention of this, a look of grief flickered across Firren's face. Hopper knew that the memory of hiding in the hunting ground was something that haunted her. As a very small rat she'd been held in the camps and delivered to the hunt as part of one of Titus's so-called "colonization" projects. In reality, she and her family, and many other innocent and unsuspecting rodents, were being sacrificed to the feral cats. Mercifully, Firren had been saved by concealing herself in a silver cup, but sadly, her parents were lost to the appetites of the enemy cats. Hopper didn't know any more than that, but from the depth of the pain he saw in Firren's eyes now, he suspected there was a lot more to her story.

"And another point . . ." Dodger stroked his whiskers thoughtfully and continued. "I don't think we can rule out the possibility that Pup is already here, in the city, watching and waiting."

At this, Hopper's ears pricked up. This had never even occurred to him. Could his tiny brother actually be that close, hiding among them, plotting his revenge? If that were the case, then perhaps Hopper could find him before DeKalb and Dev and the others did. . . . Perhaps violence could be avoided if Hopper had a chance to reason with Pup.

He was about to suggest this to the others, but he caught himself. They would never consent to it—they all believed that Pup was out for blood and would surely forbid Hopper to approach him alone. Fine, then. He'd just have to do it in secret. And the sooner the better. Because somewhere deep in his heart, Hopper still had faith that he could change Pup's mind. Of course, that hadn't worked out too well when he had confronted Pup in the wingtip loafer. But that didn't mean he couldn't hope.

Hope. The word, the name, gave him an idea. He had to get out of this meeting and into the city to search for his brother without letting anyone know what he was about, and Hope would be his alibi.

"Pardon," he said suddenly, "but I must leave."

Pinkie scrunched an eyebrow low and scowled at him. "What could you possibly have to do that's more important than this?" she demanded. "We're planning an enemy takedown here, Hopper, not a potluck supper."

Hopper gave his sister a glowing smile. "Actually, if we do find Pup, I think a potluck supper would be a lovely way to celebrate. For now, I have an errand to run in the city."

"An errand?" said Firren.

Hopper nodded. "I made a promise to my godchild, and I'm not about to disappoint her." He reached out to shake Zucker's paw, then gave Dodger a hug. "Now, if you'll all excuse me, I have to see a chipmunk about a whirligig."

Chapter Six

I HAVE LINGERED ABOUT THE *palace steps for the better part of the morning, waiting to see if my note—with its crucial information—would inspire any immediate action. I am just preparing to leave when the palace doors open.*

But it is not a group of soldiers, spurred on by my letter, marching out on the hunt to locate Pup.

It's the royal heirs.

I smile as I watch them taking to the streets of Atlantia with excitement and pride. This is their city and each has a vested interest in seeing it grow, thrive, and prosper. They are the future of this place. Each one is dear to my heart, and has been since the moment of their birth.

They follow their tutor, and my eyes follow them until they disappear into Atlantia, scampering away in a disorderly but exuberant line.

I glance up again to the window and see that Hopper, too, has spotted the children setting out. His eyes light with joy at the sight of them.

But there is still no visible reaction to my news. Perhaps the meeting's agenda is full and they have not gotten to it yet. Odd, since it is of such an important nature.

Suddenly the Chosen One bursts excitedly through the palace doors and bounds down the steps. The glint in his eyes tells me he is on a mission.

This leads me to believe that my information has been delivered after all! For what, besides the news contained in my note, could have inspired such zeal in Hopper?

This development frees me to occupy myself with a far more entertaining pursuit.

I will follow these darling children on their excursion.

I keep to the shadows, as always, and watch as this most celebrated of litters explores the city. Verrazano marches with his head high, like the soldier he hopes one day to be. He holds his sword ever at the ready, not because he anticipates danger but simply because he loves the feel of it in his paw. He is most gifted when it comes to wielding a blade. Pretty Gowanus turns this way and that, batting her eyes at the smitten young rats who gaze at her with dreamy eyes and blush when she bestows a smile. Fiske is his usual comical self, pretending to stumble over things, barking out silly observations, and expertly juggling pebbles to the delight of his sisters. But when he is not being a clown, he studies his surroundings with the eye of a philosopher; perhaps I, La Rocha, will one day be looking to him for mystical insight and guidance. Brighton—oh, Brighton, our bespectacled little scholar—has her tiny pink nose in the guidebook her tutor has provided. She takes notes on his every word, eager to learn all there is to know about the history, architecture, and politics of our fair city.

Tagging along at the end of the line comes Hope. My heart swells just to see her, small but healthy, determined to keep up with her siblings. Her entrance into this world was a difficult one and for this reason she will always hold a special place in my heart. She alone is dressed as a royal, in a cut-down version of an old ball gown, and her prized possession, the former empress Conselyea's tiara.

The tutor shows them the market square where not too long ago their grandfather Titus stood in chains, owning up to his evil deeds and offering his apology to a widely unforgiving crowd. When they pass by the library and the medical center, I realize that their schoolmaster is leading them to Fulton's forge.

Fulton has created every sword Zucker has ever owned. He labors on the outskirts of Atlantia, for safety's sake since his fires burn incessantly; to have his shop any closer to the buildings (some of which are fashioned of cardboard human castoffs) would be much too dangerous.

I follow the class as they hurry toward the sound of heavy hammering, of hot metal hissing and spitting as it cools.

Hissing and spitting. Funny how a newborn sword makes the same sounds as an angry cat.

"Good afternoon, Fulton," says the schoolmaster.

The stocky swordsmith looks up from his anvil, his fur damp with sweat. "Young majesties!" he booms in a jovial voice. "Welcome to my forge!"

Around him, flames blaze.

"Hello, Uncle Fulton," says Gowanus to the large, soot-stained rat.

Fiske makes an elaborate show of dragging his paw across his forehead. "Hot enough for ya?" he quips. Then he observes, somewhat incongruently (but that is his nature), "If only we could conceive of a world in which we had no need for weaponry. Rats living in peace with all creatures. This should be our goal."

"It is," Raz reminds him. "That's what the emperor and empress are working toward."

"They don't like to be called that," Go-go reminds him.

"Uncle Fulton," says Brighton, motioning toward a fire pit. "Precisely what temperature is required to melt steel?" She makes this inquiry with her quill poised over her notebook, ready to add this information to her ever-growing store of knowledge.

"Who cares?" says Raz. "As long as the sword comes out razor-sharp and pointy. Speaking of which, Uncle Fulton, my blade could use a sharpening."

"I don't like swords," says Hope. She is watching in wonder as the fabric tent above the smithy shop flutters and swells, billowing upward every time one of the fires flares up. "Why does that happen?" she asks. "There isn't any breeze down here."

Brighton gives her sister a condescending sneer. "Because hot air is lighter than cool air, so when the flames increase, the increase in temperature causes the tent to lift." She lets out a disgusted snort. "Everybody knows that!"

"Everybody but Hopeless," jokes Go-go. "She doesn't know anything."

I wish I could scold her for her cruelty. Her tutor should reprimand her, but he hasn't even heard Gowanus's unkind comment, due to the fact that the old rat is rather hard of hearing. Clearly, he is also severely myopic. Because he doesn't notice when Hope, sniffling and sad, slips quietly away from the group and dashes back toward the city.

But I do.

I follow the little princess all the way from the smithy shop to the palace, and still none of her siblings come looking for her. It isn't any wonder, since they mostly just consider her to be a nuisance. And that half-blind old schoolmaster is not at all qualified to supervise five sprightly young royals.

So from my anonymous distance, I see the youngest heir safely home. I watch as she stomps up the palace steps and slams the heavy door behind her. I suspect she will go straight to her bedchamber to fling herself onto her bed and sob into her royal pillow. And who could blame her? Her brothers and sisters treat her with such cruelty! My own two brothers were never unkind to me when we were growing up, and I have always been thankful for that. But Hope is not so lucky. Maybe she has gone to the kitchens to drown her sorrows in a plate of warm cookies fresh from the oven. She has been known to charm the royal chefs out of such treats on several occasions.

Perhaps while I have been off following the heirs around the city, the soldiers in their whimsical pink uniforms have

set out to begin their search for Pup. Or perhaps Hopper himself has located him. I suppose I will find out soon enough.

I suppose we all will. I only hope the news will be good. For I have lived long enough in these tunnels to know that even when things seem to be going as hoped, obstacles, misunderstandings, and even intentional evil can scuttle the best-laid plans. I, for one, shall not rest until this situation has been brought to a satisfying conclusion.

With Hope now safely back inside the castle, I decide that I am long overdue in paying a visit to the runes. The state of the tunnels improves daily, but the wandering rodents always welcome new words of inspiration to guide them. Today I know exactly what I shall write to calm their fears and give them hope. It will be the very same message I sent, via the soldier, to Hopper and the others.

PUP IS NO LONGER A THREAT.
HE IS TRULY SORRY AND WISHES
TO COME HOME.
THINK OF HIM NOT AS A VILLAIN
BUT AS A FRIEND.

CHAPTER SEVEN

HOPPER SCOURED THE CITY. He searched every corner, every market stall, and every partially rebuilt building in search of his brother. He asked merchants and construction workers if they had seen an extra-small sand-colored mouse, with a marking like a storm cloud around his eye. But of course this only succeeded in frightening them.

"Is this the 'tiny villain' you speak of?" asked a chipmunk, halting his hammer in mid-swing. "The one from La Rocha's warning?"

"Um, well . . . technically . . . yes," Hopper sputtered. "But if I can just find him and talk to him . . ."

The chipmunk was already packing up his tools. "I must alert my mate. We must bring our young ones to safety."

"No!" cried Hopper. "That's not necessary at all. Believe me, I won't let him hurt anyone. I just need to find him."

But the chipmunk was on the run, his tool belt jangling as he scampered for home.

This simply would not do. If Hopper continued to ask about Pup, he would alarm the entire city. It would be chaos.

He decided he would continue his search, but he would keep his questions to himself.

As he made his way through the city, he heard snatches of conversations, whispers among the citizens that Pinkie had just sent out a small band of her most trusted soldiers to search for her wayward brother, in hopes of ending the threat and bringing him to justice.

"Good news travels fast," Hopper muttered to himself, listening as similar discussions swept from city worker to market vendor to mousewife. Some of these citizens seemed fearful of Pup's wrath; others were comforted by the fact that an active military search was now underway. But one thing was certain: if DeKalb and his corps did manage to bring Pup back alive, no banquets would be thrown in his honor, as Titus had done for Hopper. Within the sturdy walls of Atlantia, Pup would surely be a most unwelcome guest.

Hopper moved from street to street, searching the shops and parks, but found no sign of Pup. When he happened upon a field mouse and a gray squirrel outside the barber shop and overheard their heated debate about what should be done to Pup if, in fact, he were captured, he stopped to listen. He was so wrapped up in his eavesdropping that he didn't even notice the tiny rat rushing past him until he had stepped on her tail.

"Ouch!"

"Oh, I'm so sorry!" cried Hopper. When he looked

down, he was surprised to see that the tail in question belonged to Hope.

"Uncle Hopper!" she squeaked, fumbling awkwardly with the hefty bundle she was carrying.

"Hope? What are you doing here all by yourself? I thought you were with the schoolmaster, touring the city."

A guilty look flashed across Hope's tiny face. "I . . . uh . . . I guess I wasn't paying attention," she confessed, "and I got separated from the group." She lowered her head in shame, causing her tiara to slide slightly askew between her dainty ears.

There was nothing unusual about the presence of the tiara, but that bundle she clutched so tightly gave Hopper pause. The way she'd folded it up made it look almost like a sleeping bag. It took Hopper a moment to realize that Hope had fashioned it out of the patchwork quilt he himself had sewn using scraps of fabric he'd collected as mementos. The Atlantian army had marched out under that flag on the day they'd defeated Queen Felina. How in the world Hope had come to have it, he couldn't guess. And why had she turned it into a bedroll? And what was with all her nervous squeaking?

He would have asked, but at the moment, he was far too preoccupied with overhearing the grumbling field mouse and squirrel to completely process his concerns. The barber had come out of his shop to join them now, stating decisively that "hanging was too good for the likes of Pup." The squirrel (whose whiskers were in serious need of a trim) seemed to be in full agreement, although the field mouse looked as though he possessed at least some small measure of sympathy for Pup.

Hope's voice interrupted his eavesdropping.

"I'm going to find the schoolmaster right now!" she assured her uncle. "I think they're over on the north side of the city, observing the construction of the new monument honoring those rodents who lost their lives during the Battle of the Camps. It's a history lesson. Or maybe civics? Engineering, possibly. Whichever. I'm heading right over there."

Hopper, straining to hear the gray squirrel's perspective on Pup's punishment, merely nodded. "Good girl, Hope," he said vaguely, still training his ears on the conversation outside the barber shop. "Be careful. Watch for speeding carts."

"Yes, Uncle Hopper," said Hope, quickly adjusting her dainty crown and hoisting her patchwork bundle onto her shoulder. "Well, I'd better hurry before the schoolmaster notices I'm gone."

"Gone . . . right . . ." Hopper squinted at the barber, who was now flailing his arms in agitation while the field mouse shook his head and stomped his paws in disagreement.

Suddenly Hope threw her arms around Hopper

and squeezed with all her might. "I love you, Uncle Hopper," she whispered against his midsection. "Don't ever forget that."

Then the tiny rat let go and ran off as fast as her little legs could carry her.

Hopper was about to call after her that she was heading the wrong way—east, toward the city's main entrance with its immense iron gate. The battle memorial, as she herself had just mentioned, was being built on the north side of the city.

But just then a scrawny chipmunk approached the barber and his customers to offer *his* thoughts on the Pup debacle.

"I say we tar and feather the little traitor!" the chipmunk hollered.

Hopper's stomach soured at the thought of it; he was glad that tar was not readily available here in the tunnels. For that matter, feathers were in short supply as well.

And besides, the Chosen One had searched high and low, far and wide, and as best he could tell, his angry, misguided little brother was presently nowhere to be found within the boundaries of Atlantia. Hopper took some comfort in knowing that if there were to be any tarring and/or feathering, it wouldn't be happening anytime soon.

With a heavy heart he turned and headed back to the palace.

CHAPTER EIGHT

PUP HAD SEETHED.

He had stomped his paws and bared his claws and tugged at his whiskers in frustration. He had pouted and complained and made rash choices based on anger and fueled by an inflated sense of his own capabilities.

Back at the Mūs village—how long ago, it seemed—Pinkie had refused to provide him with a uniform. She had humiliated him. But he recognized now that her refusal was not because she didn't believe in him. It was because she knew that he was not yet ready for such responsibility. Moreover, she had wanted to keep him safe. And how had he responded?

He had abandoned her. Escaped.

Now he understood that it hadn't been an "escape" so much as a desertion. After all, one only escapes from a bad situation. And what Pup had known under Pinkie's care had not been bad at all. He'd only convinced himself it was.

It had taken some time and an arduous journey, but he'd finally realized how wrong his perception had been. Now all he wanted was to go home.

Home. Once a nest of aspen curls in a rusting cage on a counter in Keep's pet shop, upland in a world called Brooklyn. Then, briefly, a comfortable barracks in a well-run and seemingly friendly camp that, in reality, had hidden a brutal and ugly secret.

Most recently home had been a gargantuan black steel engine buried deep in the earth behind a gray brick wall in the center of the safe and welcoming Mūs village. But Pup had thrown that away because he had bristled at the thought of being loved and protected and cared for.

Imagine! The idiocy of wanting to forsake such comfort just to prove that he could fend for himself. In fact, he *had* managed to survive in the tunnels for more days and weeks than he could count. But what did he have to show for it, save a single friend and ruined ear?

Pup gazed into the distance at Atlantia, and all his pride and bravado melted away. He had not succeeded in killing Felina, but that didn't matter anymore. What mattered was that he desperately wanted to apologize to his family and help them reach their goal of bringing safety to both the Mūs village and Atlantia. No longer would he shrug off Hopper's assistance, or resent Pinkie's authority. Pup wasn't ready for authority, not yet. If he'd proven anything, he'd proven that. Authority, autonomy, maturity . . . These were things one grew into. One couldn't simply claim self-sufficiency; one had to earn it.

Protection sounded awfully good to Pup right now. A pair of loving arms to enfold him, a wise sibling to educate him, a hot meal, a warm bed . . . All these things added together meant home.

And now, it seemed, home would be Atlantia.

But only if Atlantia would have him.

Hacklemesh stood beside him on a sloping knoll overlooking the city. Below, they could see the wall that encircled Atlantia with its gleaming iron gate. Pup, of course, knew nothing of the history of this gate—he was unaware that it was the place where his father, Dodger, had first met the young prince Zucker and together they'd set a revolution in motion; he had no idea that it was also the portal through which his brother had entered in utter terror and ignorance only to learn that he was the Chosen One of a proud mouse tribe and that he had a magnificent destiny to fulfill.

Gazing at the entrance now, Pup knew that the imposing iron gate would lead him either to salvation . . .

. . . or to doom.

But this was a risk he was willing to take. Because Pup, the upland pet shop mouse, was ready to accept full responsibility for his actions and tell whosoever would listen that he was sorry to the depths of his soul. The only balm that might soothe the ache of his regret was forgiveness. And forgiveness, he dearly hoped, was just inside that gate.

"I assume there's a warrant out for my arrest, Hack,"

Pup whispered to his arachnid companion. "Do you think I should try to disguise myself and make my way to the palace, where I can turn myself in directly to Hopper? Or perhaps it would be better to just present myself at that big old gate and announce my surrender. . . . With any luck, I'll be able to get the words out before the guards have a chance to draw their swords."

Hack blinked his many eyes and raised one craggy leg, pointing to the gate.

"You think I should just give myself up to the guard?"

Hack's expression said that this was exactly what he thought.

"Well, it's as good a plan as any," said Pup on a long sigh. "I guess it'll work . . . that is, if they don't kill me before I get a chance to open my mouth."

Hacklemesh, as always, was silent.

"Might as well get to it," said Pup, trying to sound brave. With a deep breath he drew himself up to his full height, and took the first step in the direction of Atlantia.

Then he stopped.

Not because he had changed his mind.

But because there was a blade pressed to his back.

A voice came out of the darkness, close to his ear; a voice that was very familiar to him:

"You are under arrest," said General DeKalb, "by order of Emperor Zucker and Pinkie the Chosen."

Pup heard the scrape and whistle of three more swords being drawn and wondered if this moment would be his last. In point of fact, he wouldn't blame these Mūs soldiers if they ran him through without another word.

But the tip of DeKalb's sword did not press deeper into his pelt; no attempt, for the moment at least, was being made to harm him.

This was a good sign.

There was a long pause, and then the steady pressure of the blade against his fur softened, as did the general's tone.

"Will you come quietly, Pup?" he asked. It was as much a plea as a question. DeKalb, Pup realized, had no wish to kill him. His heart bloomed with hope.

Slowly he raised his paws above his head in a gesture of compliance. "Yes, General," he said. "I will absolutely come qui—"

But before he could finish this heartfelt surrender, he sensed a flash of motion to his right; in the next second he felt something warm and liquid splatter across his back.

Blood.

Pup was knocked to his knees in the dirt, blinded by the dust swirling wildly under four pairs of stomping boots.

"Hack, run!" he commanded, fearing his friend

might be injured in this unexplained scuffle. Pup was small, but Hacklemesh was even smaller and, despite the strength of his spider silk, far more fragile than a rodent. "Run! Now!"

He felt Hack's hesitation, the pull of loyalty keeping him close. Eight frightened eyes blinked with indecision, but Pup refused to allow his friend to be hurt on his behalf.

"Run!" Pup cried. "Save yourself."

To his relief, he heard the delicate patter of eight slender legs as Hack fled the scene. As Pup turned his head to watch the spider disappear into the murky distance, a subway train screamed past, its headlight brightening the tunnel. And as a part of that brilliance, he could have sworn he saw a glinting prism of colored light trembling against the tile of the tunnel wall.

In the silence that followed the thundering of the train, he thought he heard a gasp. A tiny, far-off gasp. But this was not the time to think about who or what might be lurking in the shadows, because right around him a battle had erupted. Pup kept low, closing his eyes and covering his head. He had no idea what was happening. He hadn't resisted DeKalb's arrest. He hadn't so much as flinched or frowned. To the contrary . . . he'd offered himself as a compliant captive. So what had gone wrong?

Above him he heard a deep grunt, followed by a

yowl of pain. DeKalb fell, landing with a sickening thud beside him.

"Dev, have you gone mad?" came a voice Pup thought he recognized.

The answer was the whistle of a sword slicing through the air, then another dull thump as a second rodent fell facedown in the dirt on Pup's other side. Pup opened one eye—just a slit. The victim was close enough so that Pup could make out the nametag pinned to his uniform: PITKIN.

Pup closed his eye again fast; his head spun. He knew Pitkin; he was one of Pinkie's most valued soldiers. So it had been Pitkin's voice he had heard, challenging this unknown Dev.

Now a female voice cried out in a growl of fury. "Drop your weapon, Devon!" she screamed. "Drop it immediately!"

Wyona, he thought. Another member of Pinkie's personal guard. One of the bravest and most talented, if he recalled.

Wyona's demand was met with brittle laughter.

"That's just not how this is going to go, Wy," came a cold voice. *Dev.*

"I will run you through," Wyona assured him, "if you don't stand down this instant."

There was a sharp crack. Metal on bone. Wynona fell, landing in a heap just beyond DeKalb.

Pup was going to be sick.

Worse: he was going to be killed.

Shaking, he kept his eyes squeezed shut and braced himself for a sword to the back. But instead of the hiss of a swinging blade, he heard the sound of footsteps, circling him, slow and menacing.

Deciding he had nothing to lose, he opened his eyes and lifted his head.

And there above him loomed Dev, smartly dressed in Pinkie's pink military regalia, buttons shining, epaulets shimmering with fringe. His boots were polished to a high gleam.

And his face . . . looked astonishingly friendly.

"Sorry about that, Pup," said the soldier, holding out a paw. "Here, let me help you up."

For one crazy moment, Pup thought he might be hallucinating, for in addition to the bewildering sight of Dev's outstretched paw, he thought he spied another pale splash of light, shimmering on the tunnel wall and ceiling.

"It's all very disturbing, I know," said Dev breezily. "But I had to do it. You see, they were traitors. All of them."

"Traitors?" Pup took hold of the stranger's paw and stood, giving himself a moment to let this incredible accusation sink in. "Wyona and Pitkin?" He stared at the fallen soldiers with wide eyes. "I . . . I can't believe it."

Dev's face was somber.

"And General DeKalb?" Pup shook his head in disbelief. "That's just not possible. I refuse to accept it. I need to talk to Pinkie. And Hopper. Right now." Gathering his courage, he took one purposeful stride in the direction of the Atlantian gate. But Dev caught hold of him before he could take a second step, clutching his arm and stopping him in his tracks. When Pup whirled to face him, he saw an urgency in the soldier's expression.

"Listen to me, Pup. I have just saved you from a terrible fate. Pinkie sent us out from the palace at Atlantia to find you. Her orders—as far as Hopper and the emperor and that haughty, self-important wife of his were aware—were for DeKalb to bring you back alive. But you know Pinkie. She had her own designs."

Pup felt his whiskers begin to quiver. "What kind of designs?" he asked, his voice hollow.

"She wants you dead. She gave us this order in secret, long before our meeting with the Atlantian delegation. She told us to ignore whatever she might say when we met with the Chosen One and the others, because she'd only be lying to appease them." Now Dev gave Pup a grin. "She's always been a sneaky one, that Pinkie, hasn't she?"

Pup could only nod.

"Pup, you embarrassed your sister when you ran off like you did. She loathed the idea of the Mūs thinking she was unable to exert control over someone so puny and harmless as you. Her words, not mine. The point is, you made a fool of her, so she vowed to destroy you." Dev surprised Pup with a chuckle. "Only fair, I suppose, since you had already vowed to destroy . . . well, basically everyone else."

Pup bowed his head, ashamed, and he felt his knees buckle; suddenly he was back on the ground again, his shoulders shaking as he sobbed. This was too much to take in. "I don't understand. Why did DeKalb ask me to come quietly, then? Why didn't he just run me through and be done with it?"

"Ah, well, that brings us to the traitorous part of our story. DeKalb, as it turns out, is no fan of Firren's—"

"Firren?" Pup interrupted. "You mean Pinkie's?"

"Right." Devon's face flushed beneath his fur. "Yes, yes, of course I meant Pinkie." He took a deep breath, then gave another mirthless cackle. "DeKalb was no fan of *Pinkie's*. And do you blame him? I mean, she really can be something of a pink nightmare when she wants to, can't she?"

He would get no argument from Pup on that point.

"DeKalb's plan was actually quite ingenious," Devon continued.

"What *was* his plan?" Pup asked.

"To disobey Pinkie and keep you alive."

At this, Pup felt a small flutter of gratitude. "So DeKalb was acting in my best interests."

Dev snorted. "Hardly. One does not become the most powerful general in an army without being possessed of certain self-serving tendencies. His counterplan was to keep you alive because your hatred of Pinkie and Hopper could be of use to him. He wanted to overthrow both the Mūs village *and* Atlantia. Pit and Wy were behind him in this, and his hope was to enlist you as well."

"Me?"

"Well, you'd already made your enmity known, hadn't you? DeKalb intended to use that to his advantage. He would let you continue to terrorize the tunnels, causing all the trouble, taking all the risks. You would blaze forth with all your rancor and determination and set the coup in motion, then he and his cohorts would sweep in and take all the glory. He was giddy over the thought of seeing Pinkie driven out from behind that big gray wall in a giant pink cloud of disgrace."

"Pinkie would have hated that," Pup remarked.

"And his plot to destroy Atlantia was even uglier," Dev explained, "because he wouldn't have merely banished the emperor and empress. He wanted to see them suffer. Zucker would go quickly, but Firren's end would come slowly; he would listen to her cry out for help, knowing that not a single paw would reach forth to save her. For once, these tunnels would not echo with the sound of her arrogant battle cry . . .

'Aye, aye, aye!'" Dev curled his mouth back to show his pointy teeth. "Then the victor would be free to rule the tunnels, with absolute power over every rodent who dwells here." He examined the lethal edge of his sword. "Oh, and did I mention that when all was said and done, he would have killed you, too?"

"Who would?"

"The victor."

"DeKalb?"

Dev just smiled an icy smile.

Pup swallowed hard. "No. You didn't mention that."

"That was the plan, Pup. DeKalb was going to trick you into joining forces with him, then betray you just as he betrayed Pinkie, Hopper, Zucker, and . . . Firren."

The empress's name trembled in the air as Devon began to circle him again, in lazy, unhurried strides.

"Can we go back to Atlantia?" Pup pleaded. "I want to see my brother and sister. I want to make amends."

Devon let out a long rush of breath. "Nothing would make me happier than to reunite you with your family, Pup. You see, I know how important family can be, and how much one yearns for them when they are gone."

"Good. Let's go."

Again, Dev caught Pup's arm and held him back. "Unfortunately . . . this new turn of events does present something of a bigger problem." He nodded toward the three dead guards. "I'm sure that Pinkie will blame you for these deaths. Even after I explain to her that it wasn't you."

Pup's heart sank in his chest. "She can't falsely accuse me of something and then punish me for it, can she?"

"My, my, you are a bit slow on the uptake, aren't you?" Dev snickered. "Of course she can. Don't you know, Pup, that you can't fight City Hall?" He spoke these words as if they were some kind of inside joke.

"City Hall?" Pup repeated.

"What I mean is that Pinkie is in charge. She, for all intents and purposes, *is* City Hall." Again, Dev's eyes twinkled as if there was some dark humor behind his choice of words. "And she'll use that power to get what she wants."

Dev was right. If Pinkie wanted him out of the picture, she could charge him with these deaths and use the crime as an excuse to publicly execute her own brother.

"It does sound like something Pinkie would do," Pup acknowledged. His stomach rolled over and his mind whirled in search of a solution. "What should I do, Devon?"

Dev gave him a piteous look. But before the soldier could explain further, he was interrupted by the sound of a faint scuffling along the wall. His ears pricked up as he yanked his sword fully out of its sheath. His eyes darted back and forth, his senses alert, his weapon poised.

And then Pup saw the tail. It was just a flick, a swish in the dirt. A second later, a tiny face, tinier even than his own, peeked out of the shadows.

Pup thought he recognized the face, but it ducked back into the darkness as quickly as it had appeared. So quickly, in fact, that Pup was left wondering if he'd actually seen it at all. Perhaps, under the stress of the moment, his mind was playing tricks on him.

"Help me, Dev," Pup begged, springing up to his hind paws, his arms outstretched in a pleading gesture. "Whatever you can think of that might keep me alive, I'm prepared to do it. I want to live . . . at least long enough to make Pinkie and Hopper understand that I'm really, truly sorry."

"Sadly, Pup, I think you've reached the point of no return. I just don't think merely apologizing to Pinkie is going to work."

Pup felt a lump form in his throat. "What are you saying?"

"Just that you might want to rethink a few things, that's all."

Pup was about to ask what the soldier was getting at when another subway train rocketed past, shaking the walls so that a drizzle of dust rained down from above. He felt the tunnel's gloom closing in on him, despite the glow cast by the train's headlight. Out of the corner of his eye he again saw the trembling prisms splash across the wall, but this time he ignored them. He had to focus. For all he knew, Pinkie was already putting together a second search party with the same orders she had given DeKalb:

Kill Pup on sight.

When the train had passed, a voice seemed to come out of nowhere, a pretty little voice, filled with conviction and innocence. "I have a great idea!" it said.

Pup recognized it instantly by its sweet musical squeak. It was the voice of the tiny ratling who'd been talking to Hopper on the ledge. But what in the world was she doing way out here, so far from Atlantia? Perhaps she was lost.

She bounded across the gravelly expanse toward them.

"I know what you have to do!" she cried, skidding to a halt, just inches before colliding with the tip of Dev's blade.

Instinctively Pup's arms reached out to pull her back before she impaled herself.

"What is this fluffy little piece of nothing?" Dev demanded.

Her tiny chest was still heaving from her wild sprint, and her eyes were bright with excitement. "My name is Hope," she answered. "And I'm a spy."

CHAPTER NINE

"So where's the whirligig?"

Hopper looked up from his writing desk to find Zucker leaning casually against the doorframe of his bedchamber.

"Huh?"

"I asked where the whirligig was," Zucker repeated. "You said you were going out to get one for Hope." He glanced purposefully around the room, but of course, there was no spinning toy to be found. "Were they out of them in the market square?"

Hopper gulped, thinking fast. "Uh, yes," he blurted. "Yes they were. All sold out. But don't worry. I've placed an order for a custom one to be made especially for her. The merchant said it should be ready later in the week. I ordered it with sparkles if they could arrange it. I also asked that it be made to spin extra fast because I thought she'd enjoy that." The Chosen One finished his less-than-honest ramble with another loud gulp, giving the emperor a wobbly smile.

"Sparkles, huh?" Zucker folded his arms and grinned. "How long you gonna keep this up, kid?"

"Keep what up?"

"The lying. Because frankly, you ain't all that good at it. In fact, you're basically incapable of telling so much as a fib. And I know you plenty well enough to know that you would never leave the Conflict Room—"

"Strategic Planning Area."

"Whatever. I know you well enough to know that you wouldn't have left such an important meeting for something as trivial as a pinwheel, even if it were for Hope. So why don't you come clean and tell me what's what?"

Hopper let out a long rush of breath. Zucker was right. He couldn't lie to save his life. Especially not to his best friend.

"I went out to see if Pup was, as my father had suggested, already in Atlantia. Lying in wait, you might say. In hiding. Because I thought if I could find him before Pinkie's soldiers did, I might be able to talk some sense into him."

"Didn't you try that already?" Zucker pointed out gently. "In that old shoe?"

"I did, and I failed miserably," Hopper admitted. "But I'm not ready to give up on him yet. And you heard what Pinkie said: dead or alive."

"Personally," said Zucker, "I'm hoping for alive."

"Me too!" cried Hopper. "Which is why I went searching the city. But there was no sign of Pup anywhere."

"I'm sorry, kid."

"Has there been any word yet from Pinkie's search party?"

"Sorry again."

Hopper slumped low in his chair as Zucker stepped into the room that had once been his own royal sleeping quarters.

"So . . . ," Zucker began in a lighthearted tone. "I like what you've done with the place."

Hopper smiled in spite of himself. He knew his friend was trying to cheer him up by changing the subject. "Thanks. I really like having your old desk. It reminds me of when you taught me to read and write."

"Good times," said Zucker with a nod. "Well, sort of."

Hopper laughed. "Yeah. Titus's evil treaty and Felina and the refugee camps did put a bit of a damper on our fun, didn't they?"

"Sure did. But it all worked out." Zucker dropped onto the foot of the bed and stretched out his legs. "Just like this whole Pup problem is gonna work out. You'll see."

There was a pause as both the rat and mouse tried to make themselves believe it.

"You've done some redecorating, I see."

"Redecorating?" Hopper glanced around the chamber. A chalk portrait that Firren had drawn of himself, Dodger, and Pinkie hung on the wall above his bed; his purple jerkin with the silver *Z* embroidered over the heart was draped from a hook near the door; and his newest and most favorite sword, fashioned in an emergency out of a lost human key, glittered proudly in its glass display case atop Hopper's dresser. "My room is the same as it's always been."

"Not exactly," said Zucker. "The blanket's gone. The one you stitched together from Beverly's apron and that old Dodgers pennant and those other scraps you gathered. It's usually right here"— Zucker patted the place beside him—"folded at the end of your bed."

"Oh, right. Hope took it."

"What for?"

"I have no idea," said Hopper. "But I'm sure she'll bring it back when she's done with it. She knows how I treasure it."

The room went quiet and Hopper bent over his desk to read the words he'd just inscribed. He felt a tad silly, composing something so frivolous as a love letter at a time like this, but frankly, it was the only thing he could think to do that would lighten his miserable mood.

"Whatcha writin' there?" Zucker asked.

"A letter. To Carroll." Hopper felt his cheeks grow warm; just saying the upland mouse's name out loud tended to have that effect on him. "I'm inviting her for a visit. She's never seen the tunnels and I'd really like to show her around. Of course, I wouldn't have her come until after all this business with Pup has been settled."

"Wise choice," said Zucker.

"I thought so." Hopper surprised himself with a grin.

"Maybe sometime you and I can take a trip above-ground so I can show *you* around Brooklyn."

"No way, kid." Zucker shook his head and waved his paws. "Forget about it. I'm a tunnel rat, born and raised, and I have no interest in visiting the daylight world."

Hopper laughed. "So you really do like it down here in the muck and mire?"

"I like it a lot. And nothing in this world could ever get me to go topside."

"Oh, fine," said Hopper, rolling his eyes. "But you really don't know what you're missing. There's this stuff called eggplant parmigiana that would make your mouth water."

"According to you, there are also vicious alley cats and a giant bridge, neither of which sound like things I'd put at the top of my to-do list."

Hopper turned back to the letter on his desk. He was just about to sign it—*Much Love, Hopper*, or possibly *Hope to see you soon, Hopper*—when a sudden uproar arose outside, just beneath his window.

His first thought was that Pup had decided to show himself, and the wary citizens had taken matters into their own paws. He sprung from his chair and bolted for the window; Zucker was right beside him.

But what he saw was not his brother bound and gagged, being hauled up the palace steps by a mob of rodent vigilantes.

What he saw was the old schoolmaster, hobbling up the broad staircase with a panicked look on his wrinkled face. Hurrying alongside him were the royal heirs—Go-go weeping, Fiske shouting, and Brighton struck dumb by abject terror. Raz looked more frightened than Hopper had ever seen him. Hopper's pulse raced as he looked from one child to the next, silently ticking off their names in his head:

Brighton, Gowanus . . .

Raz, Fiske . . .

"What's going on?" Zucker demanded. "Why are all of my children so frightened?"

It was then that Hopper realized what was wrong. His heart seemed to freeze in his chest. As the hysterical children stumbled through the palace doors, he did another quick head count. The number hit him like a subway train.

Four.

"Zucker," he choked, turning away from the window. "Those aren't *all* of your children."

"What are you talking about?" Eyes wild, Zucker thrust his head out the window to look for himself, but the children were inside now, out of view. He whirled back to Hopper with a look of pure horror. "What do you mean?"

"I mean . . . one of them is . . . *missing.*"

The words felt like fire on Hopper's tongue; their meaning made his fur stand on end.

"Missing? Which one? *Who's* missing?"

Hopper could only shake his head in reply. He wanted to crumble into a million heartsick pieces. He felt the wind go out of him as he dropped onto the foot of his bed, onto the place where his blanket should have been. "I just saw her!" he cried. "I saw her with my own two eyes, out in the city, just a little while ago. I should have asked her why she was alone . . . I should have told her to come home. Oh, Zucker! It's all my fault. She was alone. She was all alone!"

"*Who* was alone?" Zucker prompted, his voice rising to a fever pitch. "Hopper, who's missing?"

"She said she was going to join the others. I should have realized something was wrong . . . but I was so preoccupied with looking for Pup!"

In two long strides the emperor came to stand before Hopper and placed both of his trembling paws on the Chosen One's shoulders.

"Hopper, listen to me!" he said, struggling to keep his voice steady. "You've got to get it together, kid. I know you're upset, but I need to know . . . *who* did you see in the city? Which one of my children is missing?"

Hopper's shoulders sagged; his legs felt as if they'd turned to jelly. With a jerk he lifted his face to Zucker's and saw his own incomprehensible fear mirrored on the emperor's face. "It's Hope, Zucker. Our Hope . . . is gone."

CHAPTER TEN

"A SPY," SNEERED DEVON, CONFOUNDED by the sight of this tiny stranger in her fancy dress and bejeweled crown who had just materialized out of the gloom. "That's absurd. You're nothing but a child." He lifted an eyebrow and looked down his snout at the jewel-encrusted tiara she wore perched between her ears. "A ridiculously overdressed child, but still . . . a child."

Pup, too, was shocked by the sudden inexplicable appearance of a royal princess. She was dusty and her dress was torn, probably from her long trek through the tunnels, and for some reason she was carrying a patchwork quilt like a bedroll. She looked more like a wanderer than a royal.

"I think I can help you," she said.

Around her, what pale light remained in the wake of the train danced upon the tile walls in a splatter of translucent color. It was a moment before Pup realized that this was the result of the light bouncing off her tiara. She was like her own miniature fireworks display.

For the life of him, though, Pup still couldn't figure out what she was doing here.

"I don't understand what you mean by 'spy,'" he said.

"Are you sure you mean 'spy' and not 'thief'?" scoffed Devon, still eyeing her crown. "That's quite a pricey little hat you're sporting. I doubt a waif like yourself could come by such jewels honestly."

"I'm not a thief or a beggar," Hope assured him. "I'm a spy. And I've been watching you right from the beginning. I saw all of it, and I bet you didn't even know I was there. My brothers and sisters always said I was a good spy. I guess they were right!"

She looked so pleased with herself that Pup didn't have the heart to tell her that her flashy little tiara had nearly given her away.

"You saw all of it?" Dev repeated slowly. "You mean you saw *Pup* murder these three Mūs soldiers in cold blood?"

Pup frowned. "*What?!*"

"No . . ." Hope calmly shook her head at Devon. "I saw *you* kill them."

The soldier responded with a scathing look that made Pup's fur bristle.

"And is that what you would tell the authorities if they asked you, little spy?" Devon's paw was suddenly tightening around the pommel of his sword. "That *I* killed the soldiers?"

Hope nodded. "Isn't that what I should tell them? The truth?"

"Not necessarily," Dev muttered.

"Why would you want her to lie?" asked Pup, a tremor of alarm shooting from the tips of his ears to the point of his tail. "You killed them because they were traitors and conspirators." He slid a step closer to Hope, feeling compelled to maneuver himself so that he was standing between the tiny rat princess and the Mūs soldier, shielding her from his steady glare. "Didn't you?"

Devon said nothing—he merely continued to stare at Hope. A cold tingle crept up Pup's spine; he was beginning to get a bad feeling about this soldier.

"Don't you want to hear my brilliant idea?" Hope gushed, clutching her patchwork blanket excitedly.

"Oh, by all means," drawled Dev.

"Okay." Hope turned a beaming smile to Pup. "This soldier can go back to Atlantia and sneak into the palace. He can go directly to my daddy and Uncle Hopper before Pinkie sees that he's returned, and he can tell them the truth about you wanting to apologize and the Mūs general's nasty plan and he can explain why he—not you—*had* to kill him and the others. That way, Pinkie can't turn the story around to suit herself."

Dev gave her an impatient look. "I will say this: you do think like a spy."

"But how do we ensure that Pinkie won't spot Dev before he gets to Hopper and the emperor?" Pup asked. "More importantly, how can we be certain that they'll even believe Dev when he explains that I'm innocent?"

"Proof," says Hope. "Dev would have to prove to

Daddy and Uncle Hopper that you're good again. If you were really a villain, you wouldn't have just killed the other three soldiers, you would have killed this one too, right? So if he can prove that he saw you and you didn't do away with him, they'll have to believe him. The proof will be a secret code."

"A secret code?" Dev repeated dryly.

Hope shrugged. "It's a spy thing."

"Of course."

"What kind of secret code?" Pup asked. The plan was sounding awfully good to him.

"Something Dev can tell them that only *you* could have told him. This will prove that he spoke with you and lived to tell the tale."

Dev twitched his tail. "Seems like a lot of bother to me."

"Saving my life seems like a bother?" Pup was growing more wary of this soldier by the second.

Dev ignored the question. "The problem remains," he huffed. "If I can't get to Hopper and Zucker without first crossing paths with Pinkie, she's bound to spin this incident to her own advantage. Which is why, little scamp, before you so rudely interrupted us, I was going to propose that Pup and I—"

"But you *can* get to them!" Hope informed him. "That's the brilliant part! You see, there's a secret passageway."

This got Dev's attention. Pup's too.

"What secret passageway?" Pup asked.

"My brother Raz found it once. I followed him, so that's how I know about it. It's a long, dark corridor with doors on each end, but the doors are built to look like part of the wall, so they're almost invisible. It leads to a forgotten little cubbyhole near the throne room. My daddy and Hopper have important meetings there all the time. So if this soldier takes the passageway, he can avoid being spotted by Pinkie and get to Daddy and Uncle Hopper to tell them you surrender."

"Amazing!" cried Pup. "That will work perfectly." He took a moment to gather his thoughts. "All right, I know exactly what the code should be . . . what Dev should say to Hopper when you see him, to prove I'm on his side now." He cleared his throat. "Say this:

We lived in a cage that was cozy and clean
But then Mama was taken and Pinkie was mean
Just when we thought we'd had all we could take
We were forced to escape from the jaws of a snake
I took quite a fall, but I went right on livin'
Now I want to come home . . . please say all is forgiven."

"Wow," said Hope. "That's perfect. La Rocha couldn't have said it better. When all this is over, you should write it down because the library has a whole collection of rodent verse."

"Thanks." Pup felt his cheeks turn warm. "I guess it was kind of inspired, huh?"

"It was downright lyrical," Dev said in a mocking tone. "But before I set off for Atlantia to perform this delightful little poetry recitation, I have one question." He narrowed his eyes at Hope. "How is it you know so much about the palace? You're only a child!"

"A royal child," Hope informed him, tossing her tail proudly. "I am *Princess* Hope of the House of Romanus."

There was an immediate shift in the soldier's bearing as every muscle in his body seemed to tighten at once. Pup watched as a storm of emotions passed over Devon's face—shock, happiness, even a flash of disgust. Why the soldier would have such a complex reaction to hearing that Hope was a princess was beyond him.

"A royal heir," he said at last. "A princess. The daughter of Firren herself."

Hope nodded. "And don't forget . . . spy."

"Well." Dev chuckled. "This changes everything." His next word came out in a growl. "*Everything!*"

"What are you talking about?" said Pup.

"I'm talking about vengeance!" spat Dev. "I'm talking about finally taking my revenge against that coldhearted monster Firren."

Before Pup knew what was happening, the deadly tip of Devon's sword was pressed to Hope's throat.

She let out a squeak of fear, and the sound seemed to go directly to Pup's heart.

The sickening realization that Dev was not what he seemed came hard and fast. In that instant, Pup understood that the soldier's whole story had been a lie. *DeKalb* was not the traitor with the nefarious plot to destroy and torture the royals . . . *Dev* was.

Poor Hope. The child had played right into the villain's paws! If only she hadn't announced that she was a member of the royal family! Because now Pup knew exactly what Dev meant by Hope's revelation changing everything: Dev no longer needed Pup's alliance. He had something better with which to get his revenge.

Hope.

And what better way to torture the emperor and empress than by harming their littlest princess?

Blood boiling, whiskers quivering with anger and fear, Pup prepared to pounce on the armed soldier. He bared his claws and summoned his strength . . .

"I wouldn't do that if I were you, Pup," Devon advised, a chill calm in his voice, his steady, hateful gaze never wavering from the trembling little princess. "I've waited too long for this moment. Truth be told, I'd much prefer to take my revenge slowly, perhaps by sending Firren first a chunk of the child's ear, then maybe a swath of her fur, followed by half of her pretty little tail."

Hope clutched her blanket and let out a horrified whimper. Pup's claws itched to sink into the soldier's flesh.

"Yes, I would much *rather* do that," Dev snarled, his eyes still boring into Hope's. "But . . ."

"But what?" croaked Pup.

"But if you're entertaining any heroic delusions about attacking me . . . if you make so much as a single move in my direction . . . well, I'll simply have to kill the child right here, right this minute. This blade is sharp, you see."

To demonstrate, he flicked his wrist, effortlessly slicing her blanket in two; one half landed in the dirt. She clung to the remaining piece.

"You see? She will be dead before she hits the ground," Dev promised. "And I shall take great joy in delivering her bloody corpse to her empress mother, perhaps even with that ridiculous diamond crown still perched atop her lifeless little head."

Pup could see the tears streaming down Hope's face. He had to do something. But he was smaller than Dev and unarmed.

Now in the distance he heard the faint growl of a subway approaching. As it sped nearer, the noise grew to a roar and the blinding glare of its headlight brightened the tunnel, faintly at first, then with more intensity.

Pup wasn't sure if Dev was even aware of it, focused so raptly as he was on his trembling captive. The soldier surely didn't notice the spray of prisms her tiara was suddenly splashing across the tunnel.

In that moment, Pup knew what to do.

He waited . . . one, two, three more seconds as the train raced closer . . . then he cried out, "Hope!"

It was an automatic response; despite the lethal weapon pressed against her throat, hearing her name caused the child to jerk her head around to face him . . . just as their gloomy section of tunnel filled with dazzling white light.

The reflection that burst forth from her diamond headpiece was like a flash of gunpowder exploding in Dev's face. Shocked and blinded, he dropped his blade and covered his eyes. "Ahhhh!"

It was just the opening Pup needed. He lunged forward and sunk his teeth deeply into Dev's leg. Then he grabbed Hope and her severed blanket, swung her into his arms, and ran.

Dev's howl of pain and outrage followed them into the darkness.

"Where are we going?" Hope asked, her voice muffled against the sweaty fur of Pup's chest.

"As far from Atlantia as we can get," he answered, rounding a corner. "I want to keep you safe, but I can't show my face in the city until I'm sure Pinkie won't kill me on sight. I have to find a way to prove to Pinkie that I'm innocent before I can even think about entering Atlantia."

"Oh. Well, I guess that makes sense."

Hope's dainty paw clutched the tiara to keep it from falling off as Pup barreled on. "But you're running *toward* the city," she cried.

"I know that," he panted.

Pup ran until he reached the spot he'd been looking for. He placed Hope carefully on the gravelly ground and took her hand. "Don't worry, Hope," he said. "I won't let anything happen to you."

"Thank you. But why did you bring me *toward* the city?" Hope asked. "If everyone wants to kill you, shouldn't you be running *away* from Atlantia?"

Pup smiled, lifting his eyes upward to the chipped

tile and moldering earth of the tunnel's ceiling. "You are a smart little spy, aren't you?"

"Well, I try."

"I brought you here because this is the only way to get where we need to go." There was a brief silence as Pup continued to study the wall. He was vaguely aware of Hope picking up a stone—a sharp one, from the sound of it scratching against the wall. She kept herself busy with this for several moments. When she'd completed her task, she spoke again, her words filled with trust.

"So where exactly are we going?"

"To the only place where I know that neither Dev nor Pinkie will ever find us," Pup replied. "The place they're least likely to come looking."

"Sounds mysterious."

Pup squinted hard, scanning the boundary where above met below. At last he found what he was looking for—a hole carved into the dirt near the very top of the tunnel wall. Relief washed over him as he lifted the princess onto his shoulders.

"Here we go," he said, forcing a note of hearty confidence into his voice. "To our mysterious hiding place."

"Where exactly is that?" Hope wondered.

"Back where I came from," Pup told her. "Back to Brooklyn."

CHAPTER ELEVEN

AS I ARRIVE AT THE IRON *gate that separates Atlantia from the Great Beyond, I see one of Pinkie's soldiers making his solitary way back to the city. It is Devon.*

And he is limping.

I approach him anxiously, keeping my hood close around my face.

"What happened?" I ask, eyeing the bandage that is wrapped primitively around his leg. "You're injured."

He looks at me with wild eyes. I attribute this to the fact that he must be in great pain.

"How was my news received?" I go on eagerly. "The note I gave you earlier today . . . did the emperor send you out to collect Pup safely and bring him back to the palace to make his apology?"

"I'm quite sure he would have done precisely that," says Devon slyly, "if I had bothered to inform him."

"What do you mean 'if'?"

"Come," he whispers, then grasps my arm, much harder than is necessary, and tugs. "I will tell you all you need to know." He propels me into the shadow of the wall that surrounds the city.

"I did not share your note with Pinkie and the others," Devon reveals, "because I wanted to find out for myself if

Pup planned to proceed peacefully as your message implied."

There is something bitter in his eyes, and suddenly my every instinct tells me that he is not a friend. "That was not our agreement," I snap. "You were supposed to tell them that Pup wanted to apologize."

"Apologies," snorts Devon. "They always come a day late and a dollar short, if you ask me. I've never put much stock in apologies."

For some reason, he has not let go of my arm.

"Have you a brother?" he asks me.

I nod. "Two."

"Sadly, I cannot say the same. My brother was taken from me when I was very young. In Felina's battleground, in fact."

"That is tragic," I say in what I hope is a comforting tone. I wriggle slightly, hoping he will release his grasp. He doesn't.

"We were a jovial litter, my siblings and I. There were four of us in all—Celeste, Hazel, myself . . . and Ira. My brother." He shakes his head; the gesture is one of grief, but his eyes say something different. His eyes burn with anger.

There is more to this story than he is telling me. "Wasn't it unusual for Mūs pups to find themselves in the battleground?" I venture. "I thought the elders were strict about letting anyone beside the scouts out from behind the wall."

He bares his teeth in reply.

"You have my condolences," I tell him. "About your brother. But as to my message—"

"There were so few places to hide. A moldy knapsack, a torn sneaker. A silver cup. Ira was so frightened . . ." Again, he shakes his head. "We reached for him, stretching, grasping . . . She didn't help us. She could have saved him . . ." His far-off expression sharpens to one of keenly focused fury. "And you dare to scold me for failing to deliver a note?"

"I'm sorry, soldier," I say quickly. "I did not mean to challenge your sense of duty. If you will excuse me now . . . I apologize profusely for troubling you."

I turn away and hurry toward the gate. I have already reached into the pocket of my cloak and withdrawn a paper scrap, on which I begin to compose yet another message to the emperor. This one is even more urgent than the last.

But I hear the shuffling of paws behind me. And then his chilling voice:

"I told you, I never put much stock in apologies. Even profuse ones."

His claws grasp my hood, just as I am stuffing the hastily scrawled missive back into the folds of my cape. My disguise falls away and I glance over my shoulder only long enough to see the startled expression on his face; clearly, I am not who or what he expected to find hidden beneath this cloak. Then he reaches for his sword.

Before I can even move, the heavy handle is swooping in the direction of my head. The metal pommel finds its mark, dead center on the back of my skull.

There is only the gritty scrape of dirt and stone beneath my cheek.

And then, darkness.

Chapter Twelve

Guilt overwhelmed Hopper.

Hope had run away. And the responsibility for her disappearance was his and his alone.

Everyone was gathered in the throne room, desperately trying to think of where she might have gone. No one—not Hopper, Zucker, Firren, Dodger, Pinkie, or the four distraught royal heirs—could identify a single destination.

"I should have known she was running away," Hopper said, for perhaps the hundredth time. "Why else would she have brought along my blanket? And her tiara. She took the blanket to use as a bedroll. And the tiara because . . ." His chest heaved with a shuddering sob. "Because she knew she wasn't coming back."

"I don't understand why Hope would run away," said Dodger. "She's a good girl. She's happy here."

Hopper said nothing, but his gaze went unwillingly to the huddle of royal heirs, sniffling at the foot of their father's throne. It was a piece of furniture Zucker almost never used; he was uncomfortable with such pomp and circumstance. But today was not about ceremony; today the bereft father simply could no longer bear his own weight. When he'd stormed into the throne room just moments before, he'd gone right to the oversize chair to drop his head into his paws in misery.

"But she *wasn't* happy!" said Raz.

"Not at all," Go-go confirmed. "And it was all *our* fault!"

"We teased Hope," Brighton admitted, removing her glasses and wiping her eyes. "We were bullies. She liked everything fancy and royal and we made fun of her for it."

"I guess it wasn't so funny after all," Fiske added, wiping the tears that streamed down the soft fur of his snout. "She ran away because of us."

"Because we were mean to her and called her a hopeless runt," said Brighton.

"Because we called her a spy," Go-go added.

"I'm as much to blame as you are," said Hopper. "When I saw her alone in the city, I should have insisted she come home with me."

Zucker lifted his face from his paws. "It ain't your fault, kid," he rasped, his sad eyes meeting Hopper's guilty ones. "You couldn't have known." Then he cast a disappointed glance at his litter. "The rest of you, however . . ."

"We know we were awful!" wailed Go-go. "And I'd do anything to bring Hope back."

"There's nothing you can do," snapped Raz. "So stop being such a dope."

"Don't call her a dope!" cried Brighton. "She's just trying to help."

"Enough!" said Pinkie. "This is no time to be fighting amongst ourselves. Hope is gone. The only thing we should be thinking about is how to find her."

The room fell silent but for the sniffles and sighs of the children. Hopper allowed himself a glance at Firren, who sat beside the emperor in her equally luxurious royal throne. It was due to be removed from the palace later in the week, in fact, but right now Hopper knew Firren wasn't thinking about the evils of overprivilege; right now she was thinking about Hope.

Firren hadn't said a word since she sat down. Her shoulders, as ever, were pressed back so that, even seated, her posture was regal and imposing, her paws folded in her lap, her dainty chin uplifted. Her sword leaned against the intricately carved arm of her chair, shining with power. But her eyes were dark. Ordinarily they glinted and sparked with joy, intelligence, passion. Today they were simply blank.

Hopper thought his heart might crack.

When the doors opened, every head swiveled to see who had entered. Nine pairs of desperate eyes honed in on Ketchum, the head of royal intelligence, as he made his way across the gleaming throne-room floor.

"Have you found her?" asked Dodger, springing up from his seat.

"No."

Go-go began to weep inconsolably.

"But there is news."

"Tell us, Ketch," said Zucker, his voice an agonized croak.

"One of Pinkie's soldiers has just returned."

Pinkie scowled. "Only one?"

Ketch nodded, then motioned to someone just outside the door. Hopper had a sudden flashback to a far-less-sophisticated version of himself, hiding in that very spot, peering around the doorframe at the bloodcurdling sight of the emperor Titus perched upon his throne. He imagined he could still see the scar snaking across the old rat's snout and hear his deep voice echoing through the chamber.

But Titus was gone. It was Zucker—the Zuck-meister—who sat upon the throne now, waiting for word of his missing princess.

The darker-brown mouse came limping through the door. Devon, Hopper thought his name was. Clearly, he'd been in some sort of battle, for his leg was injured. Bandaged.

With a piece of Hopper's patchwork quilt.

Zucker recognized it at the same second Hopper had. "You've seen her!"

"I have, Your Highness," said the soldier. "In the tunnels."

"Is she all right?" This question came from Firren,

although Hopper almost hadn't recognized her voice. It was high and thin, airy . . . as though it had been sliced into shreds of itself with her own sword. "Is she . . . alive?"

"Very much so," said Devon. "But . . ."

Hopper's heart seized in his chest. "But what?"

Devon lowered his eyes.

Ketchum cleared his throat. "When Devon returned from the search, I of course told him that the princess had run away. But it would seem he has information regarding that . . . misconception."

"What do you mean 'misconception'?" asked Zucker.

Devon gave the emperor a level look. "Your daughter has not run away, Your Majesty. She has been kidnapped."

The only sound was Firren's sharp intake of breath. Hopper wasn't sure when exactly he'd begun to tremble.

"Kidnapped?" Zucker repeated.

"By whom?" Pinkie demanded.

Hopper heard his own voice ringing through the room before he even realized he'd spoken. "By Pup."

He didn't have to see the soldier's somber nod to know that he was right.

Chapter Thirteen

I **AWAKE IN THE SHADOW** *of Atlantia's wall. My first thought is that I have made a terrible mistake.*

If only I could remember what it is.

There is a pounding sensation at the back of my head, and I must blink several times to clear the blur from my eyes, but it would seem that I am in one piece.

Standing, I notice a heaviness that hangs about my shoulders and a sweep of fabric around my hind paws. A cloak.

A cloak?

Why in the world would I be wearing something as cumbersome and impractical as a cloak? It is not as if I am in hiding. I shrug it off and leave it there beside the wall. Perhaps one of the poor wanderers (for there are still a number of them) will find it and put it to good use.

Ignoring the pain in my skull, I head through the gate and toward the palace steps. Perhaps my brothers will be about, although they are busy these days, training for the emperor's elite squad of military officers. One of them, Pritchard, serves under Ketchum in the Royal Intelligence Service. The other, Bartel . . . hmmm, well, for some reason, I can't quite remember Bart's position at the moment. Something to do with weaponry, perhaps? Or maybe he frosts the tea cakes in the kitchen? How odd that I can't recall. But I'm sure it will come to me eventually. All I know is that he's recently been promoted and I'm very proud of him indeed.

As I make my way toward the palace, I notice that there is quite a commotion taking place. Soldiers have assembled. A captain whose name escapes me is barking out orders. First Lieutenant something-or-other . . . Gardner? Garnet? Garfield! Yes, that's it. Garfield! First Lieutenant Garfield and Bartel are handing out fresh swords (so much for my tea cakes theory). Even Fulton, the smithy, is present. He has placed his burly self beside the emperor Zucker, who appears agitated. Even from this distance I can see he wears an expression of fury. Or perhaps it is panic I see on his face. On closer inspection I see that it is both.

I double my pace and call out to Pritchard, who stands on the bottom step with Ketchum, examining a hastily drafted document, which looks to be official marching orders.

"Are we at war?" I cry out, my blood thrumming. "What's happened?"

Pritchard looks up at the sound of my voice. "There you are," he calls back. "We've been looking everywhere for you. Your assistance is required."

"Why?" I ask, growing more frightened by the second. "What's the matter?"

Unfortunately, I am robbed of a satisfactory answer when a mouse with a white circle around his right eye comes rushing down the steps.

"Thank goodness you're here," he says, throwing his

arms around me, his voice trembling with panic.

I blink at him. He looks at once completely foreign and utterly familiar to me. The snowy-white fur marking, the wounded ear . . .

A flash goes off inside my head and I see a hazy image of myself from the past, wrapping this injury in clean gauze bandages.

"Hopper!" I cry out, amazed that I could have forgotten my dear friend, even for a moment. Perhaps it is the frantic mood that surrounds me that is robbing me of the simplest recollections. Or maybe it is the throbbing ache in my head that is playing havoc with my memory.

"We need you in the nursery," the Chosen One informs me.

"What for?"

"To stay with the children. We trust no one with them but you."

Children . . . these I do remember, for they all but own my heart. The royal heirs, Gowanus, Verrazano, Fiske, Brighton, and . . . and . . .

"Hope is missing," Hopper croaks.

Hope. Yes. The littlest princess. Her darling face appears first in a fog, then clearly in my mind.

"I . . . I don't understand," I stammer. "Please, tell me what's happened."

"Hope's been kidnapped." He closes his eyes, and I see a tear trickle through the white circle of fur that marks him as the Chosen One.

"Oh no!" Truly, I can hardly imagine more devastating

news. *My eyes search the crowd for Firren. Poor Firren.*

I find her beside the emperor at the top of the stairs. I am not surprised to see her sword drawn; she holds it poised above her delicate shoulder with the tip rotating in tiny, menacing circles. Oh, she is ready . . . ready for a fight.

Now Hopper clutches my arm and pulls me up the steps. Not harshly but urgently. It sparks a sudden memory, a recent one. I flash on a vision of myself being tugged like this . . . but where and by whom I cannot say. The recollection vanishes as quickly as it came, leaving only confusion and fear spinning inside my aching head.

Hopper brings me straight to Firren.

"Look who's arrived," Hopper announces.

Firren turns to me. She does not lower her sword. I do not blame her. This is a mother on a mission: whoever the devilish scoundrel who has taken her child is, he is going to pay. When the empress's eyes meet mine, I see a sliver of relief.

"Marcy," she breathes. "Thank goodness."

And then, with her sword still hovering above her, the empress does something I've never seen her do before:

She dissolves into tears.

CHAPTER FOURTEEN

IT HAD NOT TAKEN LONG to muster every available military rodent, palace servant, and concerned citizen. They were assembled now on the palace steps, preparing to march out into the tunnels to rescue the kidnapped princess.

Hopper had been flooded with gratitude when Marcy appeared on the steps. It had been so long since he'd seen her. She'd been stunned to learn that Pup had kidnapped Hope, and when they'd appointed her to remain behind at the palace to watch over the children, although she seemed confused at first, she'd been more than willing to accept the responsibility.

"We're afraid Pup might come after the others," Hopper explained now. He took a dagger from Fulton and slipped it into a leather pouch that hung near his hip.

"I will guard them with my life," said Marcy, gingerly rubbing the back of her head. "I'll do whatever I can to be of assistance."

Hopper saw her wince. "Did you hurt yourself?"

"I'm not sure, actually. I guess I bumped my head. But please, don't worry about me. I'm fine. You concentrate on finding . . . finding . . ."

"Hope."

"Right. Of course. Hope."

Hopper sighed, watching as soldiers conferred with merchants, consulting maps and giving instructions. "I just wish La Rocha would make contact, maybe give us some information we could use."

Marcy gave him a strange look. "Did you say La Rocha?" Her face seemed to register something, but only briefly.

"The prophet. The philosopher. You know. La Rocha always knows what's going on before we do."

"Oh yes, of course." Marcy nodded. "I'm sorry, I'm just a bit . . . scattered for some reason. But I agree. La Rocha has always known the secrets of the tunnels. Perhaps word will come soon."

"I'll tell the servants to bring any message that may arrive from La Rocha directly to you," Hopper decided. "And if you receive one, you can confer with Devon."

"Devon?"

She really is scatterbrained today, thought Hopper, feeling a twinge of concern. Then he remembered that Marcy hadn't been present in the palace when Pinkie had arrived with her soldiers. "He's one of the guards Pinkie sent out to search for Pup," he clarified. "You wouldn't believe what he told us!"

Hopper quickly relayed to Marcy everything Dev had imparted to them. First, how Dev himself had been the one to locate Pup's hiding spot—a smelly old human fedora hat, overturned at the edge of the tracks—and how he and General DeKalb had been the only ones brave enough to approach it. Dev had talked Pup out of the hat, and it appeared that they had him cornered until they heard the cries for help. Then a tiny rat popped out of the hat. Dev immediately identified her as a royal princess because she'd been wearing a tiara. But her sudden appearance had distracted the general and Pitkin, which had given Pup the opportunity to slice them both to ribbons.

"My goodness," breathed Marcy. "What did Dev do?"

"His first thought was to save the princess, of course. So he grabbed her out of the hat and ran. But Pup was on a rampage. He lunged for the third soldier, Wyona, and strangled her with his bare paws! Then he caught up to Dev, stabbed him in the leg, and grabbed the princess. Dev tried to follow him, but his wound was too severe. He was losing a lot of blood. All he could do was watch in horror as Pup disappeared into the tunnels with Hope."

"Has anyone seen to his injury?" Marcy asked.

"Probably not," said Hopper, looking around at the chaos on the steps. "Let me take you to him now."

Hopper found the wounded soldier in the Strategic Planning Area with his leg propped up on a stool. Marcy had run up to the servants' quarters to fetch her first aid kit.

"Hello, Dev," said Hopper.

"Chosen One." The soldier made to stand in a show of respect, but Hopper waved him back into his seat. "How goes the rescue mission?"

"We are about to leave. But before I go, I want my friend to have a look at that leg. She bandaged me up, once, a long time ago. She knows what she's doing."

As if on cue, Marcy appeared, smiling beside Hopper in the doorway, holding her kit bag of medical supplies.

Hopper heard Dev gasp, and saw his eyes fly open wide; the soldier's grip tightened around the arms of his chair. Hopper guessed this was due to a sudden pain from his injury until it occurred to him that Dev might also be reacting to the fact that Marcy was quite a fetching rat. He grinned.

"I'm sorry it took me so long," said Marcy, sounding flustered. "It was the most peculiar thing; I couldn't seem to remember the way to my room. I got all turned around and had to ask . . . well, never mind. I'm here now."

Hopper made the introductions. "Dev, Marcy. Marcy . . . Dev."

"How are you feeling, soldier?" Marcy asked, striding across the room to kneel beside the stool.

"Uh . . . I . . . it's . . ." He winced as Marcy gently removed the blanket bandage.

She gave him an apologetic smile, then produced a sponge from her bag and gently began to wipe away the blood crusting in his dark-brown fur. "I was impressed to hear of your brave deed, soldier," she said. "It's unfortunate to have to meet under these circumstances."

"Meet?" said Dev. "You mean . . . we haven't met before?"

"I don't see how we could have," said Marcy lightly. "You're from the Mūs village. And I keep mostly to the confines of Atlantia."

"Right," said Dev, relaxing. His shoulders went slack and he let out a long, relieved breath. "Yes. Of course."

Hopper was glad to see the soldier looking so calm. Clearly, Marcy's ministrations were soothing the pain.

"Will you be joining the others in the search for the missing princess?" Dev asked Marcy.

But Marcy did not answer, engrossed as she was in studying the wound, so Hopper spoke for her.

"Marcy is going to stay behind and look after the children. We're afraid that Pup might get ambitious and try to storm the palace to kidnap another of the royal heirs."

"Ah," said Dev. "Then I'm glad I will be here to offer my assistance."

"Soldier," said Marcy, frowning at his leg. "How exactly did you get this wound?"

Dev replied without a second's hesitation. "Pup stabbed me with his sword." He gave Marcy a crooked grin. "Please tell me it doesn't look infected."

"No." Marcy shook her head. "It doesn't look infected. But it doesn't look like a stab wound either. It looks more like . . . a bite."

Dev stiffened.

"A bite?" Hopper crossed the room to look for himself. Marcy was running the sponge carefully over the bloody punctures, which, to the Chosen One's eyes, did indeed look a lot like teeth marks. "I thought you said—"

"I did," Dev interrupted. "I reported that Pup stabbed me, which is the truth. But you see, well, I was too fast for him. I dodged the blade so that he merely managed to deliver a nick. A scratch, really. You probably can't even see it. But then, well, I didn't want to mention this before, because I didn't want to say anything that might reflect badly on the poor little victim. But Hope panicked. And who could blame her? Here I was, a perfect stranger, snatching her out of a moldy hat and dashing off into the tunnels. For all she knew, I would turn out to be a worse threat than Pup. So . . . she bit me. Sank her little fangs right into my leg." He chuckled. "I suppose one has to give the little rat princess credit for her resourcefulness."

"That sounds like our Hope," said Hopper. "Just promise me you won't hold it against her."

"I wouldn't dream of it," said Dev.

Marcy smiled and began to wrap the wound in clean cloth.

114

"Well, then," said Hopper. "I'll be off. I will try to send word back if I can. Meanwhile, take care of the children. And take care of each other."

"Don't you worry," said Dev, watching as Marcy tied off the bandage in a snug knot. "I intend to take care of *everything*."

CHAPTER FIFTEEN

As Hopper departs, I send off a silent wish, asking La Rocha to keep him and all the others safe.

I feel honored to be entrusted with the children. As I return my supplies to my bag, I hear the sound of Firren's horn outside, calling the troops. Then the thunder of a hundred paws marching.

It is a noise that is both hopeful and gut-wrenching, and it amplifies the pain in my head. I stand and head for the door, but before I exit, Dev's voice stops me.

"You know, I believe they have a valid concern about Pup coming here to harm the other children. He was quite wild when I saw him, and bent on bringing down the monarchy in a most excruciating fashion. I wouldn't be surprised if he does decide to stash his little hostage somewhere and then storm the palace to attack the rest of the litter."

This prediction sends a cold shiver through me. "What should we do?"

Dev considers the question for a moment. "I know a place where we can hide them. A place I'm certain Pup doesn't even know exists."

"Where?"

Dev's steely eyes don't flicker from my own. "It is difficult to describe. But it is secluded and secret, and a safe distance from here." He stands and grimaces slightly, shifting his weight from his injured limb. "If you trust me,

I think it would be best if we take the children there as soon as possible."

I wish he hadn't waited for Zucker and Firren to leave before making this suggestion. This is an important decision and it's not my place to make it. I take a long moment to weigh the options, the pros and cons.

"We wouldn't have to go," I say, "if we were prepared to fight him, should he storm the palace."

Dev laughs. "We could try, although remember that aside from a few chefs in the kitchen, we are the only ones left in the palace. I'm not sure how much protection a lovely maid and a wounded warrior could provide against such a determined villain as Pup."

"That's true," I concede. "But there are a million secret places in the palace. If Pup does come, we can hide the royal heirs so that he won't be able to find them."

"He wouldn't have to find them if he chose to burn the place to the ground."

A troubling observation, but an excellent point.

"You must face the facts, Marcy," says Dev, turning up his paws. "We are an easy target. The only way to ensure that Pup won't harm the royal children is to bring them somewhere he'd never think of looking."

I heave a heavy sigh, knowing he speaks good sense. At last I nod. "If you give me the location, I will alert the chefs and tell them where we can be found, should the emperor and the others return."

"No."

"No?" I blink. "Why not?"

Dev has one word for me: "Torture."

"I don't understand."

"Pup has proven himself ruthless—soulless, even. If he were to find the young royals gone, do you imagine he would think twice about torturing a common kitchen worker in order to discover their whereabouts?"

"Even if he did," I say, shaking my head emphatically, "the staff would never tell! Everyone in the palace adores those children!"

"Of course they do," Dev allows. "But loyalty and affection are no match for brutality and agony. Pup would stop at nothing. Eventually, I fear, he would extract the information he seeks."

My stomach twists into a queasy knot at his use of the word "extract."

"However, if no one knows where the children are hidden, no one can reveal their location."

Again, there is no arguing with his logic.

"I hate the idea of taking them out of the palace," I murmur, "but I see your point."

"Good." Dev steps away from his chair, favoring his bandaged leg. "So you will ready the children for the journey?"

"I will. I'll go collect them right now. Then I'll have the cooks pack up some rations. Food and water and plenty of it." My voice cracks when I add, "We may be gone for a while."

"A very long while," says Dev, his whiskers twitching.

"I'll see if I can fashion something for you to use as a crutch," I offer.

"I would appreciate that." Dev thanks me with a polite dip of his head. "But there is no need. For the majority of our travel, I will not be walking. I plan to use the method pioneered by the Chosen One himself."

"Ah!" I smile, despite the grim reason behind our travel plans. "We're going to take the subway!"

CHAPTER SIXTEEN

PUP AND THE PRINCESS EMERGED into the Atlantic Avenue station. Crossing the platform was like running a gauntlet. Pup remembered the sounds and smells of the place well (though not the sights, as he'd been clutched in the skinny boy's fist on that last visit), and every one of them terrified him. It was on a train that departed from this platform where he'd faced the fangs of a hungry boa constrictor. By sheer luck, or perhaps fate, he'd escaped when he'd fallen backward out of the subway car, only to be dropped into a twisting tunnel world of warring rodents—a world of wicked politics, malevolent treaties, and more than its share of courageous heroes.

His brother was one of those heroes.

Hopper, along with Zucker and Firren, and even Pinkie, had fought to end the violent reign of Titus, and together they had ultimately facilitated the defeat of Queen Felina. It was Pup's own father who had started it all, cobbling together the beginnings of that brave rebellion. And if Pup hadn't been so childish, so petulant, he could, at this very minute, be taking his place within this proud legacy.

Instead he was scuttling across the dirty cement floor of the Atlantic Avenue subway stop with a lost princess clinging to his neck, struggling to zig and zag

his way to what appeared to be a moving mountain, all the while trying to avoid the enormous footsteps of the rushing subway patrons.

"They're giants!" Hope breathed into his ear.

"They're humans," Pup wheezed in reply.

He ran his fastest toward the steep metal hill, which seemed to climb upward in infinite motion. Humans positioned themselves upon its shallow, squared-off cliffs and let it carry them higher and higher toward daylight. It was a kind of mechanical miracle, Pup thought. But that didn't make it any less frightening.

"Hang on," he told Hope.

Dashing faster, he leaped forward and landed on the zippered edge of a strange rolling case, just as its human owner maneuvered it onto the very bottom outcropping of the moving mountain. His claws grasped the case as the mountain rose, sliding soundlessly upward with the case perched precariously upon it. Pup knew that if the human happened to let go of the handle, even for a second, the case—with Pup and Hope clinging to it—would plummet, bumping and tumbling back down to the hard floor of the platform.

Fortunately for the mice, the human held fast and the case exited the mountain at its peak. The human rolled it smoothly out of the station and into the setting sunshine, where Pup and Hope jumped down to the sidewalk.

Hope, who had spent every moment of her young life in the dimness of the tunnels, was understandably dazzled by the fading sunlight.

"It's beautiful," she whispered, marveling at the pinkish late-day glow.

Pup would have told her he agreed unequivocally, except at the moment, he was too busy reaching out to grab her by the tail, jerking her out of the path of a different rolling contraption being pushed by a female human. The wheeled device had a smaller version of the human who piloted it strapped inside.

"That's a neat way to transport one's young," Hope observed when she was safely out of harm's way.

"It's a neat way to get yourself flattened," Pup chastised. "You're going to have to be careful up here, Hope. There are dangers you can't even begin to imagine."

Hope nodded, her face solemn.

He took her paw and guided her toward a towering building. "Let's keep to the edges," he suggested. "We'll be safer."

"Okay. But where are we going?"

Good question, thought Pup. He had no idea. He said nothing and kept walking.

Because they were both so extraordinarily small, Pup and Hope were able to travel a great distance without garnering much notice. Once, a woman in pointy shoes with spiky heels caught sight of them and let out an ear-piercing shriek.

The two runaways stopped to rest in an alleyway. Hope spread out her remaining half of Hopper's blanket so they could sit down.

"Where is the light going?" Hope asked.

Looking up into the darkening sky, Pup suddenly recalled (from having lived in the pet shop) that the term "daylight world" was only accurate part of the time. He'd seen with his own eyes through the big glass window that at the close of every day, the world willingly gave itself over to shadows, and remained thus for several long hours. He also knew the darkness would eventually step aside to allow the brilliance to once again claim the sky.

"What's happening?" Hope asked.

"Nightfall," said Pup. "At least, I think that's what it's called."

"What do we do about it?" she asked, looking up into the rectangular sliver of deep blue visible high above the alley.

"We sleep," said Pup with a big yawn. He hadn't realized how tired he was until he'd felt the softness of the patchwork blanket beneath him. He dropped his head onto his front paws and closed his eyes. He sensed Hope doing the same.

And before the first star came out to twinkle overhead, the two weary tunnel rodents were fast asleep.

Pup awoke to find Hope sitting up beside him on the patchwork quilt. She smiled.

He smiled back. Frankly, he was a bit surprised to discover that they had both survived the night. Between stray felines and humans . . . well, anything could have happened.

"Good morning, Princess," he said, rubbing his eyes.

"Good morning," she said. "I was wondering, do you by any chance happen to have a plan?"

"Not exactly. I don't know much about Brooklyn. I spent most of my life in a cage, after all."

"Well, you certainly knew what to do yesterday to keep me from getting squished by that rolling thing." She gave him a tentative smile. "You really aren't as bad-natured as everyone's been saying, are you?"

The sincerity in her words tugged at Pup's heart. "I was," he admitted. "For a little while. I didn't like the way my brother and sister were treating me, so I ran away."

"Wow." Hope's glittering eyes went round. "That's exactly what I did!"

Pup smiled. "Well, then I guess we have that in common, then."

"My siblings were awful to me. They called me a runt."

"We have that in common too," said Pup. "Unfortunately, what we also have in common is that we're stuck here in the upland world, with absolutely no place to go and no one to help us."

They were quiet, listening to the cacophony of sounds just beyond the entrance to the alley. The noises came together to form a kind of ongoing din. Pup remembered hearing occasional snatches of this same sound back in the pet store, every time the door opened. The rusty bell would jangle and then— *whoosh*—the door would swing inward and for a few seconds, the sounds and smells and the sensations of the changing weather would fill the shop, mingling with the stale air and animal scents.

How long ago that seemed . . . Pup and his family inside, Brooklyn outside.

Now he was outside, and outside was enormous. If only he had someone to help him find his way. His brother had been lucky. When he'd accidentally traveled to the daylight world, he'd made friends and found allies. Pup only knew this from eavesdropping on Hopper's conversation with Hope, of course, since he and Hopper hadn't spoken since their ugly showdown in the wingtip loafer.

If only Pup had some idea of who his brother's friends were. Perhaps he could present himself to them and ask for help.

He shook himself out of his thoughts when he realized that Hope was no longer on the blanket.

"Hope!" he screamed. "Hope!"

"I'm right here," she said, poking her face out from behind a huge metal receptacle. Pup saw that it was labeled with fading white letters: DUMPSTER. If only he knew how to read, perhaps he'd know what the giant container was for.

"What are you doing?"

"I was hungry," she said. "I smelled something wonderful and thought it might be coming from in here."

Pup sniffed. She was right. Something did smell good. In the tunnels the rodents of Atlantia and the Mūs village were lucky enough to dine on tasty crumbs and savory scraps gathered by upland scavengers who sold their haul to merchants, but this aroma was beyond tasty and savory. . . . This smell made him think that every crumb and scrap in the entire world had come together to produce the most scrumptious food smell ever.

"The smell's not coming from the Dumpster, though," she said, scampering back to the blanket.

"The what?"

Hope pointed to the letters painted on the side of the metal box. "That thing. Its name is Dumpster. At least, that's what's written on it."

"You can read?"

Hope nodded. "Yes. Can't you?"

Pup lowered his eyes, embarrassed. He remembered his attempt to change the great Chosen One prophecy in the Sacred Book with his pathetic scribbles and stick figures and felt ashamed . . . on several levels. "No," he said softly. "I can't."

Hope didn't laugh at him or even snicker. She just lifted her pink nose into the air, sniffing.

"I think it's coming from just beyond this wall," she said, following the scent to where the alley opened onto the sidewalk. A few yards down the block, a sign was propped beside a tall, glass door.

"There! The wonderful aroma is coming from right behind that door. And you know what else? I know where we are!"

Pup was confused. "How can you possibly know that?"

Hope smiled, flicking her tail at the white squiggles on the black surface of the sign. "Because I can read what that says."

"What does it say?"

Hope beamed. "It says: 'Today's Special . . . Eggplant Parmigiana'!"

Hope straightened her tiara, then picked up her blanket, brushed off the dirt, and wrapped it around her waist. "Come on."

"Come on *where?*"

"We're going inside," she said breezily.

That didn't help Pup at all. "Inside *where?*"

"Bellissimo's Deli," Hope explained patiently. "That's

where Uncle Hopper had his first taste of eggplant parmigiana. It also happens to be where his pal Ace lives."

"You could have opened with that information," Pup muttered. But he was glad that at least one of them had a plan.

They walked to the edge of the alley and looked toward the door to Bellissimo's. Entering through the front door seemed risky, with the steady flow of human foot traffic stomping in and out.

"Must be lunchtime," Hope guessed. She reversed course and headed for the far end of the alley. "I hope Ace is home when we get there."

"Ace . . . is he a mouse?"

Hope giggled. "Not exactly. And neither is Capone."

Pup followed her as she wound her way through the piles of garbage and over shards of broken glass until the alley deposited them at the deli's back door. He still had no idea what a deli was, but the delicious aromas emanating from it were so enticing, he found that he was more than willing to find out.

Hope put her nose against the glass and peered inside. "I don't see Ace," she said. "But we can go in and wait for him."

With a little wriggling and a fair amount of grunting, the Mūs and the rat princess were able to squeeze themselves through the gap below the door and into the Bellissimo's stockroom. Inside, a second door blocked their view of the front half of the deli, but still, Pup marveled at the scope of just this partial section, with its tall walls and vast floor. Again, he thought of his first home in Keep's shop. But the smells here were not of bird and rodent and fish. The smells here made his mouth water.

Except for one.

It was a smell similar to the ones he remembered from the pet store, but slightly different. Heavier somehow. Not reptile, not feline, not anything he'd ever encountered before. The smell seemed to be concentrated mostly on an enormous pillow in the corner.

Pup didn't have to wonder long about who—or what—that pillow belonged to, because in the next second a burly creature with a rippling chin and lolling tongue came waddling through the swinging door.

And this creature was most definitely *not* a mouse.

CHAPTER SEVENTEEN

IT WAS A DETERMINED AND solemn battalion of soldiers, palace workers, and civilians that set out from the palace. They were armed with everything from brooms and shovels to swords, dirks, and rapiers to sharp rocks and heavy clubs. In their minds, their quarry was the most dangerous to have ever roamed these tunnels.

Among the ranks were Firren's Rangers, led by Leetch, godfather to Raz. Hopper knew the stalwart warrior and the chivalrous young rat were fast friends, and that Leetch had taken great pride in teaching his talented protégé the art of swordcraft. The twins, Bartel and Pritchard, were godfathers to Brighton and Fiske. Go-go claimed Pinkie as her godmother. And although it was only his own godchild who had gone missing, Hopper knew in his heart that every one of these brave and compassionate rodents was as distraught over Hope's disappearance as he would have been if any of the other heirs had been taken. He could feel the connection of their shared grief and was thankful for it.

Also present and prepared for the search-and-rescue mission were Garfield, Polhemus, Ketchum, Dodger, and Fulton. In Hopper's opinion, a more loyal and capable squadron had never been assembled.

As for the rest of the army, those who had never seen Pup had been given sketches of the suspected kidnapper. Hopper had been the one to remind the artist who'd drawn Pup's "mug shot" that the once innocent, sweet-faced Mūs now had a sooty black marking encircling his left eye. The Pup depicted in the final drawing was thoroughly unfamiliar to Hopper. This was the Pup who had taken Hope; this Pup was a monster.

At the iron gate the group split into several smaller brigades, each led by an experienced soldier. They had employed this tactic in their search for Felina and it had brought them success. The more ground they could cover, the more likely they'd be to find Pup.

Raz had devised a method by which the different companies would be able to communicate, despite their widespread positions throughout the tunnels. While the searchers had prepared for their quest, the prince had hunkered down in the schoolroom and formulated a code, which was then taught with great urgency to a wise and willing group of crickets. It was ingeniously simple. Raz had assigned words to chirps.

Pinkie, upon learning that Hope had been abducted, had boarded the first appropriate subway train back to the Mūs stronghold. There she would rally her own troops to join in the search, and their instructions would be the same as those given to the Atlantians: no stone was to be left unturned; no crack in any wall or hole in the dirt should be ignored. Pup could be anywhere.

Anywhere.

But where?

Based on Dev's intel, one of the battalions was sent off in search of a fedora hat; as the regiments went off in various directions, Hopper, Zucker, Dodger, and Firren paused at the entrance to Atlantia. Hopper was glad that he and his father, along with the emperor and empress, had unanimously elected to form their own small band of hunters. What they might lack in numbers they more than made up for in conviction and personal investment.

Hopper found a kind of poetic justice in the fact that

the communications specialist (as Raz had coined his code chirpers) who would be joining them was the same cricket who had serenaded Hopper the day Zucker first rescued him from the speeding subway train.

"Are we ready?" Zucker asked.

Dodger nodded. "Yes, old friend. I am ready."

"So am I," said Hopper.

Firren said nothing. She was staring at something beside the wall. All eyes followed her gaze and immediately saw what she was seeing.

A heap of fabric, abandoned there in the shadows.

Dodger was the first to react. "That's La Rocha's disguise," he said, rushing over just as Firren plucked the cape from the ground.

"Disguise?" said Zucker, studying the garment, which was a cloak of blue felt with patches of white lettering. White lettering that, Hopper knew, had once spelled out BROOKLYN DODGERS 1955 on a commemorative pennant; he knew this because a rat merchant in the Atlantian marketplace had once tried to sell it to him. Later he'd found a piece of it in the tunnels after the camps were liberated, and it had become part of his patchwork blanket.

"Father, how do you know this cape belongs to La Rocha? No one's ever seen him."

"Her," Dodger said softly. "For now, at least."

"I don't understand," said Zucker. "Dodge, what are you getting at?"

"I know what he's getting at," said Firren, her face filled with amazement. "Zucker, don't you remember this cloak? It's the one Dodger wore when he officiated at our wedding."

The emperor's eyes went wide, going from the cloak in Firren's paws to his old friend's unreadable expression.

But Hopper understood. He could see it so clearly in his memory—the mysterious figure on the palace steps, pronouncing the new emperor and the warrior rebel husband and wife! And then the stranger's hood being thrown off, causing Zucker to go pale . . . Hopper's mind whirled. Why had his presumed-dead father been wearing La Rocha's cloak when he'd resurfaced on the steps of the palace all those months ago? Had Dodger been acquainted with the great mystic? Had he actually seen him? Met him?

Or, even more astoundingly . . .

Realization dawned on the three of them at precisely the same second. Hopper, Zucker, and Firren all spoke at once.

"*You* are La Rocha!"

"Yes," said Dodger with a sheepish smile.

"I knew it!" cried Zucker.

"Well, I *was*, at any rate," Dodger clarified. "I have since passed that honor and responsibility on to another."

"A female," said Firren.

"Yes." Dodger nodded. "Quite a capable one, in fact.

So capable, Firren, that you had no qualms whatsoever about leaving her in charge of your children today."

"Marcy!" cried Hopper, pleased by this revelation. "Marcy is the new La Rocha!" That would certainly explain her extended absences from the palace of late. "But why would she leave her cloak out here?"

"I'm not sure," Dodger admitted. "But secret identities often require fast thinking. Perhaps she sensed there was an emergency brewing and wanted to get into the palace quickly without wasting precious time returning to my old fortress to stow the cape."

Zucker looked equal parts stunned and impressed. "You have a *fortress*?"

Dodger blushed. "Well, it's more of a suitcase, really, but the point is, I'm sure Marcy had good reason for leaving her cloak behind, out here by the wall."

"Why didn't she tell us she was La Rocha?" Hopper wondered. "Why didn't you tell us *you* were?"

"It's one of the rules," Dodger explained. "It's quite a long story, for which we do not have the time right now."

Firren draped the cloak over her signature silver cape, as though it were a lucky charm, a magic talisman.

Hopper thought perhaps it just might be that.

"Dodger is right," said the empress, fastening the cloak, then flipping it behind her so that her sword was accessible. "We must hurry."

"But where do we start?" asked Hopper, still reeling a bit from so much staggering news.

"Close to the city," Dodger suggested. "The others have set out for the farther reaches, and Pinkie will be covering the area near the Mūs village. I say we begin with a sweep of the area just outside the wall."

"Agreed," said Zucker.

They all fell silent and stepped aside for Dodger to lead the way.

With senses alert and weapons drawn, the royal couple, the Chosen One and the retired rebel-slash-prophet began their search.

"Over there!" cried Hopper, pointing across the tunnel to a place on the wall. They had not traveled very far into the Great Beyond; in fact, they had yet to even reach the rise in the tunnel floor from which Hopper had once caught his first glimpse of the city. But already he'd found a clue.

At least, he hoped it was a clue.

It was a message of some sort, scratched into the wall; it made Hopper think of the runes where he'd first seen a sketch of a face he'd mistakenly thought to be his own.

He could see that Firren, too, recognized the similarity. After all, she herself was responsible for most of the artwork depicted there. The last message La Rocha (a.k.a. Dodger) had left there had directed

Firren to the grasslands of the daylight world, where she'd found Hopper and talked him into returning to the tunnels.

But the runes were far from here, deep in the outskirts of the Great Beyond. This piece of writing was much closer to Atlantia, located just below a crudely dug hole in the ceiling. And this hole was not just some random crumbling gap between the wall's upper edge and the arched ceiling. Hopper knew this small chasm was a portal that led directly to the functioning Atlantic Avenue/Barclays Center subway platform above them. He'd used it himself, on more than one occasion, but he'd never noticed a message on the wall before. It couldn't be a coincidence that words had been recently inscribed directly beneath the hole that led to the upland world.

He hurried toward it for a closer look, with the others close at his heels.

What they saw was an inscription written in childish script.

"Do you think La Ro—I mean, Marcy wrote this?" Hopper asked.

Dodger studied the words and shook his head. "I don't think so. She would have left us a message—if she had one—at the original runes, not here, where she had no reason to expect us to look."

Suddenly Firren's paw flew to her mouth; her eyes were big and round. "I know that script!" she said.

Zucker recognized it too. "Hope!"

Firren nodded and read the inscription aloud:

"We lived in a cage that was cozy and clean
But then Mama was taken and Pinkie was mean
Just when we thought we'd had all we could take
We were forced to escape from the jaws of a snake
I took quite a fall, but I went right on livin'
Now I want to come home . . . please say all is forgiven."

Hopper swayed on his feet; the short verse told an enormous story.

"Hope may have inscribed it," he said. "But surely Pup was the one to compose it! It's practically his autobiography! And look! It says he wants to be forgiven."

"Does he, now?" Zucker growled. "Well, it's gonna take a heck of a lot more than a catchy little nursery rhyme to get me to forgive that maniac for taking my child!"

"But that's just it," said Hopper. "I don't think he took her. Pup can't read or write."

"So?"

"So . . . if he were taking Hope against her will, he would have had to force her to write this for him. He would have dictated it to her, but Hope is a clever girl. She easily could have included something like 'help' or 'save me' to let us know she was in danger.

Even if Pup were holding her at"—Hopper gulped—"at swordpoint, she still could have improvised and he would have never known the difference."

Dodger frowned. "So you think Hope and Pup are working as allies? You think she went willingly?"

"I think it's a distinct possibility."

"But Dev said Pup *took* her," said Firren. "Could he have misunderstood the situation that completely?"

Hopper shrugged. "He was injured. Distracted. Maybe what he thought was a kidnapping was actually something else entirely. That's what my gut is telling me."

"An alliance would imply that they have a common enemy," Firren pointed out. "Which doesn't make sense. Pup may despise us, but Hope would never think of her family as the enemy, no matter how much her brothers and sisters teased her."

"I agree," said Hopper. "Which is why the enemy must be someone else. I think Hope was upset and decided to run away. That's what she was doing when I saw her alone in the city. Somehow she met up with Pup out here in the tunnels, where they encountered someone who presented a threat to both of them."

"That's not a bad theory," observed Dodger, stroking his whiskers thoughtfully.

"But who could this enemy be? A rogue feral?"

Hopper nodded. "Possibly."

The dreary tunnel fell silent as they all struggled to

think of anyone who might have been frightening enough to both Hope and Pup to cause them to join forces. Zucker began to pace, stomping up clouds of dust. Dodger continued to smooth his whiskers, and Firren stuffed her paws into the pockets of the found cloak.

"Could it have been another team of exterminators?" Hopper wondered.

"Not likely," said Zucker.

Hopper took some comfort in this; he hated to imagine Hope and Pup facing two giant humans in coveralls like the ones who'd coming bearing traps on a mission to destroy Atlantia. He closed his eyes to begin thinking in earnest, but opened them again when he heard the familiar sound of crinkling paper. He turned to Firren and saw that she was reading a note. She must have found it in the pocket of La Rocha's cape.

"It wasn't a feral or a human . . . ," she said through gritted teeth, holding out the scrap of paper. "It was a traitor."

Chapter Eighteen

I FEAR I HAVE MADE *a horrible mistake.*

This place that the soldier Devon is taking us to is a much greater distance than I expected, and the trek has been an arduous one. The heirs are terrified. And I'm beginning to feel the same.

As we walk, flashes of memory explode in my mind. An old suitcase; words scrawled at the runes; my own paw placing a note in an unfamiliar one belonging to someone I cannot see. I don't know why I feel so connected to these images, but they mean something . . . I know it. Sadly, I cannot stop to dwell on them now. Dev will not allow us to stop and rest, even for a moment.

First, he marched us a long way through the tunnels. I felt my first inkling of suspicion when we spied one of the search parties in the distance and Raz, budding little general that he is, suggested we chase them down and tell them of our plan. But Dev had forbidden it, rather vehemently. Again, he used the excuse of Pup employing torture to learn of our whereabouts. It had made some sense to me earlier, back in the palace when I imagined a poor, frightened cook giving in under such pressure. But soldiers? Surely they are trained to hold their tongues in such circumstances. And besides, they would have had Pup severely outnumbered, so what threat was there of torture?

I made to argue, but Dev's paw went to his sword.

So onward we went, the children in a steady line with Dev, armed and alert, at the front and me bringing up the rear.

"Where are we going?" Fiske asks now, after we've walked for what feels like miles.

"To City Hall," says Devon.

"Where's that?" asks Brighton.

Dev says, "You'll see."

"Is it a safe place for us to hide?" asks Go-go.

Dev does not reply.

"Look," cries Brighton. She stops so suddenly that her glasses slide down her nose and the siblings behind her collide with one another, nearly toppling over. This has Fiske laughing, but Dev silences him with a harsh look.

"What is it, Brighton?" I ask, forcing my voice to remain calm, although I am growing more worried by the moment.

She bends down and picks up a piece of paper that at first I think might be a page from the Sacred Book, the one the Mūs elders have compiled over time, and by which they govern most of their actions. It was the Sacred Book that told of Hopper's eventual arrival in the tunnels. I am plagued with the feeling that I actually know more about this than I think, as though I am privy to some secret regarding the book and its esteemed author, the prophet La Rocha. But right now I just can't recall what that is. I suppose this is due to my relentless headache, not to mention my concerns about Dev's motives.

"It's the prettiest paper I've ever seen," says Brighton,

running her paws reverently over the once-glossy page. She hands it to me and I examine it. It has seen better days, to be sure. . . . It is wrinkled and dusty and the corners are beginning to curl. One edge is rough, as though it has been torn out of a bound volume.

"It's a page from a human book," I tell the princess, pointing to the title printed in the top right corner. "A book called The Rise and Fall of the Roman Empire."

Now Go-go has huddled close and her curious eyes pore over the page. "I see a word I recognize," she says. "'Titus.' That was our grandfather's name!"

"Here's another one," cries Verrazano, using his wooden sword to push aside a few stones and pebbles covering a second glossy page in the dirt. "And there's a name on this one too: Cassius."

"I remember him from our history lessons," says Brighton. "He was Grandfather Titus's best soldier."

"Worst soldier, you mean," Raz corrects. "He killed Uncle Dodger. Or tried to, at least."

Fiske, who's been kicking at a pile of rubble, produces several more pages and hands them over to Verrazano.

"These are all about the Roman emperors," he says, "whoever they are. And how they rose to power."

"Emperors like Daddy?" asks Brighton.

"Sort of," says Raz. "Except these were human."

"It must have been a lovely book," says Go-go, taking a page from her brother and eyeing the colorful illustrations. "Well, I mean, for a story about dumb old politics."

"Enough dillydallying," barks Dev. "You are right, little princess, there is nothing lovely about politics. Power corrupts. And your family is the perfect example."

Raz narrows his eyes, taking offense. "Hey!"

"Quiet!" snaps Devon. "Now all of you, back in line. And march." His face contorts into a sinister smile. "We have a train to catch."

My heart is in my throat for the entire ride.

The marking on the forehead of the serpentine beast identified it as the 5 train. Dev allowed three other trains to pass before choosing this one, which we boarded just minutes ago. Getting the four heirs safely onto the narrow step at the rear of the last car was a complicated feat. Brighton was petrified; Fiske kept shouting, "Look, no hands!"; and Go-go worried the whole time that the rushing wind would leave tangles in her fur.

My only consolation is that, for the moment at least, they do not suspect that Dev might be out to cause them harm.

Raz is the only one who is beginning to wonder.

As we disembark, I try to pull him aside, to share my concerns with him. He is only a child, I know, but he already displays the makings of a great military leader. Perhaps if we put our heads together, we can come up with a plan to escape Dev.

If only Raz's sword were made of steel and not wood. If only . . .

"Come along," Dev commands as we scamper across the

cement floor of (according to the words printed on the wall) the Brooklyn Bridge stop. "We change trains here. But this ride will be much less grueling."

The children are in awe at the sight of so many humans being expelled from the belly of the train. Something tells me that these are not the first humans I have ever seen; a word circles in my brain: exterminators. But at this anxious moment, I can't seem to pull the whole of the recollection into focus. All I know is that I feel compelled to pull the children close to me and do my best to keep us from being noticed.

When the last human has exited the beast—whose name, I see from its markings, is 6—Dev gives Raz a shove and orders, "Inside!"

"You're kidding," I blurt out. "You want us to feed ourselves to this serpent?"

"Inside," Dev repeats, entering the train easily with a powerful jump.

For one crazy instant, I consider bolting, taking the children and running away. I know the jaws of the train will close on Dev any second now, trapping him inside. If we flee, we will be free of him and whatever nefarious plan he has for us in this place called City Hall.

But Raz has just leaped into the belly of the beast beside Dev. I can't leave him behind. And besides, there is still a chance that I am only imagining Dev to be a villain. Perhaps his gruffness and agitation is due to his own stress over having to travel such a great distance with such precious charges in his care.

I ask La Rocha for guidance. But the only voice that returns to me in my heart is my own.

"You must follow," it says.

And so I do.

With a gentle nudge I urge the other children toward the gaping mouth of the monster, the interior of which glows with a sickly, green-yellow light.

Go-go and Fiske scuttle in, leaping over the narrow divide. Brighton's the last one and her hind paws just barely make it, slipping and scratching. Her brothers reach out and grab her before she falls backward. Her glasses fly off, skidding across the floor of the train.

But she is safe. Alive. I heave a sigh of relief as Raz gallantly returns her spectacles to her.

"Now you," says Dev, pointing to me.

I am about to leap aboard when the train gurgles ominously, then belches; suddenly the yawning mouth begins to slide closed.

"Marcy, jump!" cries Raz.

I do exactly that, hurling myself toward the swiftly narrowing space between the monster's jaws. I feel my hind paws connect with metal, and scrabble to gain purchase on the slick, flat surface of the train's innards.

But the mouth bites closed, catching my tail. I muffle the scream of agony that wants to rip from my throat. The hold is viselike, the pain indescribable.

Raz lunges toward me, taking my paws in his and pulling with every ounce of might in his body. Brighton, Fiske, and

Go-go join him; they huff and grunt and tug, struggling to rescue me. Dev just stands there, watching, offering no aid, lending none of his strength to their efforts.

I feel a searing pain shoot through my tail, just before I jolt forward, breaking away from the grip of the train to be released into the collective arms of the children. Every one of us is crying.

Go-go examines the severe crimp in my tail but pronounces that there is no blood. It has not been shorn off, or snapped in two.

That is good news. But it hurts to the point of making me dizzy.

Of course, I refuse to let them know this. So I smile.

"Thank you, my darlings," I breathe. "Thank you for saving me."

We do not disentangle ourselves from the knot of comfort we have formed. In fact, the only move I make is to lift my head and slide a glance at Dev.

His eyes are dark, his face hard. He does not rejoice in the slightest for my rescue.

And it is at this moment that I understand with absolute certainty . . .

. . . he is our enemy.

It is a short ride, made interminable by the violent sting in my tail.

The train slows, but there is something in the rumble, the squeal of the metal wheels on the track, that tells me *it is not going to stop. Dev confirms this.*

"The train is about to turn around," he explains in a clipped tone. "It makes a loop but does not come to a halt. We are going to have to jump while it is still in motion."

"We'll be killed!" squeaks Go-go.

"Oh, please. I've done it plenty of times," Dev assures her coolly.

"But you're bigger than we are," Raz reminds him.

Dev glares, then gestures for us to follow him. Again, I position myself at the end of the line of children, who are now exhausted, both physically and emotionally. I am glad to come behind, where they cannot see how difficult it is for me to walk. The crimp in my tail, not to mention the shimmying and lurching of the train, makes it nearly impossible for me to maintain my balance.

Dev leads us to a door at the very end of the subway car. It is a human door, therefore enormous, and it leads outside into rushing nothingness. He enlists all of us to assist him in opening it, ordering Verrazano to pry it with his toy sword. The noise and wind that enter through the sliver of space we manage to create is deafening. Terrified, we file through and find ourselves on a platform, though this one is far less roomy than the first on which we rode. This one juts out like a flattened tooth, or fang, and I can only assume that it is the joint by which other cars might latch on to this one.

Dev says nothing, just places his paws on Raz's shoulders and shoves.

The unsuspecting prince drops over the edge. I let out a shriek, which joins with the screams and shouts of the others.

Next Dev tosses Fiske. I watch in horror as he bounces and rolls away from us along the rusty track.

"Now you girls," Dev snarls. "Hurry up."

I take Brighton by the paw and offer my other one to Go-go. Without giving them a chance to think about what we are doing, I tighten my grip and leap.

We hit the track hard. As we tumble, I catch a glimpse of Dev flinging himself from the hitch. We roll a ways, finally skidding to a stop in the gravel and rust. By some miracle, I am able to stand. We are scraped and filthy, but we are whole. I take a quick accounting of scratches and bruises, but no bones appear to be broken. Brighton's glasses, however, are bent and one of the lenses is cracked.

Now that we are out in the open, I wonder . . . can we escape? Can we run from this devil, who has brought us so far from home under such a false pretense?

But my question is answered when I feel Dev's hot breath on the fur of my back; I know we would not get far. Even if we scattered, even if he could only catch one of these beloved children, it would be one too many. We are (as we have been without knowing it from the start) trapped. He withdraws his sword and points to a ladder fashioned of old rope dangling over the edge of the platform.

"Up," he commands.

The heirs do as they are told, their tails swishing as they

climb the makeshift ladder, and assemble on the cement expanse of the station floor.

And then they merely stare.

Upward and around they look, gasping, widening their eyes, allowing their mouths to drop open in awe.

I am the last one up the ladder. I am the last one to see.

And when I do, I know why they are all so flabbergasted.

I feel as if I have just entered a work of art. For City Hall is nothing short of sensational, with its tinted glass and tile and iron work, boasting graceful arches and varying levels.

Unbelievably, it is empty of humans. Indeed, judging by the relative cleanliness, I surmise that there have not been humans here in years. Perhaps decades. Maybe even longer.

There is a hush, a reverent silence that seems appropriate to the grandeur of the place. After the din of the train, I am grateful for it. The peacefulness is almost welcoming.

Almost.

But I know that Dev has not brought us here to enjoy the beauty of what, under other circumstances, I would say is the most elegant place I have ever seen.

The point of this journey was not for us to admire the aesthetics of this forgotten, magnificent station called City Hall. Nor was it to protect us from a vengeful Pup, hell-bent on destroying us. I know that now.

Yes, City Hall is without doubt a stunning spectacle, but with every passing heartbeat, I feel its beauty vanishing, *draining away like blood from a fatal gash. Slowly I turn to Dev, to look into his glassy, unfeeling eyes, where everything seems to be reflected back to me. And it is there that I see City Hall for exactly what it is:*

A prison.

CHAPTER NINETEEN

"CIAO, PICCOLI."

Hope let out a squeak of shock. Pup quickly stepped in front of her, spreading his arms wide to shield the little princess from the strange beast that had just sauntered into the room.

"Who are *you*?" Pup demanded. "*What* are you?"

The creature let out a sound that might have been a chuckle. "I am Capone," the animal said. "Bulldog. And you?"

Pup puffed out his chest. "I am Pup. Hopper's brother."

"Are you, now?" The dog's face turned grim. "Would that be the same brother who ran away and terrorized the tunnels? The brother who broke his heart?"

"Yeah." Pup cast his eyes downward and sighed. "That'd be me."

"But he's a good mouse now!" Hope piped, peeking out from behind him. "He was going to apologize for all of it, but the bad soldier tried to kill me and we had to run away."

Capone studied them a moment, then shook his head. "I don't know if I should believe you. When Ace came back from the tunnels, he told me that Hopper had tried to reason with you while you were holed up in some old . . . combat boot, was it?"

"Dress shoe," Pup grumbled. "Close enough."

"Ace said that it didn't go well."

Pup reached up to touch his torn ear. "It didn't."

"But that was before," Hope persisted, stepping out of Pup's shadow to smile at the gargantuan canine before them. "He's had a change of heart since then."

"You have to believe me, Mr. Capone," Pup pleaded. "I was out of my mind with anger and confusion, and it caused me to make some very bad choices. But I've worked through that, and there's nothing I want more than to patch things up with my family."

Capone took some time to consider Pup's story. "I do believe you, *topo*," he said at last, giving Pup a sympathetic look. "I was once a fugitive myself, so I know that it is possible for one who has strayed to see the error of his ways and want to make things right."

"We're looking for Ace," explained Pup. "He still lives here, doesn't he?"

"Oh yes." The dog nodded, causing the folds of his chin to wag. "He does. But he is at work right now."

"Work?" Hope gave Capone a quizzical look. "I thought his job was relocating mice and other rodents."

"It still is," Capone assured her with a drooly grin. "Only now he commutes."

"Can we talk to him?" Pup asked. "We really need his help."

"Sure," said Capone. "He'll back in a few hours. Benito gives him a ride."

Pup's heart sank. He had no idea who or what a Benito might be, but he understood what "a few hours" meant. He honestly didn't think he could wait that long to ask for the cat's assistance in returning them safely to the tunnels, and possibly convincing Hopper to forgive him. "Please, Mr. Capone. We've come such a long distance, and I really think Ace might be able to help us. Isn't there a way we can see him now?"

"Hmmm." Capone considered the request. "I think maybe I *can* help you out. Follow me."

The dog waddled to the back door and pushed it open effortlessly with his big head. "Ace's workplace is a ways from here, though. I'd carry you there myself, but I'm not allowed on the sidewalks without a leash."

"Then how are we going to get there?"

Again, the dog's face broke into a sloppy smile. "How do you feel about bicycles?"

Ace, it seemed, had branched out. Not only did he relocate rodents from the houses and establishments up and down Atlantic Avenue, but now he was also working part-time at a place called the New York Transit Authority Museum on Boerum Place.

According to Capone, the exceptional cat had

gotten the job by sheer luck. One of the museum's tour guides was in the habit of indulging herself every Friday at noon with a takeout meal from her favorite delicatessen—Bellissimo's. Every Friday morning she would call and speak to either Vito or Guido to order what she called her "usual"—a small antipasto salad, a meatball sub with roasted peppers and extra cheese, and a serving of tiramisu for dessert—all to be delivered.

The brothers would prepare the meal, and then one of them would whistle out the back door to their third, much younger brother, Benito, who'd come screaming up on his bicycle, which had a deep wire basket attached to the handlebars.

The tour guide's meal would be placed carefully in the basket and off Benny would go, careening through the streets of Brooklyn, dodging pedestrians and taxicabs, to deliver the food. One day Benny arrived to find the tour guide looking pale and very shaken up.

What'sa matta? Benny had asked.

Trembling, she told him she'd seen a mouse in the museum and it had frightened her so badly, she'd nearly lost her appetite; she'd almost decided to skip her customary Friday luncheon.

Benny had told her that it was a darn good thing she hadn't, because he was pretty sure he could help her rectify this rodent problem. As it happened, he and his brothers were the owners of a tuxedo cat who held the title of Best Mouser in all of Brooklyn.

"Is there really such a title?" Hope asked.

"Nah," said Capone. "Benny likes to exaggerate. But the point is, the very next day he put ol' Ace in his wire basket and peddled him to the transit museum, where our feline friend was able to successfully relocate not only the mouse but three squirrels and a rat as well. The museum folks were so happy, they decided to make it a regular gig. And now, every Friday morning, the tour guide swings by on her way to work and picks him up in her car. In the afternoon, when Benny finishes his deliveries, he swings back by the museum and brings *il gatto* home with him on the bike. Pretty classy, no?"

"Very," Pup agreed.

"That's all very interesting," said Hope. "But what does it have to do with us?"

Capone chuckled and motioned to an odd-looking two-wheeled machine propped against the wall of the back alley. "Today's Friday," he said. "Guess who's ridin' with the meatballs?"

Capone boosted them into the basket. Hope was so tiny, she had to cling to the wires to keep from falling through the holes. Then the dog covered them with a white paper napkin that had the BELLISSIMO'S DELICATESSEN logo emblazoned on it in red and green letters.

Just as Capone finished tucking in the corners to conceal them, the back door of the deli opened and Vito—or perhaps Guido—came out and whistled.

"Stay low," Capone whispered. "And hold on tight." Then the dog trotted away, barking a friendly greeting to his owner.

"Yo, Benny! *Vieni qui!*"

Pup heard a scuffling sound. He peered out from beneath the edge of the napkin and saw a human in torn blue jeans and a BELLISSIMO'S T-shirt jogging toward the bike. He was glad to see that this boy, unlike Bo the Snake's scrawny, mean-spirited owner, had a cheerful face and no reptile companions.

"Museum order's ready to go. Now move it, before them meatballs get cold. And remember ya gotta bring Acey back wit'cha."

"Don't I always remember? Jeesh."

There was a crunch of gravel, then a skidding sensation as Pup felt the bike lurch forward.

They were off.

Pup gave up peeking out after the first five minutes of the ride.

It was simply too terrifying to watch. The world flew by in a blur as Benny weaved and darted in and out of the paths of huge yellow creatures with round black feet and shrill honking voices. Other similar creatures in duller hues cut in and out as well, but Benny didn't seem to mind. He merely steered his rolling vehicle sharply out of the way and kept right on pedaling.

"This is fun!" cried Hope.

Pup strongly disagreed with that assessment. His only comfort was the warmth emanating from the white paper bag perched beside him in the basket. He pressed himself against it, trying to imagine how wonderful its deliciously scented contents would taste. He was tempted to nibble through the paper and help himself to a bite, but with the way Benny's bike was lurching and swerving, Pup was pretty sure anything he put into his stomach would not remain there for long.

Fortunately, Benny managed to make it to the museum without incident. Hope peeked out from her side of the napkin.

"We're here!"

The bike wobbled as Benny dismounted and leaned it against a tall post.

"Wait until he takes the bag out," Pup directed. "Then we can climb down and follow him inside."

Hope nodded. A moment later, the bag was lifted out of the basket. Pup waited until the delivery boy had turned away, and then he took Hope by the paw. They pressed themselves through the square holes in the wire basket and made their way down to the sidewalk. Running as quickly as they could, they reached the door right as Benny disappeared inside and slipped in just before it closed.

Pup blinked.

For one mad second he thought he was back in the subway tunnels.

"This place is so cool!" breathed Hope, taking it in with eager eyes. "It reminds me of home."

She was right, of course. The museum seemed to be a cleaner, better-lit replica of the tunnel world below. An upland twin. A mirror image.

This made him think of Pinkie and Hopper, with their white markings and wounded ears, and his heart hurt in his chest. The sooner they could find Ace, the better. He was Pup's best—perhaps only—

chance of convincing his brother to forgive him.

Again, he took Hope's hand and guided her out of the flow of foot traffic, which luckily, was minimal. Only a few humans were to be found wandering around, exploring and posing with big smiles near the older train cars and turnstiles on display. The tour guide, Pup imagined, was probably halfway through her antipasto right about now.

The walls were adorned with all sorts of memorabilia pertaining to public transit. Old advertisements, maps, artwork, and photographs.

"I get the feeling the humans are very proud of their subway system," Hope observed, pausing to gaze up at a black-and-white rendering of a bustling station from the recent past—a photograph, Pup thought it was called; he'd seen a few affixed to pages of the Sacred Book when he'd lived in the locomotive with Pinkie. They were marvelous, he realized now, studying the much-enlarged image on the wall. A photograph, essentially, was a way to freeze reality, to capture humans exactly as they were at any particular moment in time.

Pup blinked. Make that humans *and* (unless Pup's eyes were deceiving him) rodents!

There in the corner of the enormous photograph, he saw the most astonishing thing. Three rodents . . . rats, judging by the size of them, crouching close to the wall. Two were burly, clearly male, but the third had a kind of feminine grace about her. She wore what appeared to be a necklace, fashioned of shining gemstones and filigreed metal. Pup wished the photo wasn't black and white; he had a feeling those stones would be beautiful in color.

"Hey," said Hope, taking note of Pup's steady gaze and following it to the photo. "The lady rat in that picture is wearing a chain just like the one my daddy wears for special royal occasions."

"Really?" Pup turned to the little princess, who nodded exuberantly.

"It belonged to his mother. I don't know the whole story, but I think Grandfather Titus gave it to her as a gift when they were courting, long before he was emperor, long before the founding of Atlantia."

This revelation caused Pup's fur to prickle and actually stand on end. Could it be? Could he really be looking at what he *thought* he was looking at?

He whipped his head around to examine the photo again. He was sure the human who took it—the human who had the magical power to freeze time into a single image—probably hadn't even known the three rats were in the picture. Something about the posture of the two male rodents—the position of their paws, the hunch of their backs—seemed to indicate that they were burrowing, digging, creating a hole in the slim crevice where the base of the wall met the floor.

It made perfect sense. The portal he and Hope had climbed through . . . the jeweled necklace . . .

Pup was about to point out his amazing discovery to Hope when he felt a presence behind him. Heart pounding, he turned slowly to look over his shoulder and saw a large, handsome cat. Like the photograph, the cat was a study in black and white, his dark ears contrasting with the dazzlingly white fur of his chest.

When Pup's eyes met the feline's clear green ones, the rhythm of Pup's heart changed from a fearful pounding to a rapid flutter.

A flutter of absolute joy.

"Hello, Ace," he said, extending a paw to shake. "I'm Pup. And I'm hoping you can help me."

CHAPTER TWENTY

FIRREN HELD THE NOTE AS though it were burning her paw. Zucker reached out, gently took the scrap of paper from her, and read it to himself.

"What does it say?" asked Hopper.

"Not much," said Zucker. "Looks like she wrote it in a hurry. But the gist of it is that Devon is not to be trusted."

"Devon . . . ," Hopper said, his mouth going dry. "Devon who we left behind to protect the children?"

Zucker nodded. "Yeah," he said, his muscles tightening. "Him. We need to get back there, right now."

"Wait," cried Hopper. "We can't all go back. What about Hope? She's gone upland, obviously. And believe me, that place can be hazardous." He pointed to the message on the wall, the one that hinted at Pup's forthcoming apology. "Even if Pup hasn't taken her away in anger, even if they've becomes allies somehow, she's still in danger." He looked at the note in Zucker's fist and struggled to make sense of it. "I don't understand what La Rocha . . . I mean, Marcy . . . means about Dev being untrustworthy. When I left her with him, she didn't seem worried at all. She didn't even seem to recognize him."

Zucker turned to Firren, his expression desperate.

"Tell me what you want to do," he said. "I'll do whatever you say."

Firren was perfectly still. Hopper knew her heart was breaking with worry for her children. It was bad enough when they'd thought only Hope was in peril, but now, to know the whole litter was at risk . . .

"Hopper," she said at last, her voice strained but steady, "you and Zucker go to the daylight world. You are the only one among us who knows the lay of the land up there. You have the best chance of finding Hope." She turned to nod at Dodger. "You and I, old friend, we will make our way back to the palace . . ." She drew her sword and held it above her shoulder, twirling it slowly. "And we'll see what this Devon has to say for himself."

"There's no point in that."

The four friends spun as one in the direction of the voice, but it was Hopper who recognized the soldier first.

"Wyona!" he cried, running to her just in time to catch her before her legs gave out. "What happened?"

"Devon attacked us," Wyona reported. "DeKalb and Pitkin and me." Her voice broke when she added, "They're dead. But I only pretended to be." Her paw went to her head, where the fur was bloody and matted. "I suppose I came pretty close. I've been on my way back to Atlantia, but the pain has made it slowgoing. Then I spotted pawprints heading in this direction, so I followed them."

"You are an intrepid warrior," Dodger noted. "And for that we are grateful. Now, what do you know of Hope's disappearance? And Pup?"

"They got away. Pup acted with exceptional valor. He distracted Devon with the princess's tiara, then bit him and took the princess away."

"So he *did* kidnap her?" Zucker growled.

"No," said Wyona, shaking her head, then grimacing at the pain it caused her. "He saved her. When we found him, Pup was prepared to come peacefully. Devon murdered the general and Pitkin and clobbered me, and then he launched into some elaborate lie about DeKalb and the rest of us being traitors, and about how Pinkie was furious with him for shaming her. He tried to get Pup on his side by saying Pinkie would find a way to blame the murders on Pup if he ever showed his face in Atlantia again. But then Hope arrived and when Dev realized that the child was actually one of the royal litter, he changed his plan completely. He held his sword to her throat. I believe he had every intention of . . . well . . ." She flicked a glance at Firren. "You know."

"But they got away?" Firren asked anxiously. "Yes? You said they got away."

Wyona nodded, wincing once more. "The bite Pup gave Devon was pretty bad. It kept him from chasing after them. Devon had to wrap it before he could walk, and while he did, he went off on a wild, crazy rant. I was right there, faking my own death as it were, so I heard all of it."

"A rant?" said Hopper. "What do you mean?"

"A tirade. Yelling and screaming—vowing he would destroy Atlantia and the Mūs village entirely, and raving about how he wouldn't rest until Hope and every one of her siblings had been . . . slain."

Zucker clenched his fists, snarled, and said nothing.

"He knew the minute you heard that Pup had kidnapped Hope, you'd send every soldier and servant out to find them, leaving the palace virtually unprotected and making it simple for him to take the royal heirs hostage. He said he knew exactly where he would hold them captive. He was crazed! All I could do was lie there, listening, holding my breath so he wouldn't know I was alive. He was out of his mind with fury, going on and on and on about . . . well, I don't know what! Half of it didn't make sense—he was muttering about something silver . . . and his sisters . . . and *skylights*, of all things. I thought he'd gone off the deep end, until he started raging about . . ." She paused to nod at Firren. "About you, Your Majesty."

"Me?" said Firren. "What could he possibly have said about me?"

"He said if it weren't for you, he would be a prince himself, reigning from a splendid and magnificent place called..." She paused again, trying to remember. "What did he call it? City Hall station."

"City Hall?" Firren lowered her weapon and swallowed hard. "Are you *sure* that's what he said?"

"I'm positive. He said his father's dream was wasted, and his family suffered, thanks to you. He said you were a selfish, useless coward. And he talked about the hunting ground. He said something about meeting you there."

"A duel, is it?" seethed Zucker. "Well, that's just fine by me. If this nut job wants to arrange a meeting at the old hunting ground, I'm all for it. I doubt he'll think Firren's a useless coward when he finds himself with her sword aimed at his heart."

"Wait a minute," said Hopper. "Wyona, did Devon mean Titus's hunting ground?"

"I assume so," said Wyona with a shrug.

"But there is no more hunting ground."

"Hopper's right," said Dodger, turning to Firren. "You had the soldiers destroy it. So how can this madmouse expect to meet you at a place that no longer exists?"

Firren let out a long, ragged breath. "Because he's not talking about meeting me at the hunting ground *now*. He's talking about having already met me there. Before."

"You mean during the battle to liberate the camps?" Hopper guessed. "When Pinkie led the Mūs army and

169

I found Pup and hid him in . . ." He let his words trail off; now was definitely not the time to mention the silver cup where Firren had hid as a pup, the cup that had saved her life, protecting her while she watched her parents disappear forever.

"No, Chosen One," said Firren. "Devon wasn't present to fight that battle. I'm talking about my first trip to the hunting ground, a long time ago."

"What are you saying?" asked Zucker.

"I'm saying," said Firren, her voice a raspy whisper, "that I suddenly remember where I've seen Devon before."

"Where?" Hopper ventured softly.

Firren closed her eyes, as if she could see it clearly in her mind. "Right beside me in that damned silver cup," she answered softly, "where together we watched our families die."

Chapter Twenty-One

It was difficult to admit it all to Ace. Saying it out loud—to a friend of Hopper's, no less—made Pup burn with guilt all over again. And with Princess Hope interrupting every few seconds, sweetly and loyally pleading his case, it took twice as long to explain.

But in the end, Ace understood. He believed that Pup had been, for lack of a better term, rehabilitated and that his motivations for turning himself in to Emperor Zucker and the Chosen One were pure.

"I'll have to go to Atlantia alone, first," Ace decided. "It's not safe for you to go back until I've had a chance to clear your name. I'll find Hopper and tell him everything. Then we'll send for you and you can return home to the tunnels. Or maybe Hopper will come up here and escort you back himself."

"You really think he'll be willing to come get me?" said Pup.

"Of course," said Ace, grinning. "And besides, I happen to know there's someone not too far from here who's been very anxious to see him."

"Carroll!" Hope cried. "Right?"

Ace nodded. "She's missed him."

"Oh, he's missed her too. He's missed her like crazy. He talks about her all the time."

Ace laughed. "She'll be glad to hear it. Make sure you tell her."

"Me?" Hope smiled. "I'm going to meet her?"

"Absolutely. I can't leave you two tiny . . ." Ace shot Pup a quick glance and cleared his throat. "I mean, you two *brave* tunnel dwellers all alone up here to fend for yourselves while I'm gone, can I?"

Pup was grateful for the cat's sensitivity, but the truth was, he'd moved beyond those petty insecurities regarding his diminutive stature. He was small. He could live with it.

"So does this mean you're taking us to the grasslands?" asked Hope, bouncing excitedly on her hind legs, tugging happily on the silky black tail that had once saved her beloved godfather's life.

"I am!"

"Yippppeee!"

Ace smiled at Hope's enthusiasm. "Right after I finish my shift here at the museum, I'll bring you to the park. I've still got some rounds to make, but you two are free to roam around and enjoy the exhibits as my guests. It's a pretty interesting place."

Pup agreed. Seeing those rodents in that photograph had really ignited his imagination.

For the next hour he and Hope explored the museum. Her ability to read was hugely helpful. At one point they had to duck out of the path of a group of schoolchildren who were being led by a tour guide.

Pup had to giggle; he was reasonably sure she was the one who had the weakness for meatball grinders, judging by the splotch of marinara sauce on the front of her blouse.

"And now, boys and girls," the guide was saying, "I'm going to let you all in on a very big secret. The secret of . . . City Hall."

At the sound of these words, Pup's ears pricked up. Devon, that vicious turncoat, had used that very same phrase . . . twice. Pup remembered, because there was something about the way he had said it that made him wonder if there was more to it than the villain had let on.

Now this meatball-loving tour guide was talking about it being some kind of "big secret."

Pup motioned to Hope to keep quiet, and together they crept along after the group, listening.

"The City Hall station," the guide explained, "was a subway station, just across the river in Manhattan."

"What's Manhattan?" Pup asked Hope.

"I think it's an island not far from Brooklyn." Before he could ask, Hope added, "'Island' means 'surrounded by water.'"

Pup grinned. "Thanks."

"It was built by the Interborough Rapid Transit Company," the guide went on, "and it opened a long time ago, at the turn of the century."

"You mean Y2K?" one of the children asked.

The tour guide smiled and shook her head. "The century before that," she said. "In the year 1904."

The children appeared to be very impressed by this.

"City Hall station was originally going to be the southern terminus of the first Manhattan Main Line. And it was truly the pièce de résistance of this marvelous feat of engineering known as the subway system. While the other stops were more utilitarian in design . . ."

Pup glanced at Hope for clarification.

"Useful but ordinary," she translated. "Practical."

"City Hall looked more like the lobby of some grand hotel or perhaps even a royal palace. It was built on a curve, and had shiny brass fixtures, even skylights."

"I ride the subway all the time," said a little girl. "How come I've never seen this beautiful station?"

The guide's eyes lit up and she smiled at the girl. "That's the secret! Sadly, the City Hall station was not functional for very long. It closed on December 31, 1945."

The children seemed disappointed to hear this. Pup felt a bit sad about it himself. It sounded like a beautiful place. So why would such a scoundrel as Devon know about it? He killed three Mūs soldiers in cold blood; he certainly didn't strike Pup as the sort who bothered himself with architectural marvels.

Suddenly Pup's imagination was churning again. If this were the same "City Hall" the villainous soldier had been hinting about, he must have been doing it for a reason. This place meant something to Dev. Could City Hall be his hideout? Perhaps it was his lair—in Pup's experience, all menacing creatures had one, Felina being the most glaring example, and then, of course, there was his own stint in the wingtip. Maybe this old City Hall station was the place Dev went to brood and scheme and devise sickening plots to murder his comrades and take down benevolent monarchies. It certainly had all the qualifications of being a lair. It was both luxurious and abandoned. And, as the guide had said, it was a secret.

So maybe Dev *was* hiding there, nursing the bite wound Pup had inflicted on him and cursing Pup *right now*!

If Pup could sneak up and capture him, it would go a long way toward making Hopper proud of him again. Bringing in the monster who planned to overthrow Atlantia would certainly make up for all the trouble he himself had caused . . . when he'd attempted to do the same thing.

The thought of having something in common with the diabolical Dev made Pup squirm. But Hopper would surely forgive Pup for all of it, if only he could catch the wicked traitor and bring him to justice.

"Come with me," he whispered to Hope. "There's something I saw on the wall that I want to look at a little more closely. And I need your help."

"Okay," said Hope. "With what?"

Pup grinned. "How are you at reading maps?"

He made Hope promise to say nothing to Ace about his plan to find the City Hall station. The princess wasn't exactly comfortable with that, but when he pointed out the importance of the mission, she consented.

"On one condition."

Pup gave her a wary look.

"I get to come with you."

"Absolutely not," said Pup, waving his paws and shaking his head. "Uh-uh. No way. Not happening."

She gave him a pout. "Why not?"

"Because it's dangerous. You could get hurt."

"So could you."

"But I promised to protect you."

"And for that, I am thankful," she said, dipping a polite curtsy. "But why can't I protect you right back? I'm the spy in our little duo, remember?"

"Yes, I do remember," said Pup, placing a brotherly paw on the tiny rat's shoulder. "And for that, *I* am thankful. But if anything ever happened to you, I'd be distraught. In fact . . ." He sighed heavily. "In fact, since we've become a duo, as you call it, I've finally come to understand what Hopper and Pinkie were feeling all those times they told me they had to watch out for me, or that I was too small to do something on my own. What they really meant was that I was too precious. To them."

"So . . ." Hope gave him a knowing smile. "Are you saying that I'm precious to you?"

"I would defend you with my life," Pup vowed. "For you are my friend."

"And I am honored," said Hope, pausing to straighten her tiara. "But I'm still going."

"Going where?"

Both rodents jumped when Ace padded up behind them, his tail swishing.

"To the grasslands," Hope said quickly. "Now that you're done working, that is."

"Okay. Everybody ready?" asked Ace.

Hope checked to be sure she still had her scrap of Hopper's patchwork quilt wrapped safely around her middle. "Ready!"

Ace lowered his shoulder so they could climb onto his sleek back, and they set out onto the sidewalks of Brooklyn.

"Uncle Hopper told me the grasslands were snowy and cold," said Hope. "Will they be like that when we get there?"

"Not today," said Ace. "The seasons have changed since Hopper visited us. It's spring now. The grasslands will be bright and warm and sunny."

"What's spring?" asked Pup.

"Spring is when things begin anew. It's a happy,

hopeful time when the whole world gets a chance to start fresh."

Pup smiled. Starting fresh was exactly what he had in mind.

Hope knew all the grassland residents by sight. She'd made Hopper tell her his upland story so many times, and in such minute detail, she was able to pick out Valky and the basketball rats (who still lived at the Barclays, but had come out on this beautiful day for a picnic in the park) and, of course, Carroll without Ace even having to tell her their names.

Hope remembered her manners and presented Pup to each of them as though he were royalty himself.

"Last we heard, you were causing trouble down there in the tunnels," Valky observed, taking a cautious step back from the Chosen One's now infamous little brother.

"I was," said Pup, flushing with embarrassment. "But I've changed." He gave the chipmunk a sheepish grin. "It's spring."

The upland rodent, who knew the magic and the power of the seasons, understood perfectly. "Glad to hear it," he said. "And welcome."

"It's very nice to meet you," said Carroll, shaking Pup's paw warmly. "I know how much your brother cares for you, and I'm sure you'll be able to work things out."

Pup could only nod. He had never seen anyone like this lovely, pink-eyed, white-furred mouse. Her face was filled with kindness and intelligence. No wonder Hopper adored her.

Ace explained to the grasslanders that the two tunnel rodents were going to stay for a bit, while Ace would venture down to the tunnels to tell Hopper all about Pup's new outlook, and to warn him about Dev's betrayal. He smiled at Carroll and added, "I'm hoping to bring our little Chosen friend back up with me. You two are long overdue for a visit."

"I agree," said Carroll. "But I have a better idea. I'll come with you."

"To the tunnels?" Ace sounded surprised. "It's dangerous."

Carroll rolled her pretty pink eyes. "Please, Ace. With your help, I escaped from a laboratory where they performed scientific experiments on mice like me. I'm okay with danger."

When Ace and Carroll were gone, Pup turned to Valky. "I was wondering," he said in his most casual tone, "if you could possibly lead me to the East River."

"Ah," said Valky. "In the mood for a little sightseeing, are you?"

Pup nodded. "Yes. Yes I am."

"Then follow me."

Pup and Hope exchanged glances, then followed

the chipmunk as he loped across the broad expanse of fresh, green grass. When they reached the edge of the park, they both drew in their breath at the strange sight before them.

"There she is," Valky announced, beaming. "Our river."

Water. And lots of it. Blue and choppy and very deep. The springtime sun glistened on its surface, putting Pup in mind of a subway train lighting a dark tunnel, only far more beautiful. On the far side was a toothy skyline of glass, brick, and steel buildings.

Manhattan, Pup surmised. Just as the map in the museum had promised.

"Thank you for guiding us here, Valky," said Hope politely. "If you don't mind, we're just going to admire the river for a while. It's very relaxing and we've had quite a long journey."

"Take your time," said Valky. "I'll come back for you later. Mind the humans and keep your eyes peeled for felines." The chipmunk chuckled. "Although, since Hopper showed a few of our nastiest strays who's boss, we don't have much trouble with cats anymore."

He gave a quick bow, then scurried on his way.

When Valky was gone, Hope turned to Pup. "Okay," she said. "So we've found the East River."

Pup nodded. "Indeed we have."

"Now all we have to do is find the fairy."

According to the princess, fairies were tiny, winged creatures with glittering hair and magical powers, who existed for the sole purpose of entertaining human children.

"Are you sure about that?" asked Pup doubtfully. "That doesn't seem like the sort of thing a human would put on a map."

"Pup," said Hope, rolling her eyes. "It was the *transit* museum. As in *transportation*. And what better way to be transported across a big, wet river than by having an East River fairy fly you there?"

"How do you know all this stuff about fairies anyway?"

"I've seen pictures of them from a human book. Go-go found some torn-out pages fluttering over Atlantia and brought them home for me." At the mention of her eldest sister, Hope's lower lip quivered. "I guess she wasn't always mean to me. Sometimes she could be very sweet."

"And these pages," Pup went on, "they talked specifically about the East River fairy?"

"Well, no," Hope admitted. "Not exactly. The fairy in the book was called Stinkersmell, or Blinkerwell, or something like that. But I'm sure the East River fairy is very similar." She went on to give him a quick description of the drawings in the book.

Pup tried to picture himself clinging to a pair of

gossamer wings while strands of shimmering fairy hair whipped in his face.

"I hope you're right," said Pup.

But she wasn't. Not even close. They discovered this when they saw an enormous sign reading EAST RIVER *FERRY* TERMINAL. And it was nothing like the sparkly little being Hope had described. This ferry was an gigantic buoyant conveyance, stocky in shape with a double-decker design. And it didn't fly; it floated on top of the water.

"So much for tiny winged creatures," Pup joked.

Hope glared at him. "How was I supposed to know that a 'fairy' was something entirely different from a 'ferry'? When I read the map, I thought it was a spelling error."

"Oh, I'm just teasing you," said Pup. "Look at all the other things you've been right about."

The princess seemed to take comfort in this. Together the mouse and the rat mounted the long, slanting bridgelike apparatus that led to the bobbing ferryboat.

"It's like a subway train that can swim," Hope observed as they approached the entrance. There they stopped short at the sight of a squat, bristly-backed animal blocking their path.

He had a narrow snout, small black eyes, and a roly-poly shape. He wore a funny hat with braided trim; its bell-curve shape made it look like a blue-and-gold version of something called a taco, which Pup had once seen Keep order in for lunch back at the pet shop. But even weirder than that hat was the fact that most of this critter's plump little body was rippling with pointy quills.

"Ahoy, there! Commodore Wallabout, at your service."

"Hello," said Hope. "Will this fairy … I mean, *ferry* … take us to Manhattan?"

"Not *us*," Pup reminded her. "*Me. You're* going back to the grasslands to wait for Ace, remember?"

When Hope rolled her eyes, Pup turned back to the commodore.

"She lands at Pier 11," Wallabout explained.

"Is that anywhere near City Hall?" asked Pup.

"Depends on what you mean by 'near,' mate. Long walk for someone of your size." The commodore grinned. "But it's a pretty short sail."

Before Pup could ask what he meant by that, Hope piped up again.

"I beg your pardon," she said, motioning to his pointy quills, "but what sort of creature *are* you?"

"Hedgehog," said Wallabout. "Born just a short way from here in the Brooklyn Navy Yard. Swam here, I did. Hedgehogs are good at that."

"Oh," said Hope. "I thought maybe you were just a prickly rat."

Wallabout's response was a great loud belly laugh.

"No, miss. I am hedgehog through and through. The only rats on this ship are a band of swashbuckling brigands who live below in the hold. A rascally bunch, they are. Love to frighten the human passengers, scare them so they drop their snacks and munchies all over my nice clean deck. Oh, they're a rowdy crew!"

"Brigands?" said Hope. "You mean pirates?"

"I mean pi-*rats*!" the commodore corrected. "Complete with eye patches, hooked paws, and peg legs. Most of them used to live along the docks and wharfs, but they found they could gather more booty out on the high seas."

"You mean river," Pup pointed out.

"Aye," said Wallabout. "The point is, they're a mischievous lot." He eyed Hope's jeweled tiara and frowned. "Now there's a treasure they'd surely want to plunder."

Pup wasn't sure what pi-rats (or for that matter, pirates) were and he certainly didn't want to know the meaning of the word "plunder." But it didn't matter. Because Hope would not be setting sail on the East River Ferry, not if he had anything to say about it.

"Time for you to go back to the grasslands," he told her firmly. "I will send word when I can." When she opened her mouth to protest, he cut her off. "Go, Princess!"

"All ashore that's goin' ashore," said Wallabout.

"All right, all right, I'm going!" Hope huffed, then

threw her arms around Pup and squeezed with all her might. "Please be careful, Pup."

"You too, Princess."

She pulled away and used a corner of the patchwork quilt to wipe a tear from her eye. "*Bon voyage.*"

"Good day, miss," said the commodore, snapping the princess rat a formal salute. "Happy landings to you."

Pushing aside his sadness, Pup watched his little friend scamper down the gangplank. *The spirit of La Rocha will keep her safe*, he assured himself. After all, Hopper had made it home from the grasslands in one piece. Valky had looked after the Chosen One there, and he would care for Hope as well.

Pup almost wished he could stay too, and get to know his brother's friends. But Dev needed to be found and brought to justice. And it was up to Pup to do it.

He followed the waddling hedgehog across the deck, being careful to avoid the human passengers. "I need to get to Manhattan," he reminded the commodore. "To City Hall station. Can you help me?"

"I think so," said the commodore. "This vessel will take you at least part of the way. But when we get to the middle of the river, you're going to have to jump ship."

Pup was sure he hadn't heard the hedgehog correctly. "Did you say 'jump ship'?"

"Aye, aye, mate. But don't worry. You don't have to

swim. You can float." With a smile he pointed at a round object with a hole in the center, hanging on an interior wall of the ferry. "That is what old salts like me call a life preserver. All you have to do is toss it into the drink, hop on, and let it carry you to land." He frowned. "'Course, you'll have to hope the current is working in your favor. And there's always the question of wind. But it's the only way to get you where you need to go."

"Fine," said Pup, heading toward the life preserver. "Let's get it down from there."

"Oh no," said the commodore, shaking his prickly head. "Not that one. That's for decoration, mostly. The human crew would miss that one. But I know where we can find another."

"Where?"

"Below," said the commodore, looking suddenly nervous. "In the hold."

Pup gave him a sideways look. "Didn't you say that's where the pi-rats are?"

Wallabout nodded. "Which is why you're going to need this!" The hedgehog reached up and, with a little grimace, jerked a single, sharply pointed quill out of his back. "Here you go, sailor. It's not a sword, but it's the best I can do. Now, the human crew is ready to remove the gangplank. We should get going."

He hurried off in the direction of the stairs, waving for Pup to follow.

Shuffling along behind the hedgehog, Pup was so involved in examining the quill, he didn't notice that one final passenger was making a mad dash up the gangplank, preparing to take a giant leap across the water.

A giant leap that would turn out to be just a hair too short.

"Help! Pup! Help me!"

Pup whirled and saw Hope . . . or more accurately, the tips of her tiny, grasping paws . . . clinging to the edge of the ship, dangling precariously above the churning river.

MIDLOGUE

SOME TIME AGO, IN THE SUBWAY TUNNELS BENEATH
BROOKLYN, NEW YORK...

THE LITTER OF UPLAND MICE were fascinated by the enormous Manx cat who gave them their tour of Titus's refugee camps. His name was Horatio, and his coat was a swirl of light gray and charcoal. His eyes were such a pale yellow that they were nearly colorless. And he was without a tail.

At first, the pups were afraid. Upland, they had been taught to fear cats. But clearly, here in the tunnels—thanks to Titus and the feral queen—things were different. Horatio was cordial and businesslike, explaining the political and societal aspects of the camps to Fiorello, who seemed impressed with the emperor's accomplishments.

"Ah," said Horatio when he spotted a line of rodents exiting the camp under the leadership of several Atlantian soldiers. "It seems there's a colonization about to begin." He grinned his feline grin at Fiorello. "Are you interested in tagging along?"

"I don't know," said the father mouse, glancing at his litter. "It's been a long day and I think my pups are much too tired."

"We're not tired, Father," said the eldest. "We can march. I'd like to see the new city where these rodents will be taking up residence."

Fiorello eyed the smallest of his children. "Ira, do you feel up to it?"

Ira nodded. "A-a-absolutely, Father."

"I'll carry him," the eldest offered. Then he pointed to the last of the colonists who had just exited through a gate in the wire fence. "Please, Father. I want to go where they're going."

Horatio laughed. "A brave lad," he remarked. "So willing to tread into the unknown."

"That will serve me well when I am a prince of City Hall," the pup said, lifting his chin high.

Horatio's eyes gleamed, but he said nothing.

"Very well," said Fiorello. "Take us to this new, promising city. I want to learn all I can from Titus's achievements, in order to make a success of my own colony."

"Follow me," said Horatio.

As they exited the camp, Ira took a deep breath, summoning his courage to inquire of the enormous Manx, "D-d-did you lose your tail in a f-f-fight?"

"No," the cat replied. "I was born this way. It is a trait unique to my breed."

Ira smiled. "I-I-I'm glad to hear it. I would h-h-hate to think of fights taking place in these t-t-tunnels. We are hoping our new h-h-home will be a peaceful p-p-place."

190

Ira's older brother thought he heard the Manx chuckle and mutter something that sounded like "keep hoping."

They walked on until they reached a cat-size door, outfitted with heavy locks and chains. The eldest mouse thought it odd that a door would have locks on the outside, but he didn't mention it.

"Here we are, mice," Horatio announced. "Right behind this door is where a rodent's life changes. Go right in."

He opened the door, just a crack.

Fiorello hesitated, his eyes sliding from the open door to the grinning cat. His son noticed the sudden look of alarm, as though some instinct were warning his father to rethink this adventure.

"Perhaps we'd better not," Fiorello said. "Maybe I should meet with Titus again before I—"

"Inside!" the cat hissed, then flung the door wide, swatted Fiorello and the four pups through, and slammed it shut.

The pups heard the locks fastening on the other side.

"Where are we?" the eldest asked.

"Father, I don't like this place," said Celeste.

"Neither do I," said Hazel, sniffing the air. "I smell something strange. It seems to be everywhere."

"Fear," her father whispered. "What you smell is fear."

Ira yelped.

"Quickly!" Fiorello cried. "We must find a place to hide." His frightened eyes darted around the dark, dismal place, where rodents were huddling, crying, and scrambling into corners in a desperate attempt to conceal themselves.

But from what, was anybody's guess.

"Over here!" came a nearby voice. "We have room in here!"

The brown mice spun in the direction of an overturned drinking vessel. It looked sturdy and sound, crafted of some shining silver metal. Inside, a male rat and his mate were waving to them.

"Hurry!" cried Fiorello, herding his litter toward the cup. When they reached it, the two rats slid out and the male introduced himself in an anxious voice.

"I am Vigneault," he said. "Something terrible is about to happen! They call this place the hunting ground. Our only chance is to hide. Put your young in this cup. They'll be safe in there."

"B-but if w-w-we get in," Ira stammered, "there w-w-won't be room for y-y-you."

"It's all right, little one," said the female rat, lifting Ira and slipping him into the cup. "We are big enough to fight."

Fight whom? the eldest wondered, beginning to tremble.

Vigneault lifted both Hazel and Celeste at once and

placed them into the cup while Fiorello hoisted his eldest son in beside them.

It was even darker inside the silver cup than it was in the hunting ground, but as his vision adjusted to the gloom, the eldest spotted a pair of bright eyes shining from the depths of the cup.

Vigneault poked his face in, grinning (although to the mouse pups his smile looked strained). "There is our little girl, tucked way into the shadows. I'm sure you will all become fast friends."

The girl mice gave the young rat tentative smiles. The eldest mouse noticed that she held her shoulders back in a most confident way. He found himself trying to copy her proud posture.

"Now," said Vigneault, "I want you all to be very brave. Cover your ears and try not to listen. It will all be over soon."

"What will be over?" the eldest mouse asked.

Vigneault's answer was a courageous smile. Then he turned to Fiorello. "Now, let us see what we might find to protect ourselves. Stones, perhaps. Blades lost in the dirt during previous battles . . . anything with which we might fight off these hungry ferals."

Hungry ferals. The eldest mouse's heart flipped over inside his chest.

Vigneault and his mate paused only long enough to give their daughter a loving glance.

Fiorello, too, allowed his terrified eyes to fall upon

each of his children in turn, lingering for the space of a heartbeat first on the eldest, then on the girls, and finally on Ira, who had curled himself into a quivering ball of brown fluff. "I love you all," he whispered.

"We must hurry!" said Vigneault's mate.

Without a backward glance, the two rat parents and Fiorello sped off to prepare for battle.

For a while the hunting ground bustled with rodents seeking places to hide, and searching for artillery. Some wept; others cried out in fury. To the disgust of the young mice watching from the cup, some even fought amongst themselves, shoving each other out of hiding spots or stealing found weapons for their own protection.

And then, without warning, the whole place fell silent.

The sudden absence of sound was an eerie presence inside the cool, shadowy cup. The eldest mouse imagined he could hear the rat child's heart beating beside him. He knew he could feel Ira trembling.

Then, to his surprise, the rat smiled and held out her paw to shake. "I'm Firren," she said.

He shook her paw and introduced himself. "Devon."

"I'm Celeste."

"My name's Hazel."

Firren turned to Ira, who had peeked up from his cowering position with curious eyes.

"Hello," Firren said.

"H-h-h-hello," Ira squeaked.

"What's your name?"

"My n-n-name is . . ." Ira swallowed hard and squeezed his eyes shut, struggling to coax his own name to his lips.

"His stutter gets worse when he's afraid," Hazel whispered to Firren.

Before Ira could try again, the hush outside the cup was broken by the sound of locks clicking and chains clanging. The scent of terror filled the hunting ground as a voice rose from the throng of rodents. . . . It was Vigneault's, Devon was certain.

"We won't go down without a fight," Firren's father bellowed. "Be brave, all of you. We must fight for our lives! And for the lives of our children."

And then came the whoosh of the heavy door opening to allow the ferals entrance. The last word Devon heard before the battle rang out was his brother's name.

"My name is . . . I-I-Ira."

CHAPTER TWENTY-TWO

FIRREN FINISHED HER STORY WITH tears in her eyes. Zucker went to her and held her close.

"I had no idea," he said softly.

"So Devon's parents and his brother, Ira, were lost to the ferals," said Hopper, sickened by just the thought of it.

"He blames me," said Firren with a shudder. "And I suppose he has every right."

"Oh no he does not!" scolded Dodger. "You were a mere pup, and a terrified one at that. There was no way he or anyone else could have expected you to save Ira."

Firren gave Dodger a grateful smile, then turned to Wyona. "Do you really think he's taken my litter?" she asked.

The soldier hesitated, then gave the empress a grim nod.

"There would have been no one to stop him," Hopper realized. "Nobody's left in the palace except a couple of chefs. And Marcy . . . who would have believed anything he told her, since I was the one who said he could be trusted."

"Where do you think he's taken them?" Dodger asked. "The remains of Felina's lair, perhaps? Pup's abandoned shoe?"

"City Hall," said Zucker decisively. "That's where this lunatic is holding them. I feel it in my gut." He turned to Hopper. "If it's a station, that must mean that one of the metal beasts can take us there, right?"

"I think so," said Hopper. "But I wouldn't know which one, unless I had some clue as to the location. Pinkie might know where it is, what with all the traveling she's been doing." He turned to the cricket. "Find Pinkie," he commanded. "Chirp her this message: 'Urgent. We need to find a station called City Hall.'"

Wyona had mentioned that Dev had described the place as "long forgotten," which made sense—he would want to avoid working stations.

"Likely abandoned," Hopper added. "Send word back to me at the Mūs village."

The dutiful cricket flicked his antennae and scampered off on his mission.

"Why the Mūs village?" Firren asked.

"Because," said Hopper, who was already in motion, nudging his friends toward the track in the distance, "on the chance that Pinkie doesn't know the whereabouts of this City Hall station, I'm going to need a subway map. Probably an old one."

"Yes," said Dodger, "and fortunately for us, the Sacred Book is filled with them."

Since their brave and loyal cricket had already been dispatched, Dodger volunteered to deliver a second message; this one would not be encoded in chirps, tweets, and whistles, rather it would be written upon the tunnel wall:

"Old school," Zucker had observed. "But always effective."

Dodger would rush to the runes, where he would inscribe the following information:

WE HAVE REASON TO BELIEVE THAT
THE MŪS SOLDIER DEVON
HAS ABDUCTED THE ROYAL HEIRS.
WE BELIEVE WE KNOW WHERE HE HAS
TAKEN THEM.
ALL ARE TO REASSEMBLE AT THE PALACE
TO AWAIT FURTHER INSTRUCTIONS.

With any luck, the searching parties would see the notice and discover the change in plans. From the runes, Dodger would then escort the still-reeling Wyona back to the palace to administer medical attention.

It wasn't long before the appropriate train appeared;

Hopper, Firren, and Zucker scrambled onto the hitch, and they were off to the Mūs village.

On the way, Hopper found himself wondering about Dev's description of City Hall station. According to Wyona, living there had been Dev's father's "dream," and the place itself was "splendid and magnificent." Hopper had been in the tunnels for quite some time now and, with the exception of Atlantia, he'd yet to see anything that fit that description. Dirty and musty, yes. Gloomy and frightening, absolutely. But splendid and magnificent? No.

When they arrived at the gargantuan gray wall that sealed off the Mūs village Firren knocked urgently on the door and, for the first time, the pink-uniformed sentry posted there did not hesitate to allow them entrance.

Ignoring the startled looks of the civilians who leaped out of their way, Hopper, Zucker, and Firren bolted through the village, toward the locomotive engine. There, they knew they could count on the newly reinstated elder tribunal to offer their assistance.

"We need to see the Sacred Book," Hopper called out, even before he had finished clambering up the metal ladder. "Sage, Christoph, Temperance . . . we need to examine every old subway map we can get our paws on!"

They burst into the engine, panting and sweating,

and found Sage obediently laying the book on a battered table in the center of the cavernous room. Reverently he opened the tome to which the Mūs unfailingly turned when in need of inspiration for how best to govern their lives.

This was the book that had foretold of Hopper's arrival.

The book, the Chosen One now understood, had been lovingly compiled from gathered pieces of lost human communication—letters, playbills, coupons, storybook pages, and so many other things—which were interpreted to offer a kind of mystic guidance to the civilization of rodents. There were also a number of pages that had been inscribed by La Rocha himself.

Or herself.

Hopper leaned over the table and began to rifle through the book. A birthday card from Jack to Shannon, dated August 12, 2013; a newspaper clipping dated February 7, 1964: BEATLES ARRIVE AT JFK; a lengthy set of handwritten notes scribbled by someone who went by the name of Truman, for a story called *Breakfast at Cartier* (the last word had been crossed out and changed to *Tiffany's*).

Hopper turned page after page until he found what he sought. A subway map, like the one he'd used when he first deciphered the workings of the trains. But this one was much, much older. He reasoned that if Dev's City Hall station was out of com-

mission, it might not be noted on one of the more current maps.

At last he found a brittle, yellowed one dated 1905. Hopper had no idea how long ago that was, but the condition of the map suggested it was hardly recent.

And after several frantic moments of squinting, scanning, and searching, he located a stop called City Hall station!

"This says we take the 5 train," he explained, "then switch at Brooklyn Bridge."

"Isn't that the bridge we were hanging off not too long ago?" asked Zucker.

Hopper nodded. "Except that time I was traveling

over it. This time I'm pretty certain we'll be going under it."

"That's a relief."

"When we get to Brooklyn Bridge station," Hopper continued, "we'll have to change to the 6 train. And then…" He frowned at the map, hoping he understood it correctly.

"And then what?" asked Firren.

"Well, if this is the right station, according to this map, there's a loop."

"Loop?" Zucker repeated. "What does that mean?"

"It means that City Hall is—or was—the end of the line. In the old days the train would have stopped to let the passengers off. Then it would have continued around the loop to go back the way it had come. But if the station is abandoned, and I'm pretty sure it has to be, this train probably isn't going to stop. It's just going to keep moving around the loop. So we're going to have to jump off while the train is in motion."

Zucker sighed. "I was afraid of that."

"It's not like you haven't done it plenty of times before," Hopper reminded him.

"I know, kid. I guess it's just one of those things a rat can't ever get used to."

Now the cricket messenger appeared in the doorway, exhausted but determined as he began to chirp out Pinkie's reply. Apparently, there were two stations called City Hall, but only one was functioning. The cricket tweeted the specifics to Hopper, who listened carefully, then compared Pinkie's instructions to what he'd found on the map.

"That confirms it," he said. "This old station here in Manhattan is the one we want."

With a quick nod to the elders, Zucker turned and made it to the locomotive's door in two long strides. "To Manhattan!" he commanded. "Wherever that is."

Moments later, Hopper found himself again running as fast as he could through the Mūs village. This time, the citizens cheered them on, wishing them luck and invoking La Rocha's blessings upon their quest.

"Chosen One!" A voice rose above the din. "Hopper! Wait."

Hopper didn't want to slow down. He didn't want to waste even a single second in getting to the kidnapped royal heirs. But the voice that called out to him was so insistent.

And so familiar.

"Whadaya stoppin' for, kid?" Zucker shouted from up ahead. "C'mon, buddy. Let's go!"

"I'll catch up!" Hopper yelled back, waving for the emperor and empress to go on without him. Then he turned to the elderly female Mūs who had called out to him. She was the old lady mouse who had fed him a warm meal on his first visit—as Firren's captive—to the Mūs village. She was also the midwife, Maimonides, who had delivered the royal litter.

"Mamie," he gasped, catching his breath. "What is it?"

"I have something for you," the old Mūs explained, "something I want you to have with you on this quest . . . for luck." She extended her paw; in it was a carefully folded scrap of paper.

Hopper, who was all for taking every bit of luck he could get, took the scrap and unfolded it. What he saw astonished him. It was a drawing. An exceptionally artistic and thoroughly surprising drawing. For a moment, Hopper could only stare at it.

"You recognize them, I see," said Mamie with a smile.

"I . . . I think so," said Hopper, unable to pull his eyes from the beautifully rendered portrait. "I only ever met one of them in person. As for the other . . . well, I can guess who he is. The white marking is pretty unmistakable." He lifted his gaze from the sketch and looked at the midwife. "Where did you get this?" he asked. "Who drew it?"

"Your grandmother."

"My grandmother?" Hopper could only blink in amazement. "You knew my grandmother?"

Mamie nodded. "Your father's mother. Myrtle, her name was. She was an upland mouse. Grew up in a wonderful place called Pratt Institute, where only the most artistic of humans come to study. I suppose that's how she came to be such a talented artist herself. I was with her the day she sketched this portrait

of her husband—your grandfather—Ebbets . . ." She pointed to the second face in the sketch. "And his friend."

Hopper frowned. "They were *friends*? That can't be right."

"But it is," said Mamie, sighing. "Difficult to believe, I know. But there was a short period of time when they were very close. As it happens, this was the very last thing your grandmother ever drew. You see, we were in the tunnels, Myrtle and I, with her newborn litter. Your father, Dodger, was very small and weak, and—" She stopped herself with a sad shake of her head. "There isn't time to go into it all, Chosen One. It's a long and heart-wrenching tale. But I have kept the drawing all this time, as a memento of your mother, who was *my*

dearest friend. Now I want you to have it."

"For luck," said Hopper over the lump in his throat.

"For luck," the midwife repeated with a nod. "Now, you must hurry. Keep that safe and send good thoughts to La Rocha."

"Thank you, Mamie," said Hopper, tucking the artwork into his vest. "I will treasure this. And so will Zucker."

Then the Chosen One was once again racing toward the big gray wall.

This time, though, he carried with him a charm to bring good fortune, a faded portrait tucked close to his heart. A sketch, drawn by his artistically gifted grandmother, of her beloved Ebbets, looking hopeful and determined as he stood smiling beside a friend. Hopper almost hadn't recognized this friend at first, for he was much younger in the drawing and had not yet received his scar. But once Hopper had made the connection, he'd been utterly shocked, astonished.

As he barreled on toward the gray wall, it occurred to him that perhaps it shouldn't have come as such a surprise after all. Perhaps somehow he should have known it, *sensed* it, all along.

Perhaps it made perfect sense that the friend in Myrtle's drawing, smiling so genuinely at Ebbets and looking ready to take on the world, was none other than Zucker's father, the former majesty of Atlantia. Titus.

CHAPTER TWENTY-THREE

THE FERRY GLIDED AWAY FROM the dock, chugging and wheezing, with the royal princess hanging precariously over the side.

"Hold on!" Pup commanded, dropping his quill sword and rushing back to the door to grasp first one of her straining arms, then the other. With one great heave that sent both of them tumbling backward, he managed to yank her into the boat.

She was safe.

Unfortunately, the same could not be said for her tiara. The jolt of their landing knocked it off her head, sending the glimmering crown sliding across the deck, where it spun to a stop ... right beside what, if Pup didn't miss his guess, appeared to be a peg leg.

"Seriously?" he muttered, gaining his feet. "*This* is happening?"

"Arrgghh! What have we here?" The owner of the wooden leg crouched down, picked up the jeweled headpiece, and peered at it, a task made slightly more complicated by the fact that one of his eyes was covered by a patch. "Ain't this a pretty bauble, now," he drawled. "And mine for the taking."

"Give that back!" snapped Hope, standing up, checking to see that the quilt was still snug around her waist, then tossing the pi-rat (for surely, what else could this peg-legged, eye-patched, arrgghh-uttering rodent possibly be?) a contemptuous look. "Give it back this instant."

"Says who?"

"Says me, Princess Hope of the House of Romanus."

"We're in open water now," the pi-rat snarled. "So I don't recognize any such authority." He smiled at the gem-encrusted treasure in his grasp. "Although I am bloody impressed by the crown jewels."

Thanks to the pi-rat's preoccupation with the haughty little princess and her pricey piece of headwear, Pup had quietly succeeded in locating his quill. He leaped forward, brandishing his weapon with a flourish.

"I'll take that tiara!" he shouted. "Hand it over."

"Arrgghh! You'll have to catch me first."

"Catch you?" Pup repeated, throwing up his paws in frustration. "*Seriously?*"

The pi-rat's answer was to take off at a run.

"Told you they're a rascally bunch!" said the commodore, trotting off after the scoundrel. "Come on!"

Pup paused only long enough to grab Hope by the paw; clutching his weapon, he followed the hedgehog to a short flight of metal steps. Down they clambered into the depths of the ferry, where the light faded quickly to a murky mist and the stench was horrendous.

"I've never been down here before," Wallabout

admitted. "So I'm not sure what to expect. Just be sure to—"

Whoosh!

Pup watched in surprise as the pudgy commodore was swept off his feet and into a well-placed trap.

"Are you all right?" cried Hope, gaping at the hedgehog, who was now caught in an old fishing net, swinging back and forth in a wide arc above their heads.

"Shipshape, no harm done," the commodore assured her. "But watch out!"

This advice came a split second too late. Hope squealed when the point of a pi-rat's cutlass shot out from a pile of rope and stopped short, just a hairsbreadth from her tiny pink nose.

The pi-rat who held the blade was not the one with the bum leg and missing eye. This one was shaggier than the first and wore a red rag tied around his head. There was a hook where his right paw should have been.

Hope didn't so much as whimper. Perhaps she was becoming used to being on the business end of a sword.

"Give me back my tiara!" she demanded.

"Well, ain't you the bossy little wench," the pi-rat snickered.

"I'm not a wench, I'm a rat. A royal rat."

"Are ye now?" said the rat, waggling his whiskery

eyebrows. "That's good to know. For it's the royal ones that fetch the greatest ransoms."

"She's not your hostage, pi-rat!" spat Pup.

"Be still, runt!" barked a third brigand, dropping down from an overhead pipe and pulling a dagger from its sheath. "If we say she be, then she is."

"Well, I say she isn't!" Pup shot back. Summoning all his strength, he sprung upward off his hind paws, grabbed onto the net that held Wallabout, and swung himself at the pirate with the dagger, kicking him hard in the gut and knocking him off his feet. Catching one of the knots of the net between his teeth, Pup managed to open a hole just big enough for Wallabout to drop through. The commodore landed—prickle side first— right on top of the hook-pawed pi-rat!

"Owwwwwcccch!" The pi-rat dropped his rapier and howled as the pointy tips of a thousand quills connected with his fur.

Now a fourth pi-rat appeared, hopping out from behind a pile of moldering life preservers. This was by far the biggest one yet, with rotten teeth and a face full of scars.

And he was holding the most lethal-looking sword Pup had ever seen.

Pup raised his quill.

The big pi-rat laughed out loud. "Ye plan to fight me with that? A hedgehog quill? Why not just try ticklin' me to death with a seagull feather?"

"I would," Pup growled, "if I had one."

He lunged at the pi-rat, who deftly dodged the point of the quill and laughed even harder.

"So that's how it's going to be, eh?" The pi-rat swung his sword with startling force.

Pup leaned out of the way just in the nick of time, then parried again.

The pi-rat blocked the strike.

By now the other two pi-rats had righted themselves and, to Pup's distress, several more had appeared, popping out from under tarps and behind crates, every one of them menacing, and every one of them armed.

Pup was going to need more than one measly hedgehog quill to get out of this mess.

He shot a look at Hope, who was huddled with Wallabout near the metal stairs. Then with a mighty roar he ran at the largest pi-rat, wielding his meager weapon.

Unfortunately, he didn't get far before the hook-pawed rat shot out a leg and tripped him, sending Pup toppling to roll across the slick floor. The quill went flying.

He hoped it might by some miracle lodge itself in the big pi-rat's heart.

But it didn't.

Lying there in the slime of the ferry's hold, Pup knew he had lost. He closed his eyes and waited to feel the dagger across his throat. Or perhaps they'd do something more dramatic like toss him over the side of the ship and into that cold, bottomless river.

Mice weren't known for their aquatic skills, after all. He'd sink like a stone and be dead in no time.

And Hope would be alone. Helpless. Vulnerable.

This thought sickened him most of all.

The moments ticked past, but no hook jerked him up from where he was sprawled, and no peg leg kicked him in the backside.

Cautiously he opened one eye . . . and yelped when he saw the eye-patched pi-rat staring down at him.

"Yer quite the scrappy little mouse, ain't ye?"

Pup sat up gingerly and sighed. "Scrappy . . . or stupid . . . it's a tough call."

The pi-rat let out a raucous peal of laughter. "I'm thinkin' you be both. And ya know what? We like that combination."

"You do?"

Still laughing, the half-blind pi-rat reached down, offered Pup a paw, and helped him up. "Well, now, one don't come to be a pi-rat by being timid and smart, do he?"

"I suppose not."

Hope scurried over to where Pup was standing beside the pi-rat. "Can I have my tiara back now?"

The pi-rat looked down at her and grinned. "No. But you can have your lives."

"Fair enough," said Pup quickly, scooting the princess behind him. "We'll be on our way now."

The pi-rat laughed. "I'm only funnin' with ya, missy," he said, handing her the crown. "Here's your hat back."

"Tiara," Hope corrected primly, placing it on her head. "And thank you."

The commodore cleared his throat, then pointed to the pile of life preservers.

"Oh," said Pup. "Right, I forgot!" He pushed his shoulders back and lifted his chin. "I need a favor . . . mate."

"Aye? And what might that be?"

"I'd like you to relinquish one of those flotation devices to me. I need it to carry me to the island of Manhattan. Maybe you can think of it as a reward for my exemplary scrappiness and excessive stupidity?"

The big pi-rat considered the request, then smiled at Pup.

"We are proud to call ourselves pi-rats," he said. "Buccaneers! Gadabouts! High-spirited rogues, the whole motley lot of us. But know ye this, lad, for it be the truth: there is not a single unkind soul among us. We have lived hard lives, and seen our share of disappointment and pain. 'Tis why we've joined together here, to start anew. Here, where we can live a carefree, rollicking seafaring life, causing trouble and making mischief, but our antics are all in fun. We pi-rats of the East River are naught but an honest, merry band of harmless vagabonds. So aye, little mouse, you may have your float. And 'tis my wish that it carries you safely to whatever port of call ye little varmints consider your home."

"Touching," said Hope with a sniffle.

"Yeah," Pup agreed, blushing. "Too bad he didn't give that speech *before* I dropped the hedgehog on him!"

The peg-legged rat selected the least battered of the stowed life preservers and, under Wallabout's direction, two others hauled it all the way to the ferry's stern. There they dragged it out onto a low-slung platform hovering over the water, skimming the choppy surface.

Another pi-rat appeared to hand Hope a shiny foil bag with colorful letters printed on it, then scampered off with an "arrgghh" of farewell.

Hope read the words printed on the foil. "Buttered popcorn."

"Ah," said Wallabout. "A treat from the snack bar. He must have scared it away from a human."

"What is it?" asked Pup.

"Food," the hedgehog explained. "For your voyage. Quite a thoughtful gesture, I'd say. I guess those pi-rats really aren't the rough-and-tumble bandits I imagined them to be."

Pup was in full agreement with the commodore's

improved opinion of the pi-rat band. At the moment, however, Pup was more concerned with the unimpressive flotation device balanced on the edge of the ferry.

"You really expect us to ride this thing?" he asked.

"It's the only way to get to Manhattan," Wallabout assured him. "Unless you'd rather do the backstroke."

"It'll be fun!" cried Hope, lifting her smiling face into the watery spray off the river. "An adventure!"

"You two board the life preserver," Wallabout instructed, "and I'll shove you off. It'll be rough at first, but just hold tight until you clear the wake. Then you should have smooth sailing all the way past South Street Seaport. Just watch out for seagulls."

"What are seagulls?" Pup asked.

Wallabout declined to elaborate. Instead he plucked another quill from his back and handed it to Pup. "You might need this," he said in a serious tone. "Gulls prefer fish to mice, but you never know."

Pup didn't like the sound of that. He took the quill. "Thank you, Commodore," he said, offering the hedgehog a crisp salute. "Thank you for everything."

Then he and Hope climbed onto the foam ring and held tight.

"Good luck, mates," cried Wallabout, giving the float a hearty shove.

It slid into the river with a splash, bouncing and

spinning across the ferry's powerful wake. Pup gripped the circle until his claws were digging into it.

"Wheeeeee!" cried Hope.

After a few turbulent minutes, the life preserver found its way out of the roiling path of the ship and into calmer waters.

"This is incredible!" said Hope, her whiskers whipping in the breeze as she gripped the bag of popcorn that was more than twice her size.

Pup had to admit, there was something both relaxing and exciting about being on the water. He almost envied those pi-rats, spending their days just cruising the East River, with nothing to do but poke fun and frighten humans into giving up their popcorn. With a twinge of longing he watched the ferry disappear, enjoying the sensation of the float bobbing gently on the open river. But his peaceful respite didn't last long.

Now that the ferry was gone, the water had stilled considerably. Although they still rose and fell over the shallow crests of the chop, their little float was no longer covering much distance. Hope noticed it at the same time.

"We're not getting anywhere."

Pup frowned. "I see that." But that wasn't the only thing he saw. Out of the corner of his eye he sensed motion. Turning, he spied another boat—this one was shaped like a smile with two tall triangles rising out of its middle—slicing swiftly across the river.

Headed right for them!

"We need to get out of the path of that thing!" Pup screamed, dipping his paw into the water and slapping at it frantically. His thought was to push the water behind them, and propel the craft in the direction of Manhattan. But the river was immense and his paws were the size of sunflower seeds. Even as he splashed and paddled, he knew the effort was useless.

Hope, meanwhile, was frowning at the tremendous boat coming closer by the second. "Fulton's forge," she said.

"What? What does the bladesmith have to do with anything?"

"The fire in his forge did something to the tent. It made it flutter. Billow. Brighton said it had something to do with hot air being lighter than cold air, but to me it just looked like breeze."

Pup leaned away from the edge, shaking the river from his hands in a splatter. "And?"

Hope pointed to the sky. "We've got breeze. And that boat is using it to wonderful effect. Just like Fulton's tent. The wind is pushing against those big triangular sheets, and making them billow. The boat is traveling in the direction the wind is blowing. It's pushing them."

The observation was spot on. "Quick!" said Pup. "We need something that will billow."

He looked around at the flat, paint-chipped surface of the life preserver, but there was nothing that might flutter in a stiff breeze. There was only the quill Wallabout had sacrificed for their defense against seagulls. Whatever they were.

"I've got it!" cried Hope.

When Pup saw her paws go to her waist, his eyes lit up. "Yes! Brilliant!"

Hope made fast work of untying the blanket from where it was knotted around her midsection, while Pup shaded his eyes from the glare of the sun reflecting off the river for a better look at the boat. The fluttering triangles appeared to be secured to a tall post.

"Here!" he said, snatching up the quill and sticking the pointy end into the life preserver so it stuck straight up.

He didn't have to tell Hope what to do—she was already tying the blanket to the quill, knotting it at the top and the bottom with plenty of slack between.

"Okay, wind," she invoked, delighted. "Do your best!"

Sure enough, the little swatch of blanket caught the breeze, puffing itself outward, billowing, whipping, and

carrying Pup and Hope safely out of the path of the approaching sailboat.

Carrying them across the calm blue waters of the sun-splashed East River.

Carrying them toward Manhattan.

CHAPTER TWENTY-FOUR

DEV HAS FOUND A WAY *to do something so mystical that even the great La Rocha himself scarcely could have imagined it; this vindictive traitor has managed to bring the illusion of daylight into the tunnels.*

I have never seen daylight, of course. But the way the glow emanates from the strange, bent-armed objects that hang high above our heads to flood the place with gilded brilliance, I am sure genuine daylight could not possibly be more beautiful than this.

How sad that I must experience such a glorious sight while my arms and legs are bound and my back is pressed against the rough bricks of the station wall.

Dev has tied us up—myself and the four royal heirs— with the reluctant help of two female mice we found waiting here. His sisters, Celeste and Hazel. They are plump and sweet-faced, with fur (like Devon's) of a darkish-brown color. Not Mūs fur. It is clear to me now that Dev has only been pretending to be a member of the proud Mūs tribe.

All a part of his malicious plan.

And yet, from the argument I am overhearing between Dev and his sisters, I sense that neither of them has had any prior knowledge of his intended villainy. I gather that they have been living here in this opulent place for quite some time, and it seems, are as surprised by our arrival as we are.

"This is madness, Dev," scolds the sister called Celeste. "Impersonating a Mūs, killing a general! So this is what you've been doing all this time you've been absent from us, leaving us here to scrounge and scavenge and to endure the comings and goings of that slithering monster."

Hazel shares her sister's disgust. "Kidnapping?" she huffs. "Torture? Revenge? You're being completely irrational! Tell me, brother, what will any of that accomplish? It won't bring Father or Ira back to us."

"I know that," says Dev, his voice brittle and cold. "But don't you remember how it was in that hunting ground? Don't you remember how Ira suffered? We could have saved him, but for a single arm's length. Hers! Well, now I want to see Firren suffer, just as Ira did." He presses his snout close to Hazel's and grinds the words out through his teeth. "This is not about reason, sister. This is about retribution."

"Well, I refuse to go along with it," Celeste informs him, folding her arms defiantly. "Count me out."

"And me," says Hazel, stepping closer to her sister. A united front.

For a moment, Dev just glowers, and then he erupts in a roar of anguish and fury. The station echoes with it; the sound of his frustration pounds back on itself from the shining wall tiles to the cracked glass of the elaborate skylights overhead.

"How can my own siblings be so unreliable?" he bellows. "So weak! Just look at this place!" He flings his arms wide, *indicating the undeniable beauty of City Hall station. "Our father wanted to claim it, not only for our comfort and enjoyment but for that of all rodents. It would have outshone Atlantia, that much is certain, and it would not have been built on lies and treachery. It would not have been a place of evil."*

Hazel reaches out a tentative paw to place on Dev's outstretched arm. "And what sort of place is it now, brother? With words like 'retribution' and 'suffering' ringing off the very walls."

Dev's reply is an icy glare.

Now Celeste lifts her chin defiantly. "I won't allow you to do this, Devon."

"And how do you propose to stop me?"

"By boarding the very next silver beast that slinks around that bend," she announces, "and going to warn Firren."

"And these children . . . ," Hazel adds. "They are innocent. They weren't even in that hunting ground." She starts toward the children and me, reaching out with trembling paws as though preparing to untie us.

For her trouble, she receives a punishing blow to the back of her skull with the pommel of her brother's sword. I stifle the scream that rises from my throat, because seeing this action brings it all back to me in a flash even brighter than the false daylight that burns from above:

My disguise falls away . . . the startled expression on his face . . . he reaches for his sword . . . the heavy handle is swooping in the direction of my head . . . the metal pommel finds its mark . . .

Blending with my recollection is the sight of Hazel flying forward from the force of the attack, landing with a bone-bruising thud mere inches away from me on the hard surface of the platform.

Celeste gasps. "How dare you!" She makes to charge her brother. But he is ready for her. He wields his sword.

"I would not do that if I were you," he warns with a sinister smile.

With a grunt of helplessness Celeste changes her course and hastens to her sister's side.

"I would never do that to you," Raz whispers to Brighton, who is tied beside him. His eyes go pointedly to her glasses. "Even in a blind *rage, I could never make such a* spectacle *of myself as to* knock you off *your feet."*

From behind her shattered eyeglasses, Brighton blinks, then nods.

Raz turns his teary eyes to the others. "I couldn't hurt any of you!" he promises. "I would never take a chance on severing our family ties like that."

At this statement of loyalty, I see Fiske and Go-go exchange glances, and then they, too, nod to Raz.

Meanwhile, Hazel is not responding to Celeste's worried whispers. I fear the damage is irreversible. Celeste realizes it as well. She lifts her face and gives her brother a look of pure abhorrence. "You mourn one dead sibling, but think nothing of killing another?"

His mouth twitches. "She's probably just stunned" is his dispassionate diagnosis.

Celeste presses her ear to Hazel's chest but gives no report. Dev points his sword at her, then motions to us. "You may join the royal brats," he says evenly.

Wisely, Celeste does as she's told, crumbling to the hard floor beside me. In no time, Dev has wrapped her arms and legs in twine.

He is so busy securing the knots that he does not hear what I hear. A soft shuffling; it is the ghost of a sound, really, almost not a sound at all. Footsteps—times eight— scurrying somewhere above my head.

The noise ceases and I am left wondering if I only imagined it.

Then Dev turns to me and his dull, black eyes bore into mine. "So, pretty maid, what do you think your illustrious La Rocha would have to say about all this?"

Before I can answer, Fiske pipes up. "La Rocha would say that there is nowhere for the wicked to hide, for sooner or later evil will be found out."

"Well, I'm banking on later," Dev drawls. "After I've had my revenge on Firren."

Suddenly Brighton cries out dramatically and drops her head to her chest in despair. The action causes her eyeglasses to slip from her face and into her lap. Strangely, she does not lament over the loss of them. In fact, it is almost as if she's knocked them off her snout on purpose.

"Oh no!" Fiske shouts. "Look! There's a big ugly feline headed down those steps!"

Alarmed, Dev spins in the direction of the broad staircase, weapon raised. Both Celeste and I brace ourselves for a feline attack, until we realize there is no cat approaching.

Fiske laughs. "Ha ha. Made ya look!"

I turn to chastise him with a glare—for we do not need to anger this madmouse any more than he already is—just in time to catch a glimpse of the tip of Brighton's pink tail flicking forward from behind Raz's back . . . and also to see that the spectacles have disappeared from her lap.

There is a slight crunching noise that sounds like breaking glass.

Now beside me I feel Raz squirming, ever so gently. If our shoulders were not grazing, I would not even realize he was moving. I have no idea what this resourceful prince is up to, but instinctively I know I must keep Dev's focus elsewhere, so that he does not notice what Verrazano is about. Because it is clear that these clever children—bless their royal little hearts—are up to something.

"You cannot expect to keep this place to yourself for long," I say loudly. "It is far too beautiful. The humans are bound to come back and reclaim it."

"Humans are fools. Things of beauty and value amuse them for only so long before they move on to something they think is more beautiful and valuable. This place has been abandoned for nearly three quarters of a century."

"And how do you know that?"

"*My father told me. He heard it from his father, who heard it from his father. Our clan lived in the basement of an important upland palace called City Hall, just up those stairs. All of New York, the greatest city in the world, was governed from that building. My father understood politics. He listened to the plans and policies of the great men and women who walked those hallowed halls, and that was when his dream began. He wanted to create a proud and powerful city for himself.*"

"*Like Atlantia,*" Gowanus ventures.

"*Better than Atlantia!*" Devon snarls. "*Bigger and safer and open to any rodent, whoever chose to live there. At the time we were just pups, Celeste, Hazel, Ira, and I. Our mother, who hailed from a grassy place in Brooklyn called Marine Park, had just days before fallen prey to a spring trap left by the rodent-hating City Hall custodial staff. We were still in mourning when our father took us from that big, important building down here into the tunnels. You see, he had heard from a rodent who'd wandered up from below about a great and prosperous civilization, governed by a rat named Titus. My father's plan was to approach this emperor Titus to ask for his cooperation in colonizing this long-forgotten, splendid, and magnificent wonderland.*"

He swings his sword in a wide arc, to indicate all of City Hall, from floor to ceiling. My eyes follow the blade of their own accord, and when my head tilts back to gaze up at the ornate arched ceiling, I bite back a gasp.

Because the bent-armed light machines are not the only eerie things I see suspended from above. I look away, then, just to be sure I am not imagining what I think I've seen, I look back upward.

And eight piercing eyes look back at me.

CHAPTER TWENTY-FIVE

"**Splendid and magnificent**" indeed!

From the hitch on the back of the 6 train, Hopper gaped at the unexpected and spectacular sight that was City Hall station.

"Look at this place," said Zucker. "It's better than my old man's palace."

Hopper certainly did not disagree. If anything, the description Dev had given of City Hall (as relayed to the Chosen One and the others by Wyona) had been a serious understatement. The station into which they rolled now surpassed "splendid" at first glance and became more and more "magnificent" the longer one looked. As their train slowed to round the curve, Hopper snapped out of his awestruck daze. He thought he heard voices ahead, but they were small and muffled by the rumble of the slow-moving beast.

"This is us," he said, preparing to jump.

"Aw, man," muttered Zucker. "I really hate this part."

"Tuck and roll," Hopper advised.

"Yeah, kid. Right."

Zucker took Firren's hand and leaped from the train, with Hopper soaring through the atmosphere behind them. The three of them landed hard on the concrete slab of the subway platform, skidding, toppling, and tumbling over themselves until they hit the wall.

"Did I mention I *hate* this part?" snarled Zucker, standing and brushing off his purple tunic.

But Firren was already on her feet, sword drawn, creeping quietly in the direction of a broad staircase. She held up a paw to shush them as Hopper and Zucker followed her, pressing themselves against the bottom edge of the wall.

Now a voice came rippling toward them, a voice rising and falling with passion, amplified to a hollow boom by the acoustics of the near-empty station.

It was the lunatic Devon, ranting once again.

Inching along the curvature of the wall, Hopper could see that the incensed mouse was pacing the platform with his sword raised. He was barking out his speech as though he were some great, wise orator, lecturing before a rapt audience.

The audience, Hopper saw now, was Marcy and the royal heirs. And they weren't exactly "rapt." But they were "wrapped." In tightly knotted lengths of twine! He had to grab Zucker hard by the collar of his tunic to keep him from bursting forth to tackle the madmouse.

"Wait," Hopper whispered, motioning to indicate Firren, who, still cloaked in the blue felt cape of the tunnel prophet, was now a foot ahead of them, close to the wall, circling her sword above her shoulder in tiny loops, a sure sign that she was preparing to pounce.

Dev's voice exploded into the cavernous space. "Titus was greedy, and cruel," he bellowed. "That deceitful, pompous rat pretended to like my father's proposal, telling him they could work together to build a second metropolis, a twin city, here in the tunnels. When Titus boasted that he was already successfully establishing colonies all over the tunnels, and offered to show my father around the wonderful camps where future colonists were so comfortably and generously housed while they waited to begin their new lives, naturally, my father accepted. And then . . ." Here the mouse's voice cracked and his step faltered. "And then—"

"And then you discovered the truth?"

Firren's calm, lilting voice flooded the station, startling Dev, who whirled to face her, his eyes fiery, his muscles tense. When he realized who had spoken, he dashed toward the row of hostages and pressed the tip of his blade to the spot dead center between Brighton's eyes. Brighton let out a strangled sob.

But Firren did not flinch; her eyes stayed firmly on her daughter's captor, and her sword continued to twirl, stirring the dusty air into small, glittering motes.

"You discovered the truth," Firren repeated, not missing a beat. "That there were no colonies, only certain death. Right?"

"Yes," hissed Devon. "But not for all."

"No." Firren shook her head. "Not for all. We lived, you and I. And your sisters."

Devon's gaze flicked toward one of his captives, whom Hopper did not recognize. But Firren did.

"Hello, Celeste," said Firren, still unruffled. To Hopper's confusion, she sounded as if she were greeting an old friend.

"Your Majesty," the mouse—Celeste—choked out.

"Do not dare to call her that!" hollered Devon. "There is nothing majestic about this selfish coward."

"Hey!" said Zucker, striding forward, sword drawn, teeth bared. "That's my wife you're talking about, pal."

Now Zucker turned to his children and forced a light tone, though Hopper could see the fury and terror in his eyes. "Everybody all right?"

"We're all right, Father," said Raz, his voice level. "Well, except that Brighton lost her *glasses*. And Fiske . . . well, you know him. Even though this is a serious predicament, he's still joking around . . . you know . . . being a real *cutup*. It all has me almost at the end of my *rope*."

Hopper was amazed when Zucker's mouth quirked up. Was he actually grinning? How could he smile under such circumstances?

"And Go-go's been very disobedient," Raz went on. "She doesn't seem to understand that I'm the one in *charge*."

In the next second, Hopper was grinning too,

realizing that Verrazano wasn't simply tattling on his brothers and sisters. He was giving his father a message. He was speaking in code!

"Much as I hate to interrupt such a lovely father-and-son conversation," Dev drawled, "I'm going to have to order you two to *shut up!*"

He pulled back his sword from Brighton's face, only to thrust it toward Go-go, allowing it to hover just above her heart. Go-go gulped and her whiskers quivered, but she didn't make a move.

Dev turned his scathing glare back to Firren. "Does your family know what you did to my little brother? Why don't you tell them about it, *Empress*? Go ahead. Tell your little royal brood how, before you were a monarch, before you were even a rebel warrior in red and blue stripes, what you really were . . . was a monster."

Firren glanced away as Dev's scream ripped through the station. "Tell them, Your Highness! Tell them what you did to Ira!"

Firren took a long, slow breath, her expression turning grim and distant; to Hopper's surprise, she lowered her weapon.

"We were in the hunting ground," she began in a faraway voice. "My parents and I. My father claimed the silver cup for our hiding place, but when Devon's father—Fiorello was his name—was ushered into the stadium with his four little ones, my parents immediately offered their space in the cup to the mouse pups."

"Clearly, kindness skips a generation," Devon sneered.

"I didn't understand what was happening," Firren went on, "but I knew that something terrible was coming. I could smell the fear. The entire hunting ground reeked of it. To take my mind off it, I decided to try and make conversation with these four little mice who'd just scampered into the cup with me. I wanted to make friends."

Dev snorted.

Firren ignored him and went on with her story. "So I introduced myself. The first three told me their names were Celeste, Hazel, Devon. Last was Ira." Here the rebel empress paused to smile sadly. "He was so tiny and sweet."

"Like Hope?" asked Raz, swept up in his mother's tale.

Firren nodded. "Just like our little Hope. I said, 'Hello, I'm Firren.'"

"Yes," seethed Devon. "And tell them what Ira said. Exactly what he said."

Firren sighed. "He said: 'M-m-my name is I-I-I . . . I-I-I . . . I-I-I.'"

"Huh?" said Go-go. "Mother, I don't understand."

"Ira stuttered," Devon snapped. "My little brother had a stuttering problem."

Again, Firren nodded. "He was still trying to tell me his name when the doors were flung open. And he finally managed it . . . 'I-I-*Ira*,' he said . . . just as the first feral cat came stalking into the hunting ground."

"It was awful," Celeste recalled in a whisper. "The squealing and meowing. Claws, tails, whiskers . . ."

"And the blood," Dev reminded her tersely. "Don't forget the blood."

"Yes, there was plenty of blood," Firren agreed. "But we were safe. We huddled together inside that silver cup and we were safe. Until . . ." She trailed off as though it were simply too hard to remember.

"Until . . . ," Dev prompted fiercely. "Tell them!"

"A calico swatted our cup with his tail. Ira . . . he fell out of the cup."

At this revelation, Fiske let out a yelp of horror. Brighton gasped, and Go-go had tears in her eyes.

"Yes he did," Dev confirmed. "My little brother fell out of the cup and tumbled into the bloody dirt. He called out for help. 'H-h-help,' he cried. 'H-h-help!' Of course, my sisters and I tried to rescue him. We thought maybe we could pull him back up into the cup if we formed a chain. It was quite clever of us, really. Celeste took Hazel by her hind paws, and then Hazel grabbed on to my hind paws and I lowered myself out of the cup to try to save Ira. I reached . . . oh, how I reached . . . but we were so small, and the mouth of the cup was just a bit too high above the ground. I stretched downward as far as I could. I was close, but I still couldn't reach him. I was short, by a single arm's length." He turned to scowl at Firren. "That's all we would have needed to save our little brother . . . one more arm's length. One more rodent to attach herself to our chain."

"Mother!" Verrazano gasped. "You didn't . . ."

"You refused to help them?" Go-go's voice was a whisper of disbelief.

"I didn't refuse them," said Firren. "But I didn't help, either. I was petrified. Literally . . . petrified. I couldn't move. I wanted to. I wanted to help them save Ira, but the sounds of that battle—the hissing and yowling, the bones crunching, the thuds of rodents being tossed into walls—those noises were right outside that cup, and because of that, I panicked. I froze!"

"Coward!" Devon hollered. "Pathetic, selfish coward!"

"Child!" Firren corrected calmly. "That's what I was, Dev . . . a child, just like you were. Just like Ira. I was a child. And I was afraid."

"So that's your excuse?" Devon sputtered. "Youth?"

Firren shook her head. "It's not an excuse. It's merely a fact. A sad and tragic fact.

Devon removed the sword from where it was poised over Go-go's heart. Then he spun in a circle, again indicating the beauty of the City Hall station. "Ira would have been a prince. Here, in this wondrous human castoff. He and my sisters and I would have been royal heirs, just like your litter. My father could have built this place into a flourishing society if he'd lived. But Titus took that all away. Just like you took Ira away."

"I'm sorry."

"*Sorry?*" Dev strode toward Firren with wild eyes. "You're *sorry*? Tell me, rebel, do you ever even think about my brother? Have you even once, before this moment, given Ira a second thought?"

Firren's whispered answer made Hopper's fur stand on end:

"Every. Single. Day."

"Pssshhht." Dev waved his paw dismissively, his tone dripping with sarcasm. "And when exactly do you find the time in your busy royal schedule to trouble yourself with remembering a poor, innocent little upland mouse who died because you were, as you say, a frightened child? Is it while you are sampling sugared morsels at the royal breakfast table, or perhaps when you're enjoying a command performance in the gilded palace theater? Or maybe it's while you're having your paws manicured, or trying on the crown jewels?"

"I don't waste my time with crown jewels or sugared morsels," said Firren. "I'm more interested in making sure the citizens who trust in me to govern them are safe and prosperous."

"And you expect me to believe that you remember a little mouse you only knew for a moment?"

"Yes, Devon. Because of *all* the moments of my life, *that* is the one that haunts me the most. Which is why I wear this." She tossed back the drape of La Rocha's blue cloak to reveal her silver cape beneath it, the one she once draped over a sleeping Hopper to keep him warm so long ago. "You see, I chose this fabric for a reason, Devon. I chose it because it reminds me of that silver cup. Not that I need reminding. I wear it more as a symbol of something I have vowed never to let happen again, which is that I will never fail to help another rodent who needs me, ever, for as long as I live. That is what I offer up to the memory of your little brother."

Devon shook his head. "I don't believe you."

"Don't you? Are you not aware of the call by which to summon my rebels to arms? I have a very specific battle cry. Perhaps you've heard it echoing through the tunnels." Firren turned to her children, who were listening with wide eyes.

"How does Mommy call her Rangers into battle?" she prompted. "Tell him."

Obediently four little voices cried out as one: "*Aye, aye, aye!*" they chanted; the chorus rang out in peals through the station. "*Aye, aye, aye! Aye, aye, aye!*"

Hopper's heart quickened at the sound of it. And then he understood.

"Aye, aye, aye," he said softly. "Like . . . I . . . I . . . I. For Ira."

"For Ira." Firren nodded. "I-I-I . . . for Ira. The name I will never forget. The victim to whom I will never stop apologizing in my heart, and to whom I will never cease paying tribute . . . the only way I can. 'Aye, aye, aye' is and always will be in honor of Ira. My fallen friend."

CHAPTER TWENTY-SIX

THERE IS NOT A SOUND in the station as Devon takes in this heartfelt apology. Against the wall, beside me, Celeste is weeping softly, silently.

I fix my eyes on Dev, wondering what he will do next. For a moment, no one moves; no one even dares to breathe.

And then he speaks a phrase I've heard from him before. "I never did put much stock in apologies."

The noise he makes is unlike any I've ever heard before; it is a scream, but more than a scream . . . It is the sound of grief colliding with rage and it seems to shred itself from the deepest place in Devon's broken soul. He lunges at Firren, his sword flailing before him. But his aim is true and the weapon finds its mark.

The lethal tip of it pierces Firren, slicing into the fur and flesh just below her shoulder.

She cries out and staggers, but before she even hits the ground, the royal heirs spring to their feet—their bindings have been severed, cut clear through by the sharp glass shards of Brighton's broken spectacles. They are free! As one, the four of them charge the monster who's stabbed their mother.

Dev is so caught by surprise that he almost drops his weapon; the children kick and swat and nip at him. Celeste and I, still tightly bound, can only look on in shock and horror. Hopper and Zucker have flown to the empress's side;

Zucker cuts away a piece of the blue cloak and attempts to stave the blood flow with it. Hopper removes his own tunic and bunches it beneath her head like a pillow.

"Be gone, brats!" Dev shouts, regaining his faulty grip on the handle of the sword. He swings it once, twice. Raz ducks, evading a blow, but Fiske takes a hit; the edge of the blade glances his snout and he howls. Again, Devon swipes his weapon. This time Brighton catches the hilt. She shouts, clutching her forehead.

Now Dev flings out a paw and grasps the collar of Gogo's cotton dress. He yanks her out of the melee, separating both the child and himself from the fray. His sword sweeps around so that he has positioned it lengthwise, pressed against her neck.

The children immediately go still. They know he will slit her throat if they so much as spit at him. Slowly he begins to back away toward the wide staircase that leads, I presume, into the daylight world.

"Nobody come after me!" he warns. "Nobody move."

And of course, nobody does.

CHAPTER TWENTY-SEVEN

IT HAD TAKEN SOME DOING, but Pup finally managed to pry open a small crevice along the edge of the grate that covered what he sincerely hoped would turn out to be one of the skylights that once graced the ceiling of City Hall station.

He was exhausted, but that had not stopped him from clawing and gnawing at the board, and then at the old grate that covered the glass. He and Hope had run for what felt like a million miles, all the way from the riverbank where their life preserver had come ashore at Frankfort Street.

There they had encountered a gray-and-white creature, beaked and feathered. And hungry.

"You ain't fish," the creature had said.

"No, we're not," Hope confirmed. "We're mice. What are you?"

"Seagull."

Pup had been afraid of that. The bird was enormous, with beady eyes and a sharp bill. Pup had believed, in that moment, their journey was about to come to an abrupt and unpleasant end.

But when the gull saw Hope's foil bag, Pup discovered that seagulls not only preferred fish to mice, but given the menu option, they would also choose popcorn over rodent as well.

After Pup cajoled Hope (who was pretty hungry herself) into surrendering the foil bag, they made the trade, handing over the snack food in exchange for their lives and directions to City Hall Park.

"Head that way, 'til you see green," the seagull said, bobbing his narrow head in a westerly direction. "Take Frankfort."

Pup and Hope had done exactly that.

They'd run and run, and run some more, until their scraped and aching paws landed on the green grounds of the park.

There they'd scampered about until they'd found the grates, which, according to the literature Hope had studied back in the transit museum, covered the three wrought-iron skylights in the ceiling of city hall station.

Pup had attacked the corner of one until he'd opened a space large enough for them to slip through. Then, with a deep breath, they held fast to each other's paws. . . .

And they jumped!

Just before they hit the ground, Pup wrapped himself around Hope, sparing her the impact of the hard cement floor.

Pain shot through his body; he was certain one of his ribs had broken, and his left arm stung with pain. But Hope was safe. He'd protected her, and that had been his mission all along.

It took them both a few seconds to shake off the harshness of their landing, but the moment Hope recovered, she grabbed Pup's arm and tugged him away from the wide open center of the mezzanine level of City Hall station. Before them, a wide, short flight of stairs led down to the platform.

And on the platform there was chaos.

Quickly they'd ducked behind the brick corner of the arched wall and peered out. On the platform below, they could see not only Devon—the quarry they'd set out to capture—but Hopper, Zucker, Firren, and all four of Hope's siblings.

Pup felt a brief flash of joy at seeing so many familiar faces.

And then he saw the sword.

"Nobody come after me!" Dev commanded, his blade against a princess's neck. "Nobody move."

As the crazed mouse began to back toward the stairs, Pup saw that Dev's pink uniform was now splattered with blood. Whose he could not say, but it definitely did not bode well.

Devon continued his slow march backward toward the stairs while Zucker and Hopper remained helplessly at Firren's side. Zucker's expression was filled with loathing for the mouse who had attacked his mate and was now making off with one of his children. If looks could kill, Pup realized, Dev would

be dead already. But that was all that Zucker or any of them could do; if they even flinched, the lunatic mouse would take the princess's life. So Zucker remained still, with his hateful gaze fixed on the escaping kidnapper.

Hopper, too, Pup noticed, was staring . . . but not at Devon.

He was staring at Pup. When Pup realized that the Chosen One had spotted him peeking out from the jog in the wall, he quickly averted his eyes. He could only imagine what Hopper might be feeling—after all, in many ways this whole catastrophe was Pup's fault. If Pup hadn't threatened Atlantia and the Mūs village, they would have never sent out a search party to haul him in. A search party that included the dastardly Devon, who was now climbing backward, slowly, carefully, up the broad steps to the mezzanine.

But even as the villain drew closer to where he and Hope crouched, Pup could not seem to focus on him. Instead he met Hopper's gaze and held it, hoping that the shame and remorse writhing within him would show plainly enough on his face, to make Hopper understand how truly repentant he was.

Hopper looked back at him. And there, across the golden-lit expanse of City Hall station, Pup saw what he needed to see in his brother's eyes.

Forgiveness.

"I have an idea," Hope whispered. "I'm going to distract him."

"Brilliant," said Pup. "How?"

"Let's just say," said Hope, removing her tiara, "that I won't be needing this silly thing anymore."

"Why not?"

"Devon wanted to be royal, and look what it did to *him!*"

"So . . . ," said Pup, confused, "you *don't* want to be thought of as a royal princess anymore?"

Hope rolled her eyes. "I am *so* over it." With that, she flung her shining tiara straight at Dev's head. Her aim was true; the little crown clonked him on the back of his skull. It wasn't enough to do any damage, but it was all the distraction they needed.

Devon cried out in surprise, bobbling his weapon, and losing his hold on the princess. Feeling mighty, Pup brandished the hedgehog quill and ran full force at the stunned villain as Hope bolted forward to grab her sister and drag her back down the steps out of Dev's reach.

But Devon was quick to recover from his shock; he regained his sword almost instantly, and aimed it at Pup.

Pup waved the quill, but he knew as well as Dev did that a hedgehog spine was no match for a well-crafted sword.

And then he sensed it . . . motion, just overhead, something hovering above. His eyes shot upward. And what he saw there actually made him laugh with delight.

"Something funny, Pup?" Devon snickered. "Besides your weapon, that is?" He began to stalk Pup slowly. "Do you honestly think you can hurt me with that pathetic excuse for a sword?"

"Probably not," Pup admitted, his face breaking into a cocky grin. "But I bet a little spider silk could do some serious damage!"

Suspended by a nearly invisible filament, Hacklemesh dropped down from the ceiling and landed on Dev's head.

"Ahhhh!" cried Dev, slapping at the eight hairy legs that now enfolded him. "Ahhhh!"

"Spin, Hack!" Pup cried. "Spin."

As the astonished group of rodents looked on, Hacklemesh worked his arachnid magic, expertly encasing Dev in a tightly woven cocoon of sticky spider silk.

Devon was caught.

The battle was over. But the terror had just begun.

Because Firren had closed her eyes. And from where Pup stood, she did not look as if she'd be opening them again anytime soon.

CHAPTER TWENTY-EIGHT

IT IS A SOMBER PARTY *that jumps aboard the empty 6 train to return to Atlantia. Zucker carries his beloved Firren as though she is a priceless treasure, which, of course, she is. Each of the royal heirs takes a turn hugging their sister Hope, thrilled that she has been returned safely to them, but at the same time heartsick over their mother's precarious condition. Having retrieved her tiara she used to save Go-go, Hope carries it tucked under her arm but oddly, chooses not to put it on.*

The Chosen One and his brother flank the prisoner Dev, while Celeste and I look on. Celeste's eyes are still moist with tears for her lost sister.

What will become of Dev, we cannot yet guess. Pinkie will try him in a Mūs court for the murders of her soldiers. The elders will decide what is to be done with him. And while I am sickened by the crimes he has committed, the damage he has caused, I cannot help but feel sorry for the loss that brought him to this point of madness.

The legacy of Titus's treaty with Felina, it seems, can still bring pain. I suppose it is like that with evil. Even when we believe we have destroyed it, we must remain ever vigilant and be prepared to defeat it again and again whenever it rears its ugly head.

Before we left the splendid and magnificent City Hall station, Pup and his spider friend bid each other a fond farewell. The spider apparently liked the aesthetics of the abandoned station and elected to remain there, where he would spin webs as intricately ornate as the wrought-iron filigree work of those long-forgotten skylights.

It is a long way back to Atlantia. We must take another train to the Barclays stop, and then we are forced to run the gauntlet of human foot traffic in order to reach the portal that drops us into the part of the tunnel that we call home. All the while, Zucker's tender hold on Firren never falters.

We arrive, at long last, at the gates of Atlantia and find that for the first time in a very long while, the entrance to the city is being guarded by an enormous, green-eyed feline.

All of us, except for Pup, Hope, and the Chosen One himself, stop in our tracks. They, however, hurry forth without hesitation or fear.

This strikes me as odd, until I hear Hopper calling the cat by name.

"Ace!" he cries. "Ace, you're here!"

CHAPTER TWENTY-NINE

ACE MOVED LIKE A STREAK of black-and-white lightning toward the palace of Atlantia. With Hopper and Marcy's help, Zucker had managed to climb onto the tuxedo cat's strong, silky back without letting go of Firren.

Firren, who hadn't stirred since they'd left City Hall station.

Raz, along with Bartel and Pritchard, was sent on his first official military detail: escorting the silk-bound Dev to the Mūs village, where he would be imprisoned until Sage, Christoph, and Temperance could determine his fate.

The citizens of Atlantia watched in hushed awe as the emperor rode through the streets of the city on the back of the upland cat. At the palace Zucker carried Firren to the royal bedchamber. Marcy helped him to remove the blue cloak and silver cape in an effort to make the wounded empress more comfortable. Hope covered her mother with the worse-for-wear scrap of patchwork blanket and refused to leave her side.

No one saw any reason to ask her to.

"Mother," the tiny princess whispered. "I understand now. I understand why you and Daddy don't want me and Raz and the others to get carried away with royalty. It's what made Dev so greedy and mean. He hurt people because he wanted to be a prince. He thought being royal was more important than being good. And I don't want to be that way . . . ever! I don't need pretty dresses or shiny jewels to feel special and important. You and Daddy make me feel that way every single day . . . and not because I'm a princess. Because I'm me."

Zucker leaned down and kissed his daughter between her ears. "I'm sure Mommy is happy to hear that," he said softly.

Hopper only stayed long enough to see that the warrior empress was settled; then he tiptoed out of the bedchamber to make his way to his own quarters, where he knew Pup would be waiting.

He was halfway down the corridor when Marcy came out of the royal chamber after him.

"Hopper? May I speak with you?"

Hopper turned and saw that she was holding the blue cloak. La Rocha's disguise. He gave her a sad smile. "I don't suppose you're taking that to be laundered."

Marcy shook her head. "This is who I am now, Hopper. I had forgotten for a bit, but it's all come back to me."

"So you'll be going? Back out into the tunnels?"

"Yes, but I'll never be far. You'll see me about the palace now and again." She leaned down to kiss his torn ear, the one she herself had once washed and bandaged. "I don't like to be gone from those I cherish. And I think you know how much I cherish you, Chosen One."

"I cherish you right back," he whispered.

"There is something I want to share with you. A secret."

"Okay."

"Now that you know about La Rocha's legacy, you understand that one day in the future I will be passing on my mystic title to another."

"It's a good system."

Marcy laughed. "It is. And now I am entrusting to you and only you the name of the one I would like to see take up this duty when I have finished. The one who shall follow in my pawprints, so to speak."

Hopper's eyebrows rose with curiosity. "Who is it?"

Marcy glanced around the corridor, then pulled Hopper close and whispered a name into his ear. His face lit up.

"A wonderful choice!" he said. "Perfect, really."

"I thought so," said Marcy. "He already shows the signs. He is wise and thoughtful. A small rat with big ideas and an interesting way of looking at the world. Not to mention a wonderful sense of humor. Believe me, that comes in handy when dispensing wisdom in this often dreary tunnel world of ours."

"Can I tell Zucker? I think he'd be proud."

Marcy shook her head. "No. You can tell no one. It is part of the mystical legacy. La Rocha's identity must always remain a mystery. It was only these extreme circumstances that allowed you and the royal couple to discover that, for the moment at least, the role of tunnel prophet is mine."

"You're right," said Hopper. "I will keep this information about the next La Rocha to myself, and when the time is right, I will tell you-know-who that he has a very special destiny to fulfill." He puffed out his chest and grinned. "I have some personal experience with that sort of thing, you understand. I know a thing or two about destiny."

"That you do," said Marcy with a laugh. "Be well, little hero. I will see you soon."

Hopper watched his friend skip off down the hallway, and then he continued on to his own bedchamber. As expected, Pup was there, hunched over the desk that had once belonged to Zucker.

"Hello, Pup."

"Hello, Hopper."

Much to Hopper's satisfaction, upon their return to the palace, Marcy had directed two liveried servants to do for Pup exactly what they had done for him when he'd first come to the palace—lost and alone and very dirty, clinging nervously to Zucker's paw with no conception of the future that lay ahead of him.

As the servants had escorted Pup up the stairs that would eventually bring him to a basin filled with chilly water and soap, Hopper had called after him, "Don't worry, Pup, it's only a bubble bath. It won't kill you."

Thanks to that bubble bath, Pup's beige fur was once again clean and soft. The biggest improvement was that he'd been purged of the ugly black circle he'd drawn around his eye. He was Pup again.

Well, almost.

"What's with that rag you've got wrapped around your head?" Hopper asked. "Did you hurt yourself?"

"It's just something I'm trying," said Pup, blushing. "It's what the pi-rats wear."

"The pi-*whats?*"

"They live on a boat called the East River Ferry," Pup explained. "They're a little scary at first, but once you get to know them, they're a fine bunch of rodents. Kindhearted, and honorable. According to them, a life on the water is the most exciting life of all. Trust me, Hopper, you haven't lived until you've felt the wind in your fur and the spray of the river in your whiskers."

Hopper smiled. He felt the same way about riding the subway. "Sounds thrilling."

"Oh, it is! Which is why I was hoping . . . well, if it's all right with you and Pinkie, I think maybe I'd like to be one. A pi-rat, that is."

Hopper frowned. "Pup, you can't be a pi-rat!"

"Why not?"

"Well, for one thing, you're a mouse." But Hopper had heard the need in his brother's voice. He hated the thought of losing Pup yet again, but he also understood that destiny has an awfully strong pull.

"You're your own mouse now," Hopper said with a sigh. "All grown up and more than capable of taking care of yourself and anyone else who might need you. You proved that by bringing Hope home safely."

Pup beamed. "That means a lot to me, Hopper."

Hopper reached into the pocket of his jerkin and took out a letter, which he handed to his brother. "This was delivered for you. From Pinkie."

Pup gave him an embarrassed look. "Will you tell me what it says?"

"Oh, right. Sorry." Hopper opened the note and read it silently. Then he looked up at Pup and smiled.

"What?" asked Pup.

"She forgives you," Hopper reported. "And we know what a big deal that is for her!"

"She's changed," Pup observed.

"More than you know," said Hopper, pointing to the letter. "This goes on to say that she's turning the responsibility of leading the Mūs village back over to the elders entirely."

Pup looked as though he could scarcely believe it. "Why?"

"She wants to explore the tunnels. She's been doing that, you know. Riding the trains far and wide, collecting treasures from all sorts of places. Meeting new rodents, seeing new places."

"Sounds rather adventurous."

"Sure does." Hopper nodded. "So I guess this is how it's going to be, then. My brother is going upland to become a pi-rat, and my sister is heading out to become a great explorer. Makes my life sound a little dull."

Pup laughed. "I don't think the life of the Chosen One will ever be dull," he said. "And who knows, there may be some great big grand adventure waiting in *your* future too!"

If there was, Hopper couldn't imagine what it might be. He was about to mention this to his brother when the bedchamber door swung open and his godchild stepped in.

"Hope!" said Hopper. "What is it? How's Firren?"

"Awake!" cried Hope, her eyes glistening with tears of happiness and relief. "All thanks to Celeste. She knew exactly what to do to make the bleeding stop. When Mother awoke, the first thing she did was invite Celeste to stay on as Atlantia's physician. And she agreed."

Hopper smiled. "That's wonderful."

Now Hope turned to Pup. "You look much better without that silly smudge around your eye."

"Thank you."

"I brought you a couple of surprises," she said, handing him her tiara. "This is to remind you of the big rescue. We made a great team, didn't we?"

Pup nodded, taking the glimmering crown.

"Consider it your first official object of pi-rat doody!" said Hope.

"I think the word is 'booty,'" said Pup, grinning. "But thanks."

"Next surprise . . . ," said Hope, leaning back into the hallway and waving. Because Hopper was closer to the doorway, he saw the second "surprise" before Pup did. His heart went warm as Hope said, "Hopper, would you care to do the honors?"

"My pleasure," he said, his voice catching. "Pup, I'd like you to meet a living legend."

Dodger stepped into the room, his eyes shining as they gazed, for the first time since that long-ago night when he'd crept out of the cage in Keep's shop, at his son.

"Dodger, this is Pup," said Hopper. "Pup, meet your father."

Hopper and Hope left the newly reunited father and son alone to get acquainted. By now the whole population of Atlantia had heard the news of Firren's recovery, and the streets were filled with gleeful revelers, rejoicing over the empress's good fortune. A dinner banquet was being planned for that evening to celebrate.

Firren officially declared it a non-royal event. No bowing, no curtsying. Dress code: casual.

As the Chosen One and the young rat made their way through the palace, Hopper realized he was still holding Pinkie's letter. When he slipped it into his pocket, he was surprised to find that there was something already tucked in there. The sketch Mamie had given him that his grandmother Myrtle had drawn, so long ago. He'd forgotten all about it.

He was about to take it out of his pocket when the emperor came dashing around the corner from the royal bedchamber.

"Hopper, have you heard?" Zucker cried, clapping his friend on the back. "She's been asking for you! She can't wait to see you."

"Firren?"

"Well, yeah, her too," Zucker said, laughing. "But that's not who I mean."

"That's another surprise!" said Hope, taking her very confused godfather by the paw and dragging him across the palace lobby. "In here!"

Zucker flung open the towering door to the throne room and all but pushed Hopper inside.

And there she was.

"Carroll!"

In that moment, Hopper knew that there was, in fact, a stupendous adventure in his future. And he had a feeling it would be more wonderful than he ever could have hoped.

Chapter Thirty

A FEW WEEKS LATER, BELOW *the streets of Manhattan* ...

The ceremony took place on the steps.

Of City Hall station.

The new city, which Hopper would oversee as mayor, was mostly still under construction, but a handsome, sturdy home already had been built at the foot of the staircase for the Chosen One and his bride. At present the home was largely unfurnished, except for a gleaming wooden desk that had been brought from Atlantia and placed in the mayoral office.

Zucker's old desk, the one at which Hopper had learned to read and write.

"Think of it as a wedding gift," *President* Zucker had said when the desk was delivered.

Zucker and Firren had finally convinced the Atlantians that they no longer needed a monarchy to rule the city. The family-formerly-known-as-royal would be moving out of the palace into a more reasonably sized home so that the palace could be turned into a school for all the children of Atlantia.

Brighton was already hoping to be the valedictorian of its first graduating class. And Go-go was planning the prom.

Hopper looked out over the gracefully curved City

Hall platform where friends and family members—Atlantians, Mūs citizens, and even a handful of grassland residents—were gathered to witness his marriage. He liked that this station, which would be his and Carroll's new dwelling place, came complete with overhead chandeliers. This simulated sunlight would mean that Carroll would never feel homesick for the bright upland sky. And of course, Hopper and Carroll would be visiting Ace often, and Pup the swashbuckler, who had arrived back in the tunnels just the day before.

He'd brought Hope's diamond tiara with him as

a wedding gift. Carroll would wear it today, not as a crown, but as a beautiful accessory to her formal wedding ensemble. Like the new Atlantia, the government of City Hall station would be a democratic one, so she would not need it afterward. And because it had first belonged to Zucker's mother, the brave and selfish Conselyea, the tiara would remain forever after on display as part of the Atlantian history exhibit in the city's soon-to-be-built museum. Hope would be entrusted with the crown immediately following the speaking of the vows, over which La Rocha would officiate.

The wedding party included Pup, Hacklemesh, and all the royal heirs, who would be carried up the steps in style, riding on Ace's back. Hope would be Carroll's maid of honor, and Dodger would have the pleasure of giving away the bride.

Pinkie, sadly, would not be in attendance, being that she was off on her biggest exploration campaign yet. . . . She had gone out in search of a legendary kingdom called Grand Central Station. She'd sent her regrets, along with a wedding gift: a collection of hundreds and hundreds of book pages she'd uncovered in her recent travels, all torn from human books long-lost in the tunnels. Hopper could not have asked for a better present. He planned to use these to start the Ira and Fiorello Memorial Lending Library, which would also house pages from a book called *The Rise and Fall of the Roman Empire*. At Firren's suggestion, the front door of the library would be made of silver.

"We're ready to begin the ceremony," La Rocha whispered from the shadows of the hooded cloak.

Hopper grinned and whispered back, "Thanks, Marcy."

He turned to his best man, Zucker, who was dressed just as he'd been for his own royal wedding—in his best purple tunic with the blue gemstone-studded chain around his neck. Not because it was a royal occasion, but because it was a special one.

The chain reminded Hopper of something. He reached into his pocket and took out the drawing Mamie had given him . . . the drawing his own grandmother Myrtle had made so long ago of Hopper's grandfather, smiling with Titus and Conselyea. In the portrait Conselyea was wearing the chain.

"Remember the prophecy?" he asked Zucker. "*There shall appear One who will lead them, small of stature but brave of heart?*"

"How could I forget it?" Zucker's eyes twinkled with humor. "You dropped out of the daylight world and set everything in motion."

"That's not entirely true," said Hopper. "It was in motion long before I escaped from my cage."

He showed Zucker the drawing of their ancestors, explaining that Ebbets was Dodger's father. "I want you to have it," he said. "Hang it in your new museum.

This is *our* history, mine and yours. It's the moment when Atlantia and the Mūs village became possible."

Zucker was amazed. His eyes shone with tears as he gazed at the image of his lost mother, and at Titus, who at the time still had so many dreams in his young heart . . . dreams that were as yet untainted by fear and desperation. Hopper hoped this would be the way Zucker would remember the father who had ultimately given his own life to spare his son's.

Hopper admired the way Myrtle had so deftly captured the keen intelligence in young Titus's eyes—the same keen intelligence he now saw reflected in Zucker's. And the white circle of fur distinctively marking the gentle, hopeful face of his own grandfather, Ebbets, which still lived on in Hopper.

"Zuck-meister?"

"Yeah, kid? I mean . . . Mayor."

"I believe we were always destined to be friends, you and I."

"I believe it too."

Suddenly the station was filled with the beautiful sounds of cricket song. Ace was carrying the wedding party up the steps. At the bottom of the steps Dodger was taking Carroll's arm.

Carroll. The chosen one of the Chosen One.

Hopper's future.

It was a future he would face with confidence,

commitment, and most of all, courage. He knew this from the tops of his ears to the tip of his tail, to the deepest most joyful place in his fluttering little heart.

His Mouseheart.

A BONUS TALE
of
HISTORICAL IMPORT

REPRINTED HERE
BY SPECIAL PERMISSION OF
THE NOBLE MŪS ELDERS FROM THEIR SACRED BOOK:

The Lost Pages

As inscribed and faithfully recounted
from memory by one who was there
Atlantia Rising: How It All Began

A **very long time ago**, before Atlantia, in the cellar of the Brooklyn Public Library . . .

These rats had no names.

There were two of them; they were not friends in the traditional sense, but both were young, healthy, and united in their common desire to stay alive. They'd banded together because being alone was dangerous, and there was at least some small degree of might in being a duo. Of the pair, only one of them could be considered smart, and what the smart rat knew best was that he did not know enough. He also knew that he could learn.

He and his mean-spirited companion had burrowed their way into the underground room of an enormous structure and there made themselves a temporary home. The location was not accidental.

The place was dank, dusty, and cavernous; it smelled of drying paper and old ink (which was not unpleasant) and mold (which was). But it was warmer than being out in the gutters, and here humans appeared only occasionally; they mostly came to drop off large black bags, the contents of which would be spilled into the incinerator at the end of each week by a human called Custodian. These bags were not difficult to chew through and yielded more delectable sustenance than the rats could ever hope to gather living in the streets.

This had pleased the mean rat, and he'd taken full advantage. He'd been scrawny when they arrived in the cellar, but after months of living off the bounty of human refuse, he'd become bulky and solid. And, truth be told, a bit cocky.

But in the eyes of the smarter rat, what was even better than the constant supply of food was the fact that this cellar was a storage place, or perhaps a dumping ground, for all the books that had been deemed no longer useful to the humans who frequented the upper levels of this magnificent place called the "Library." The smart rat had purposely chosen the basement of this building, not only for shelter but also because here he could acquire the knowledge he so desperately sought. Somehow he understood that knowing and thinking could prove to be exceedingly helpful in keeping a rat safe. Possibly even happy.

At present he was poring over a thick, dusty old

volume that must have been relegated to the basement years before. The words on the book's tattered spine read *The Rise and Fall of the Roman Empire*. As usual, the rat who was not so smart was busy with the garbage bags, relishing the half-eaten lunches and open sugar packets.

As his companion rummaged through the trash, the smart rat used his teeth and claws to turn the book's broad pages, reading what he could. It was a skill he had only recently acquired, and certain words were easier for him to decipher than others. There was one in particular he liked: "peace." And another word: "power." He liked the way these words sounded when he spoke them aloud in his rodent voice, and he liked how they looked printed in bold letters alongside the other less-intriguing words on the page.

The bright-but-nameless rat had just come to a section about emperors when there arose a terrible commotion on the cellar stairs.

"Help me! Please, someone! *Help!*"

The smart rat's hungry companion immediately dove into the torn trash bag he'd been plundering. But the shouted pleas ignited a sense of duty in the smart rat, who dashed for the stairs. There he saw the loveliest female rodent upon whom he'd ever laid his glittering black eyes. She was frantically making her way downward, leaping from step to step, her whiskers quivering with terror. In a moment, the smart rat learned why: The female was being chased by a screeching human woman, an upstairs employee known as the librarian. This librarian was swinging a broom, poking and stabbing it in the direction of the fleeing female. Luckily, the human's aim was poor and the female rat was able to dodge the blows.

"This way," the smart rat called.

The female's eyes were filled with horror, but she did not question his instructions. She flung herself behind him; he could feel the warmth of her coarse fur bristling against his as she trembled.

The librarian galloped down the stairs, her broomstick flailing in front of her. Oddly, she looked as frightened as the female rat, but even in her fear she seemed determined.

"I won't stand for rat droppings in my library!" she shouted. "There'll be no disease-ridden pestilence slinking around in *my* stacks."

The smart rat did not know these words, but he did rightly take them for insults. The librarian spotted him now and let out a long, shrill shriek. She gripped her stick and swung it up over her head, preparing to bring it down mercilessly on both of the rodents at once.

But before the librarian could swing the weapon, the smart rat leaped forward, baring his claws and sinking his knifelike teeth into the human's fleshy ankle; he came away with the metallic taste of blood on his tongue.

The scream that ripped from her throat seemed to shake the entire library. Still the rat did not back down; he went up on his hind paws, ready to attack again, but the librarian had gone deathly pale. Her weapon clattered to the concrete floor as her hands clasped around her bleeding limb. The smart rat lurched toward her a second time and as she swatted him away, something jangling and sparkly slipped from her wrist. Sobbing, she turned and hobbled back up the stairs, screeching the word "rabies" over and over.

The rat spit the blood from his mouth, then turned to take hold of the female's front paw.

"Are you all right?" he asked. "Did she get you with that stick?"

"No," the female replied in a shaky voice. "But she would have, if you hadn't come to my rescue so bravely." She looked up at him with tear-filled eyes and smiled. "Thank you."

The rat felt an unfamiliar fluttering of his heart. "Glad I could help."

Then he leaned down to pick up the sparkling object the librarian had lost and saw that it was a chain fashioned of golden links, dotted with glittering stones of the deepest blue.

"What is it?" the female breathed, her eyes dancing at the sight of such a pretty bauble.

"Jewelry, I think. Humans treasure it." Feeling bold,

he draped the jangly chain around her neck and smiled when he saw how the color of the gemstones complemented her gray coat. "For you."

"Thank you." She smiled. "My name is Conselyea."

The smart rat repeated her name; it sounded like music to him. "I don't have a name," he confessed.

For a long moment, they just stared at each other. Until the smart rat's nasty companion stuck his head out from the trash bag, startling them both.

"That was a close one," he observed, munching into a pretzel. "Hope we've seen the last of her."

The smart rat was just about to say he doubted it very much when again, he heard noise on the stairs. This time the footsteps came fast and heavy. He turned to his friend with wide eyes.

"Custodian!" they said together.

The three rats scurried into the shadows just as the custodian reached the bottom step.

But today the familiar human in the blue uniform did not come bearing bulging bags of treats and nourishment. This time he carried a shovel! And a box with ominous-looking words printed on it in big red letters:

RAT POISON.

The smart rat understood immediately that their time in the cozy basement with the endless supply of food and knowledge had come to a close.

"Hey, you stinkin' rats!" the custodian barked,

banging the floor with his shovel. "Come out, come out, wherever you are!"

The noise of the metal shovel was a clattering, clanging din that made Conselyea cover her delicate, rounded ears and press her face into the smart rat's chest.

He had to admit, he kind of liked that.

The custodian set about pouring small piles of a grainy green substance from the box. The hungry rat's nose immediately began to twitch with interest.

"Eat up, pests." The custodian chuckled. "Feast! And tomorrow morning I'll be shoveling your flea-bitten carcasses into the incinerator with the rest of the trash."

Conselyea gasped. The custodian laughed and stomped back up the stairs.

The minute he disappeared, the not-so-intelligent rat made to scamper toward the closest pile of mysterious grain.

"No!" the smart rat roared.

"But it smells so good," his friend argued. "I just want to taste it."

"It will kill you," the smart rat promised. "Now that they know we're here, they won't stop until we're dead. That stuff will likely boil the blood in our veins if we so much as take one nibble. If that doesn't work, they'll set out those vicious torture devices they call traps. Either way, we can't stay here."

Conselyea looked at him as though she were sizing him up, taking his measure. Apparently, she found him worthy because after a moment she said simply, "I trust you. If you say we must go, then we must."

A tremor of joy filled him. Sad as he was to be leaving behind the warmth and the books, he knew he could live happily without those things for the rest of his life . . . as long as he had her trust, as long as she was by his side.

He had no idea where he would lead her, but the elation he felt, just knowing she would follow, was indescribable. And for her trust, he would reward her with his devotion. His protection. He would do whatever was required of him to keep her safe.

His mean, hungry companion would come along too, of course, and this would make them that much stronger. They would fight for one another, against whatever enemy they might meet.

The hungry rat slid one more longing glance toward the poison. "When do we leave?"

The smart one looked upward, toward one of the cellar's high windows. Beyond the grimy bit of glass, the brilliance of the day was fading to evening gloom.

"At first light," he decided. "We'll tunnel out the way we came."

"Where will we go?"

The rat had no answer just yet. But he'd once read a book about a sailor called Columbus who'd set out on a great ocean voyage and discovered a new world. The idea of a sailing adventure appealed to the rat. He'd heard Brooklyn was close to the water. All he would have to do was find it.

"You two get some rest," the smart rat suggested. "I'll stay awake and keep an eye out for Librarian and Custodian with their sticks and shovels."

Obediently the mean rat and Conselyea closed their eyes.

The smart rat went back to his book, *The Rise and Fall of the Roman Empire*, and read through the night. He read of strong leaders and proud cities, and wicked enemies who were conquered bravely and gloriously in the name of prosperity and peace. He let the words and their lessons take hold, drinking in their wisdom, forming his own new plan. He read of soldiers and senators from Rome, of orators and of emperors who had made history, and of the one elusive thing they wanted and fought for above all else: *power*.

Power, he realized, was what kept the shovels and the poison at bay. Power meant safety, and safety meant freedom. And although power could occasionally be won with brute force, he discovered that it could only be maintained with cunning and intellect.

Luckily, he was possessed of both.

As the night wore on, the smart rat read and studied and debated silently with himself on matters moral and points political. Rome and the Romans fascinated and enlightened him. He only wished he were large enough to take the entire heavy volume with him to whatever new place he'd be going in the morning. But since he could not do that, he tore out as many of the glossy pages as he could carry. Then, to be safe, he tore several sections from a book called *Latin: A Primer* in case any of the vocabulary on the glossy pages gave him trouble. He did this quietly, so as not to awaken his sleeping friends.

All night long the smart rat read. He read, and he learned.

And by the time the high windows had begun to glow with the first pale rays of daylight, he had chosen for himself a destiny.

And a name:

From this day forward, he would be called Titus. And he would be strong.

Titus christened his companion "Cassius." It was a name he'd found in the pages of his book about Rome, and it sounded sufficiently intimidating. Titus told the mean, hungry rat his new name as they crept out through the same short tunnel they'd dug to enter the library.

"I want to be more than Cassius," the mean rat snarled. "I'd like a title."

"Fine. General Cassius, then."

General Cassius smiled. "I like it." He had taken an armful of food from the plastic trash bags and was cradling it close to him. Titus had his tail rolled snugly around the pages he'd torn from the books, and Conselyea wore the elegant golden chain of blue stones around her neck.

"That suits you," Titus observed. "You look like an empress."

Conselyea did not know what an empress was, but she took it for the compliment it was.

They emerged from the library into the predawn light and found themselves on a thoroughfare called Flatbush Avenue. At this early hour they saw almost no humans. A stray dog roamed the sidewalks, and some squirrels skittered down the trunk of a scraggly tree. The rats followed this path for a great distance.

As they scuttled along, Titus would occasionally lift his snout into the air and sniff deeply.

"Why do you do that?" Conselyea asked.

"I'm trying to find the river," Titus explained. "I have heard that rats can prosper along the docks." What he didn't tell her was that he was seeking an adventure—for all three of them. If they could get to the river, perhaps they could board a ship that would take them far away. Titus imagined a great ocean crossing, an epic sailing trip into the warm waters of a place called Italy, the birthplace of Rome. There they could make their new home in the eternal city he'd read about and admired. Surely a rat as smart and determined as Titus would be welcome in there; he might even find a way to live in luxury, prosperity, and peace, just like the Roman emperors once had.

He glanced around but saw no signs of water. He did see a building of sand-colored bricks, less imposing than those that surrounded it. It seemed to exist as an island, just like Sicily or Capri, floating between the two black-tarred streets, which, with every passing second, were becoming more alive with zooming vehicles. And more dangerous.

Titus studied the structure; it bore the words ATLANTIC AVENUE. He liked the rounded roofline and the decorative garlands of carved fruit that draped from it. Titus imagined that no rodent would ever starve in a building made of fruit. It was cement-and-brickwork cornucopia. But it was not the river.

"Never cared much for the water myself," Cassius sneered. "I say we find ourselves one of those places where humans gather to relax and gorge themselves. A rest-or-eat-all-you-want. I bet that's where we'll find the best garbage in the city."

"Hah! Speaking of garbage . . ."

The voice had come from a gap between two tall buildings. Titus felt an instinctive prickle of worry when he saw the group of rats hovering at the mouth of the alleyway. He had read in one of the library cellar's many books that such a gathering of rodents was called a plague—*a plague of rats.*

Looking at these sloppy strangers, Titus feared the term would prove to be accurate. A quick count gave him six rats in all, every one of them burly, most of them battered. None friendly and every last one of them up to no good.

The scruffiest rat stood at the front of the mischief, baring his teeth. "Speaking of garbage," he repeated, "what's that you've got there? Smells tasty." He motioned to the food Cassius was cradling. "Give it up."

"No," snapped Cassius. "This belongs to us."

"Well, well, well," said the leader. "Somebody's got a *bad* rat-itude."

Without even realizing it, Titus stepped closer to Conselyea. But he knew there was no way he and Cassius could take on six rats and live to tell the tale. A mad dash to escape would be their only option.

The head rat pressed forward. His bedraggled little army did the same.

Titus turned to Cassius. "Give them the food," he said through his teeth.

"Absolutely not," huffed Cassius, clutching his garbage.

"Well, if you won't give it," snarled the head rat, "I guess we'll just have to take it."

Titus could see that this streetwise rodent meant

what he said. He took hold of Conselyea's paw and gave the command: "Run!"

"Where?" cried Cassius, gaping at the busy street. "We can't cross."

"We have to cross," said Titus. "These rats will tear us to shreds. Just head for that building."

He darted into the street, pulling Conselyea along with him. The cars sped past, but Titus bobbed and wove and minced and leaped, somehow managing to avoid every massive tire, every red-hot tailpipe. Cassius was right on his heels, tracing his path.

The three rats made it to the island where the Atlantic Avenue building stood, smaller than the others but still massive to them. They were panting and quivering, but unharmed.

On the far sidewalk the scruffy leader shook his head. "Idiot rats," he spat. "Crossing Flatbush Avenue at rush hour." When he realized the trio was heading into the building, he snorted. "So yer headin' underground, are ya?"

"Wouldn't do that if I were you," called one of his grubby mischief-mates. "Word on the street is them tunnels is haunted by the ghost of a bloodthirsty feline."

"We ain't goin' after them, are we?" asked another rat, who was missing half his tail. "I don't wanna tangle with no cat ghost!"

"Fuhgeddaboudit," said the mischief leader. "I ain't messin' with no undead kitty cat."

With that, the rat gang scampered off.

"So now what?" asked General Cassius, still gripping his cache of treats.

Titus considered it. Between the madness of "rush hour" and the potential for running into more hoodlum rats, it seemed that continuing on in search of the river might be ill-advised. But the gang leader had said something about this Atlantic Avenue building leading underground. Titus reasoned that if a place as deep as a library basement was good, perhaps somewhere even deeper would be better. He'd seen humans descend below the streets—why, he did not know—but who knew more about survival than they did? They were the ones who built the buildings and produced the delicious trash. They were the ones who wrote all those miraculous, wonderful books.

"Let's go in here," he said, starting toward the building's entrance.

As Titus led Cassius and Conselyea inside, he felt a wave of excitement. As omens went, these were good ones: they'd escaped a rowdy rat pack and made it safely across a busy street. It may not have been a voyage across the ocean, but it was a crossing nonetheless.

His adventure had begun.

There were humans everywhere.

They toted bags and carried cases of all sizes. The

light had a sickly quality; it bounced off the shiny walls, making the human faces glow green. Just beyond the floor where Titus and his friends crept was a chasm, a wide canyon where the floor dropped off. The humans stood perched at the edge of this, craning their necks to peer into the darkness. Titus wasn't sure what sort of beasts might live in the shadows into which the canyon stretched, but he was certain he didn't want to encounter one. So the three rats kept to the wall as far from the edge as it was possible to be, and tried to avoid being seen.

"Where are we?" Cassius asked, nibbling a chunk of old baloney from his stash. Titus glared at him, hoping he was enjoying his snack, since it had nearly cost them their lives.

A thundering sound suddenly filled the cavernous space, and a shining serpent sped out of the darkness, screaming to a stop where the humans awaited it. With an expulsion of breath the serpent opened its several gaping mouths, into which the humans willingly offered themselves. A moment later, it was gone.

Titus couldn't believe what he'd just witnessed. "What in the name of Caesar Augustus was *that?*"

"I think it was a subway train," said Conselyea.

Now Titus remembered. He had heard of these when he'd lived outdoors, before he'd moved into the library basement. The rodents on the street mentioned them occasionally, but Titus had never taken much interest.

His outside home had been a modest nest built upon one of the city's rare patches of dirt and underbrush. It wasn't much, but it was home. Cassius, who was useless when left to his own devices, was an occasional boarder at Titus's place, paying his way by scavenging for food and sharing it with his landlord. But one day the humans had come with their growling bulldozers and plowed Titus's nest into oblivion. That was when he'd moved into the cellar and discovered the joys of residing indoors . . . among *books*! Since then he'd spent as little time outside as he could, and frankly, he'd forgotten the street myth about these subway monsters, screaming around beneath the earth. Now he understood that it wasn't a myth at all.

"Let's go," said Conselyea, interrupting his thoughts. "Before another silver beast arrives."

The rats crept onward, until Titus spotted a rodent a few yards ahead. He was significantly smaller than Titus, and his coat was more brown than gray. Titus realized this was a mouse. Despite his small stature, he was working diligently, clawing at a spot where the wall met the floor.

For a long moment, Titus, Cassius, and Conselyea watched the determined little rodent at his work.

"Shall we eat him?" Cassius suggested, licking his chops.

Conselyea's expression said she found this to be an utterly repulsive question. Titus was in full agreement.

"How about we just talk to him," said Titus.

As they approached, Titus could see the mouse's tiny paws scraping away at a place where a small gap had begun to take shape. It was evident that his intention was to enlarge it.

"He's digging a hole," Conselyea observed.

When Titus's enormous shadow fell across the mouse, the pawing ceased abruptly. The mouse looked up from his task and blinked into the rat's face. He looked concerned but not frightened. Titus could see immediately that this was no ordinary mouse. There was a dignity in his face and an intelligence crackling in his bright black eyes. Most interesting was the circle of pure white fur surrounding his left eye; Titus had never seen a mouse with such a distinctive marking.

"Are you going to slaughter me?" the mouse asked calmly.

"Wasn't planning on it," said Titus.

"Good." The mouse grinned. "The name's Ebbets."

"Titus." The rat nodded to his companions. "Conselyea, and Cassius."

"*General* Cassius," the rat corrected, then gulped down his mouthful of baloney and belched.

"Nice to meet you all," said Ebbets.

"Our pleasure," said Conselyea.

Titus eyed the gap Ebbets had been digging at so industriously. "What's going on here?"

"I'm creating a portal."

"To . . . ?"

"The tunnels."

"Why would a little mouse like yourself have need of such a portal?" Titus asked.

Ebbets shook his head sadly. "Until a few weeks ago, my entire family and I were happily residing in the rafters of an empty building. But the wrecking ball came and took care of that. So we made our way into the tunnels to find a new home. My mate was very close to birthing our litter when we set out." Ebbets puffed out his little chest with pride. "I'm a father, as of two days ago."

"Congratulations," said Conselyea, offering him her pretty smile.

"Today I ventured upland to find food to bring back to them." Ebbets eyes shot to the haul of treats in Cassius's grip, but he refrained from remarking on it. "But it's a long and treacherous journey. Getting back and forth into the tunnels by crossing that track over there is a death-defying endeavor. So I thought if I could poke a hole here between the floor and the wall, I could jump and sort of free-fall my way home. It'll probably be one doozy of a drop, but I think if I tuck and roll, I can manage it."

Titus thought for a moment. "Is it safe in the tunnels?"

"No less safe than anywhere else, I suppose. And as far as I can tell, there aren't any wrecking balls. And definitely no humans, except for the ones in the trains."

"How about ghosts? Big, white, cat-shaped ones?"

Ebbets looked at him funny. "*Huh?*"

"Never mind," said Titus. "Would it be all right if we came with you?"

Cassius's eyes flew open. "You want us to go into the tunnels?"

Titus turned to Cassius, nose twitching at the stench of the general's baloney breath. "If we go back out onto those streets, that pack of rat ruffians will track us down eventually. And even if we could get far enough away from the city to build a nest, sooner or later the humans will obliterate it. I think the tunnels are worth a try." He turned back to Ebbets. "Let us come with you and we will give you a portion of the food my friend is carrying."

"*What!?*" Cassius shook his head. "That's out of the question!"

Titus flattened his ears and scowled at the general. "Either you share those rations with our new friend, or you get lost. Back to the streets . . . on your own this time."

Cassius glowered, but nodded his reluctant consent.

Satisfied, Titus crouched beside Ebbets and reached

toward the gap. Together the rat and the mouse began to dig.

So intent were they on their task that they barely noticed the human with his photography equipment, snapping shots of the bustling station. When the camera turned in their direction, Conselyea squeaked in surprise as the sudden brilliance of the flash lit up the platform.

"That's a keeper," said the human as he strode away. "Transit museum's gonna love these shots."

The rats did not know, nor did they care what a "keeper" was, and they had no idea what a transit museum could possibly be.

All they knew was that they were on a mission.

To find themselves a home.

The fall into the sub-tunnels was not exactly Titus's idea of fun, and the muck in which they landed made his pelt stiff and smelly. The air was stale and the lighting was dim. But at least there were no shovels, or poison, or crazed librarians running about. Not that he could see anyway. Still, he was wary of this new, dark place.

"Where is your nest?" asked Titus, eager to find shelter.

"My village is quite a trek from here. Three days, give or take. But we will find my mate and our litter waiting at a spot about half that distance."

Ebbets began to walk.

"Just out of curiosity," said Titus with a jerk of his tail in the opposite direction, "what's that way?"

"An abandoned platform where trains used to stop. There are still some human artifacts about, like signs and mechanicals. Mostly just trash." Ebbets eyed Cassius, who was now enjoying a crumb from a broken pretzel. "*You'd* love it there," he noted, then shrugged. "But it's basically a ghost town."

"There's that word again," muttered Cassius, gulping down the salty crumb. "Ghost."

"I'm going to go take a look," said Titus. "You guys go on. I'll catch up."

As his friends continued on their way, Titus went off to explore. It was only a short scamper to the place Ebbets had called the "abandoned platform."

And a more promising piece of real estate Titus had never seen!

He looked around at the remains of what once had been a functioning subway stop. Signs still clung to the upper parts of the tiled walls, and there was a porcelain basin attached to one wall, with pipes running from it. He'd seen one of these back in the library basement, in the custodian's closet, and seemed to recall that water could be extracted from such a device if one knew how to properly milk it.

A clever rat could really make something of such a place.

There were plenty of other human-made objects scattered about as well. He saw broken tiles, cardboard boxes, old clothing, pamphlets, newspapers, empty bottles, even a lost shoe with a high heel.

Titus marveled at it all, studying the platform just long enough to keep the image vivid in his sharp little mind. Then he raced off to join his friends.

"Ebbets," he said when he caught up to them, "that platform is truly amazing. Might I ask why you and your, um ... pack? ... cluster? ... faction? ..."

"Mischief," Ebbets corrected with a smile. "A gathering of mice is known as a mischief, which might be true in other cases, but my family is not like that. We're a more thoughtful bunch. We're strong and resourceful when we have to be, but we prefer a more peaceful, philosophical approach to life. We like to think of ourselves as a tribe."

"Okay," said Titus as they continued onward. "Why didn't your tribe just settle back there at the abandoned platform?"

"We knew that, although it was roomy and conveniently located for scavenging, in its current state it would not provide enough protection for rodents as small as we. That would require major construction, which we did not have the time nor the mousepower to undertake. So I sent scouts in search of a safer place for the tribe to settle, directing them to head south, into the depths of the depths. There they found even older, more secluded branches of these tunnels." He grinned and added, "Just as I suspected they would."

Ebbets led the rats farther and farther into the tunnels. Cassius grumbled the entire way, but Titus was gratified to discover that Conselyea was quite a trouper. She did not whine or grouse or even ask to rest. This pleased Titus more than he could say. Having such grit would be a benefit while living here in these tunnels.

After several hours of walking, Ebbets stopped. "Here is where the tribe camped while we awaited word from the vanguard."

Titus could see the remnants of the temporary encampment mixed in among the pebbles and trash. Evidence of campfires and snug sleeping spots dotted the landscape. He was beginning to develop a profound respect for this little mouse, who was so courageous and wise. He wished he could give Ebbets the name of a Roman emperor, or at least an impressive-sounding Latin moniker that would reflect his bravery and wisdom; he certainly deserved it.

"We were safe and comfortable here," Ebbets explained. "Days passed before the scouts came back with news that they'd discovered a great wall, a flat gray surface that rose up from the dirt floor and stretched all the way to the arched ceiling of the tunnel. I knew such a barrier would provide all the protection we could ever need, so I decided we would make our home behind it. The tribe packed up, ready to set out again, but just as we began the march, my mate whispered in my ear that she could not travel... it was her time to deliver. So I sent the others on ahead, asking only the tribe's midwife to stay behind with us. I built a makeshift but sturdy nest over there, by that rock, and it was there that my children came into the world. The first of our line to be born into the tunnels." A smile of genuine joy lit up the mouse's face. "As soon as they have grown strong enough to travel, we will take them to our new village behind the gray wall. Come. I'll introduce you."

The rats followed Ebbets, picking their way across the rubble to a small pile of twigs, fortified with bits of string and paper. There Titus saw Ebbets's delicate little mate sitting quietly with their napping litter.

"Ten in all," boasted Ebbets, pointing to each pup and announcing its name. "That's Koufax, Hodges, Reese, Robinson, and that one with his tail sticking up in the air there, that's Lasorda—he's got spunk. These two are Snider and Campanella, the twins, and that's Spooner, and Erskine."

His eyes clouded when the tiniest bundle of fluff began to cough.

"And this little one," Ebbets explained with a catch in his voice, "is Dodger. He's not feeling too well." The father mouse reached down to gently stroke the pup's ears.

Titus saw that of all the pups, only Dodger had the same white marking around his eye that Ebbets did. He also saw the worry in his new friend's face.

"Let's eat," he said, quickly taking the food from Cassius and doling it out. He was careful to give the best and most healthful-looking morsels to the new mother—whom Ebbets introduced as Myrtle—knowing she would pass the nutrients on to her litter when they nursed. "Myrtle's an artist," Ebbets boasted, beaming. "She went to school for it."

Myrtle, who was at the moment, sketching on a scrap of paper, gave a shy laugh. "As a pup, I lived at Pratt Institute," she clarified modestly. "I wasn't exactly enrolled."

"But you're very talented," Ebbets insisted, motioning toward her drawing. "See, Titus? She's got a real gift for portraiture."

Titus took the sketch and admired it. Indeed, Myrtle's loving rendering of her sleeping litter was a thing of beauty. "It's wonderful."

Myrtle thanked him with a smile, took up another scrap, and quietly began a new drawing. Titus realized with a bit of self-consciousness that he was one of the subjects of it, along with Ebbets and Conselyea. The artist chose to leave Cassius (who was chewing with his mouth open) out of the portrait. Titus couldn't say he blamed her.

Ebbets also introduced the midwife, Maimonides,

whom they affectionately called Mamie, who'd once resided in the maternity ward of a Brooklyn medical center.

As the little party dined on old biscuits, apple cores, and bits of cheese, Myrtle continued to draw while Ebbets told them all about his plans for creating a peaceful, thriving village behind the distant gray wall.

"Fascinating idea," said Titus. "Do you think it can be done?"

Ebbets nodded. "I do."

When again baby Dodger began to wheeze, Myrtle put down her artwork and picked him up. Conselyea asked if she could hold him. With a weary smile Myrtle handed the nearly weightless puff of brownish gray to Conselyea. Titus looked on, his heart near bursting at the sight of her cradling the sweet, fragile mouse pup.

"Look," Conselyea said. "He's got a circle around his eye, just like his father."

Ebbets beamed. "I know. Handsome little guy, isn't he?"

They continued to eat, and Titus showed Ebbets the pages he'd torn from the Latin primer and *The Rise and Fall of the Roman Empire*.

"That's exactly what I'm talking about," said Ebbets. "Great civilizations could spring up all over these subway tunnels. I've even heard of a place across the water, City Hall, I think they call it. It's fallen out of use, so it would be a perfect place to colonize. It's supposed to be beautiful, an architectural jewel in the crown of the New York subway line."

"Personally, I like that abandoned platform. I think I'd like to build a city there," said Titus.

"So it shall be!" cried Ebbets joyfully. "Me and my tribe behind our wall, you and yours constructing a grand metropolis at Atlantic Avenue. We'll be the greatest of allies!"

Titus smiled. "Of course. From our friendship will come our strength!"

Ebbets frowned. "We'll have to be careful of the trains," he said wisely. "They will always present a danger to small creatures like us. Perhaps we would do well to impose laws forbidding our citizens to go anywhere near them."

"Excellent suggestion."

Ebbets nodded, his eyes shining with hope and excitement. "I know if we pull together, Titus, we will make something of these tunnels. Something lasting, something good. For all of us."

"All?" said Conselyea. "You mean there are others down here like us?"

"Plenty," said Ebbets. "All kinds of upland rodents who've been bullied out of their homes, like you and I were. There are mice and rats, and I've even seen a squirrel or two. There are chipmunks and—"

"*Cats.*" The word rippled out of the shadows like a sinister breeze. "Don't forget the *cats.*"

The rodents watched as a shape of pure ghostly white slunk toward them.

"The bloodthirsty cat ghost!" breathed Cassius.

Titus and Ebbets were already on their feet, prepared to face off against the feline spirit. But as the white vision drew closer, Titus could see that while she was as ghostly pale and eerily colorless as a phantom, she was very much alive. A red, jeweled collar glittered around her neck, and her eyes—one blue, one green—had an evil gleam.

"Oh, look," she purred. "I'm just in time for lunch."

Myrtle's gasp of horror at the sight of the cat startled her babies; they began to wriggle, tumbling out of the nest, whimpering as they rolled in every direction.

Ebbets and Myrtle sprung into action, scampering around frantically, trying to catch them.

Titus instantly flung himself in front of Mamie and Conselyea, who was still cradling little Dodger in her trembling arms. A quick glance at Cassius told him the general was more intent on shielding his food than the females from the hungry cat.

"Help Ebbets and Myrtle!" Titus commanded. "Gather the pups! Hurry!"

Cassius grudgingly dropped his food and attempted to help collect the pups. But the frantic efforts of the rat and the mice were nothing compared to the size and speed of the vicious cat.

She swung one dazzling white paw and scooped up

all nine of the scattered pups and their mother in one fell swoop. Her mouth opened wide.

"Noooo!" Ebbets wailed, running toward her.

Without even looking, the cat swatted her tail; it collided with Ebbets like a fluffy club and sent him crashing hard into the tunnel wall.

Undaunted, he gained his feet and attacked again. This time she used the claws of her hind paw to pin him down.

"I'm beginning to understand why the humans call you rodents 'pests,'" the cat murmured.

Then, to Titus's horror, the cat raised the paw that held Ebbets's family. One by one she dropped each of them into her mouth.

Mamie shrieked. Conselyea cried out. Even Cassius looked sickened by such a gruesome display. But not Titus . . . What Titus felt was much stronger than sadness, much deeper than disgust.

What Titus felt was *fury*.

A blazing knot of it, low in his belly, burning, glowing. It seemed to take hold, becoming a part of him. He'd never known he could experience such loathing. Whiskers quivering, he glowered at the beautiful cat, who dabbed daintily at the corners of her mouth.

"Mmm, tender," she drawled. "What were they . . . two, maybe three days old? Well, that's the thing about mice. They're so much tastier when they're *fresh*."

Titus let out a roar. He was about to spring for her

throat until he realized that this would leave the midwife, Conselyea, and baby Dodger open to attack. Gritting his teeth, he stayed where he was, shielding the three precious creatures and watching the white cat preen.

Now she removed her back paw from Ebbets and looked down at him with disdain. "Thanks for being such a gracious host," she purred in a mocking tone. "In case you were wondering, I'm Queen Felina. And I assure you, you haven't seen the last of me."

The white cat gave Ebbets a hard kick and sent him rolling across the dirt to land in a bloody heap at Titus's feet.

A moment later, Felina was gone.

Titus could see that Ebbets was bleeding badly, but still the mouse dragged himself to where Conselyea was rocking Dodger in her arms.

"He's all right," Conselyea assured the worried father.

"That's my boy," Ebbets whispered. "He's a survivor."

Titus examined the injuries his friend had suffered at Felina's paws. There were four deep puncture wounds where the cat's hind claws had pierced him, and unless Titus missed his guess, Ebbets had sustained several broken bones as well.

"What should we do?" Conselyea asked, her voice filled with terror.

"Leave him for dead," Cassius muttered. "And get out of this hellhole."

"No!" Titus shook his head. "No. I won't do that. His tribe needs him. His son needs him. And . . . he's my friend."

"But we have to do something," said Conselyea. "Look how badly he's hurt. His wounds need to be cleansed and bandaged, and perhaps a bone or two will require setting."

Titus looked to the midwife. "Mamie, are you experienced in this kind of healing?"

The midwife sighed. "I am, but with no supplies I am helpless. I would need clean water, bandages, something to use for a splint . . ."

Titus scanned the area. He could probably put some of the nest's twigs and string to use for a splint, but the greater problem was cleaning out the bloody gashes. With no water to rinse them, it was only a matter of time before infection took hold.

"I think," the midwife said softly, "there is one in these tunnels who could help Ebbets."

"Who?" asked Titus. "Where will I find this rodent?"

"Not a rodent." Mamie shook her little brown head. "A cockroach."

"Yes, of course," sneered Cassius, rolling his eyes. "Because when you're looking to stave off germs and disease, who better than a filthy little cockroach?"

"This insect is different," Mamie assured them. "He

is a prophet." She reached into the pocket of her smock and withdrew a square piece of paper. It was wrinkled and stained, but the writing on it was clear and legible.

On one side was printed NEW YORK STATE LOTTERY LUCKY NUMBERS. And on the other were scrawled the words *Those who believe in La Rocha shall be healed.*

"I found this as we were marching," the midwife explained. "It seems La Rocha is a benevolent being who helps rodents in their time of need. I believe he has quite a following, or so it is written."

"Written where?" scoffed Cassius.

"On the walls, all throughout these tunnels. Words of wisdom and comfort from the great La Rocha himself. Messages of promise, messages of hope. I saw many of these writings as we marched."

Titus had seen them too, although he hadn't bothered to pay much attention. He'd thought it was just like all the other graffiti he'd seen upland. Now he looked at his suffering friend. Ebbets had already lost plenty of blood, and his eyes were beginning to glaze over.

"How can we locate this La Rocha?" Titus asked.

"I found this piece of scripture back near the abandoned platform," Mamie said. "So I think you might find him there." She reached out and gently took the pup, who'd begun to cough again, from

Conselyea. "It is much too far for this little one to travel. I will take Dodger to the beginnings of our village, where I can care for him and keep him safe. You three must deliver Ebbets to the great La Rocha to be healed. And when he is well, you can return him to his pup, who will be waiting behind the wall."

Titus frowned. According to Ebbets, the gray wall was at least a day's walk, and Titus didn't like the idea of this tiny midwife mouse traveling the damp tunnels alone with a sick pup to protect. Then again, Ebbets had said his son was a survivor. Maybe he was right.

"It's the only way," Titus said at last. "But let's bundle the child so he'll be warm."

Titus reached for the book pages he'd brought along from the library, choosing one from the Latin primer. He spread it on the ground, and his eyes fell upon the list of words printed there:

multitūdō -inis f.: **multitude, number**
mundus -ī m.: **world, universe, heavens**
mūnus mūneris n.: **gift, offering; duty, obligation**
mūrus -ī m.: **wall**
mūs: **mouse**

Titus felt a shiver go up his spine. How strange that these words should appear together on a single page. He supposed they were arranged by the order of their letters, just as the books in the library had been. But still, to him it seemed to suggest some cosmic purpose, some mystical design.

The midwife saw it too, and smiled. "You see? It is practically foretold. This is all meant to be."

Titus took the pup from Mamie. He settled him on the page from the Latin book that suddenly seemed so rich with meaning. As he wrapped Ebbets's one surviving child warmly in the clean paper, he whispered a cheerful song, a gentle litany:

"There you go now, Dodger. There you are, little Mūs. I will take good care of your father, you shall see. For this is my mūnus mūneris, my duty and my gift to you. It is the way of the world, the mundus, to be kind to those in need. And so you must be brave, little Dodger Mūs, and go off to the mūrism, to be with the multitūdō. Titus will see to the safety of your father. Titus will make everything right."

When Dodger was snugly swaddled in the list of Latin *M* words, Titus handed him back to Mamie.

"Please be careful," Conselyea said.

"Oh, I will," the midwife promised. "And I am not afraid. La Rocha will watch over us on our journey." She brought the pup close to Ebbets's face so the injured mouse could place a kiss on his son's tiny forehead. Then she crept off into the tunnel with little Dodger pressed close to her heart.

It seemed ages before they arrived back at the abandoned platform. Titus, who had carried Ebbets the whole way, could feel the blood seeping from the mouse's deep puncture wounds into Titus's own fur.

Blood brothers, he thought.

He placed his friend on a pile of soft rags. Ebbets's breath was coming in shallow gasps now; it reminded the rat of little Dodger's labored breathing.

"La Rocha!" Titus shouted, his voice ringing off the tile walls. "La Rocha, I bring you a rodent in need. Please come and assist us."

He waited.

Nothing.

"La Rocha, please! We have an injured friend who needs you to minister to him."

Still, nothing.

Titus's heart sank.

"Maybe he's not taking on any new followers at this time," Cassius quipped sardonically.

"Shhhh," said Conselyea. "Listen!"

Titus tilted his ear and heard a scratchy, scampering sound . . . the sound of six spiny legs making their way across the hard-packed dirt. Seconds later, the rat was looking down at an oval-shaped insect.

A cockroach.

"I am La Rocha," said the bug. "How can I be of aid?"

Titus quickly explained about the feline attack. La Rocha instructed Conselyea to bring him a red metal box—a human leftover—that was propped against the wall. She made quick work of dragging it over to where Ebbets lay whimpering in his semiconscious state.

La Rocha opened the box, and Titus saw that it contained all manner of human medical equipment. Relief washed over him as he watched the roach use moist wipes and ointments to clean out the mouse's wounds, and sticky bandages to bind them.

But setting the broken bones was another story.

"Is there something he can bite down upon?" La Rocha asked. "This next process will be exceptionally painful."

Conselyea removed her golden chain and gave it to Titus, who placed one of the hard blue stones between Ebbets's teeth.

"Bite," the roach commanded his patient.

From deep in his twilight sleep, Ebbets must have heard the instruction, because his tiny teeth gripped the stone.

La Rocha took hold of the mouse's limp and broken arm and, in a nearly imperceptible motion, jerked the snapped bone back into place. Ebbets squeezed his teeth against the stone and moaned in agony.

"That is all I can do for him," said La Rocha, returning the jeweled chain to Conselyea. "I will send out good thoughts and ask for the blessings of the universe to make him well. But . . ."

"But what?" Titus prodded.

"His injuries are extensive, and your journey here was a dusty one. His wounds are already beginning to fester. The human medicines can only do so much."

La Rocha then bowed his head and crawled away.

To Titus's surprise, Ebbets's eyes fluttered, then opened. "Titus?" His voice was a raspy whisper.

"What is it, Ebbets?"

"Tell me about your city you're going to build on this abandoned platform."

Titus swallowed hard, fighting back the emotion that threatened to overwhelm him. "Sure. What do you want to know?"

"What will you call it?"

Titus looked around and saw a sign hanging askew high on the tunnel wall: ATLANTIC AVENUE.

"How does Atlantia sound?"

Ebbets managed a little nod. "Tell me about this Atlantia."

"It's going to be wonderful! Just like Rome under the great emperors was. And the rodents who live here will be as safe and as lucky as the ancient Romans ever were. In fact, we'll call the ruling family the House of Romanus. What do you think of that?"

"Sounds pretty lofty," Ebbets choked out, "but if anyone call pull it off, Titus, you can."

"That's right." Titus forced a chuckle. "And you can rechristen your tribe the 'Mūs.' It's Latin, for mouse. Impressive, huh?"

"Very."

"And here in Atlantia I'll commission beautiful buildings . . . maybe even a palace. And there'll be special spaces where the rodent children can learn and play."

"Sounds nice. I'll bring Dodger to visit."

"He'll always be welcome," said Titus, then caught himself and added, "You both will."

Titus's planning was interrupted by a bone-chilling sound that tore out of the darkness. "Meeeooowwww."

Conselyea blanched and Cassius dove for cover as once again, the wicked white cat appeared, hovering over them.

"We have to stop meeting like this," Felina joked in her icy way.

"I couldn't agree more," Titus shot back. "So why don't you just leave us alone."

"Because that would go against nature, silly. Believe me, I'm not particularly thrilled that the main staple of my diet happens to be mangy, flea-bitten rodents, but that's just how I'm built. I like fish, too, but as you might imagine, salmon filets and tuna steaks are pretty hard to come by down here."

"Then why do you stay?" Conselyea challenged. "You're a pretty feline. I'm sure you could find a human family up above who'll take you in."

Felina's eyes flashed. "You'd think so, wouldn't you?"

"You're wearing a collar," Conselyea noted. "Maybe you already have humans. Why don't you just go home?"

"Why don't *you* just shut *up!*" Felina hissed and swung one claw-tipped paw at Conselyea.

Titus threw himself in front of her, taking a mean swipe to the snout. A welt came up instantly, snaking across his nose and mouth in a bloody trickle.

"Here's the thing," said Felina. "I'm going to eat one of you. So either *you* can decide who that's going to be, or *I* will."

Titus could not bear the thought of this monster devouring Conselyea, and he was sure Cassius was not prepared to volunteer. With an ache in his heart he began to step forward. But before he could offer himself up to those gleaming fangs, Ebbets spoke.

"Take me," the battered little mouse whispered from his bed of rags. "Take me and leave the others alone."

"Ebbets," said Titus. "What are you doing?"

"We both know I'm dying, Titus. But you . . . you still have Atlantia to look forward to. You have Conselyea, and maybe one day you'll have a litter of your own to raise."

Felina yawned. "Tick tock, rodents," she sneered, rolling her mismatched eyes.

Titus clenched his fists and gritted his teeth. He knew what Ebbets was saying made sense, but it felt wrong. He didn't want to sacrifice a friend—even if that friend was not likely to last through the night. The only other option was for Titus to give his own life—a life that suddenly seemed to have purpose. He had Conselyea now, and the dream that was Atlantia. For the first time ever, there was a sensation in Titus's heart that felt like hope.

With a ragged breath he turned his back on Ebbets and gazed up into the blue and green eyes of Felina.

"Take the mouse," he said. The words tasted like blood on his tongue.

"Very well," said Felina, padding her way toward the pile of rags. "He'll do." Then she purred and flashed a toothy smile at Titus. "For now."

"What's that mean?"

"It means I like this little arrangement. You give me mousemeat and I don't have to get my lovely white fur all dusty hunting around in these grungy tunnels. I eat, you live, everybody's happy. What do you think?"

"I think you're a fiendish beast!" screamed Titus.

"Yes, yes, of course you do," drawled Felina. "But I meant, what do you think about you and I striking some kind of bargain? A working relationship. One that will make me happy and keep the target off your back."

"Never!" Titus hurled the word at her, wishing it

were a rock or a hunk of jagged glass. "That will never happen, Felina."

The cat sighed and flicked her tail. "Fine. Be that way. But just so you know, I have a nice, cozy lair off through that curving tunnel there. If you change your mind about striking an accord, you'll know where to find me."

"Not going to happen," Titus assured her.

Felina merely laughed. Then she leaned her head down toward Ebbets and bared her fangs.

Titus allowed himself one glance—what he saw nearly undid him: The mouse's head was held high and his black eyes glinted with courage. But trembling in the white fur around Ebbets eye, there was a single tear.

Titus grabbed Conselyea's arm and motioned for Cassius to join them. As the rats fled, Titus heard Ebbets's voice following them into the darkness of the tunnel.

"Long live Atlantia," the mouse sang out.

"Long live Atlantia," Titus echoed on a sob.

And as he ran away from his dying friend and the feasting cat, he shouted the words he knew would be the last ones that Ebbets would ever hear:

"Long live the Mūs," cried Titus of the House of Romanus. "Long live the brave, courageous tribe, the Mūs."

THE END